THE HEART OF REVENGE

RICHIE DRENZ

Jamaica's Most Outrageous Author

A TRILOGY

DRENZ BOOKS

A DRENZ PUBLISHING PRODUCTION

DRENZ BOOKS
Published by the Drenz Publishing Co. (Ja.)
www.drenzbooks.com

Cover design, Interior design and typesetting by Richie Drenz
Photography by Pure Marketing
Model- Melissa Smith {Available for hire}
Editor, Dian Morgan

First Drenz Publishing Printing July 2012
10 9 8 7 6 5 4 3 2 1

Copyright © 2012 by Richie Drenz
Excerpts from "Climaxes" copyright ©Richie Drenz, 2011
All rights reserved

Published in Jamaica

Without limiting the rights under copyright reserved above, Any excerpts for review, or parts of this publication, to be utilized, reproduced, stored in or introduced into a retrieval system, or transmitted, in any form, or by any means, now known or hereafter invented, including (xerography, electronic, mechanical, photocopying,, recording or otherwise), is forbidden without the prior written permission of both the copyright owner and the above publisher , Drenz Publishing Co.

PUBLISHER'S NOTE

All characters in this book have no existence outside the imagination of the author and have no relation whatsoever to anyone bearing the same name or names. They are not even distantly inspired by any individual known or unknown to the author, and all incidents are pure inventions of fiction.

If you purchased this book without a cover you should be aware that this book is stolen property. It was reported as "unsold and destroyed" to the publisher and neither the author nor publisher has received any payment for this "stripped book."

The scanning, uploading, and distribution of this book via the internet or via any other means without the permission of Drenz Publishing Co., is illegal and punishable by law. Please purchase only authorised electronic editions, and do not participate in or encourage electronic piracy or copyrighted material. Your support of the author's rights is appreciated.

ISBN 978-976-95365-2-4

Acknowledgements

If I had a son, I would thank him, but since I don't, Mira Williams is the first person, I would like to thank after thanking God. She has been there a whole lot to listen to my buzzing nags and worry about every detail of the book thrice. Thanks Mira and I am looking forward to publish your upcoming book **'Kitty Rules'**. Patrick 'Pajujah' Anderson thanks for being a gigantic support of my literature, moral support and encouragement, without you this book would still be at chapter eleven. Likewise Shanice Steve you have been such great support. Tadreen 'Bossybratz' Segree, I swear your support knows no bounds and I too am a fan of you, Thank you. Franz Hoilette, much respect for all the strength you've given behind this project mi brother, big up **ilovebeingjamaican.com.** Lisa Campbell you have been awesome. Thank you the reader for your support and do continue.

A huge thanks to persons on facebook that from day one has encouraged me to write, this list is in no order whatsoever and some persons may have changed their names but here goes, Keda-Gaye Duffus, Shev Morgan, Sophia Shakur, Carla McClaughlin, Sugar Bear, Kimmy Simpson, Sacha Barririffe, Kim Lee Kafka, Rochelle Bosslady, Chelton Glenister, Samantha Bryant, Shawya Hudson, Stacyann Taylor, Taneisha Kentish, La Tondra, Sashell Bennett, Laurie Sanford, Tannica Brown, Ty Anthony, Pretty Nessa, Nikki Nickalicious, Lia Dimepiece, Shannika Palmer, Monique Grant, Ashoikie Saunders, Aretha Miller, Lady Jay Knight, Christina Brown, Jason Williams, Alicia McKenzie, Flawless Stop Caring

Meika, Sabrina White, Ana-Alicia Beckford, Breezy Thompson, Shanese Thorpe, Krystal Saunderson, Myesha Johnson, Anrkiss, Ronae White, Marsha Lamont, Shari Reid, Frankii Maragh, Lacey Thompson, Shanique English, Lisa Heartfelt, Camille Loren, Jelisa White, Alethia Gooden, Alessi Alexander, Kim Berly, Deveen, Lacye Hyman, Phelecia Miller, Ibrena Rebele, Antoinette Toni Brown, Lisa Marie Hydes, Lotoya Grey, Shantel Smith, Chilli Swaggerific, Shamel Lopez, Malissa Fletcher, Kandis Williams, Jhennell Trudy, Taneipoo Boost, Foxalot Variance Will, , Kelz Squire, Waldo Pitt, Sonya Henry, Tequilla, Rosa Bonfire Wood, Nathoya Smith, Nia Simone, Bella Ferguson, Kooli Badu, Shelly Simone, Cassie Blake, Ivy Ivana, Renzii Hibbert, ShanLeica, Sherita Bell, Pam-Pam Smiley, Evelyn Walsh, Monalyn Blake, Cherribaby, Kristol-Lee Robinson, Shannel Johnson, Jordiekae Bolt, Kaya Hastings, Lori Stewart, Rose Marie Shaw, Thick Chick, Faith Rankine, Le Grimm, Brigette SoHard, Elimac Evol, Tabitha Lynch-Powell, Marian Foster, Jodi-ann Superstar Mudfish, Danielle Cox, Abigail Simpson, Chevelle Campbell, Natalia Rose, Stacy-Ann 'Karamel' Johnson, Rochelle 'Bosslady' Gibson, Mitsie Charlton, Kaseka Daley, Latoya Grant, Rayphia Porter, Brenda Daley, Shantell McFarlane, Seveen Jaja, Sasha Henry, Faith Rankine-Bell, A. Divine 'Karma' Blake, Latoya Lyn, Nak'ky Curtis, Regina Bennett, Ishaku Ibu Shango, Akeila Dyer, Brenda Daley, Shannel Johnson, Simone Smith, Diamond Benjamin, Meika Skyers.

Dedicated to - Tasheka Dacres

OTHER BOOKS BY RICHIE DRENZ

The Jamaican Ninja — Release Date – 30 Sept. 2012
Read sample excerpt at RichieDrenzBlog.com/The-Jamaican-Ninja

Climaxes — Release Date - 31 Nov. 2012
Read sample excerpt at RichieDrenzBlog.com/Climaxes

The Heart of Revenge 2 - Release Date – 31 Nov. 2012
Read sample excerpt at RichieDrenzBlog.com/THOR2

Join our official facebook page at
www.facebook.com/EroticBlissByRichieDrenz

CONTENTS

CHAPTER 1
Heartburns & in-Deceptions 1

CHAPTER 2
God in her heart 7

CHAPTER 3
It Started When I was Fourteen 12

CHAPTER 4
Heart Forgives but After I Revenge 15

CHAPTER 5
Busted Or Not? 21

CHAPTER 6
Jacket Or Abortion 28

CHAPTER 7
Daddy Wishes Son Dirt 36

CHAPTER 8
Death, His Final Supper, Served As a Hearty Breakfast .. 41

CHAPTER 9
Vance Has a Big Heart 48

CHAPTER 10
Vance Has A Good Friend 52

CHAPTER 11
Ice cream for Pinky? 60

CHAPTER 12
Before I Touch it 66

CHAPTER 13
A Clean Heart, Muddy Hands and Who Breed 68

CHAPTER 14
I'm Building a Mansion On Quicksand 77

CHAPTER 15
Picture-woman Munchy 82

CHAPTER 16
An Heartfelt I Do 83

CHAPTER 17
My White Gold Wedding Ring 88

CHAPTER 18
Braveheart, I Won't Run 92

CHAPTER 19
Do This For Me 99

CHAPTER 20
The Heart of War 107

CHAPTER 21
The Broken-Hearted 112

CHAPTER 22
Full Heart Attack 113

CHAPTER 23
Emergency, Just Pick Up 121

CHAPTER 24
What Now? 123

CHAPTER 25
It's in a Nissan Sunny 127

CHAPTER 26
Use your Head 134

CHAPTER 27
Vodka in My Heart String 139

CHAPTER 28
Dig Up in Mi Mother's Business 143

CHAPTER 29
Pack Your Belongings 145

CHAPTER 30
What kind of Secret Between Them.. 154

CHAPTER 31
Pay Me or Get Shot 155

CHAPTER 32
Be Warned 157

CHAPTER 33
Keep Trying Till Never 159

CHAPTER 34
This is the Plan B 165

CHAPTER 35
Got To Go 172

CHAPTER 36
Who dead 178

CHAPTER 37
Persuasion 180

CHAPTER 38
Mr. Willie Hold the Keys 181

CHAPTER 39
Back to the Warehouse 185

CHAPTER 40
Heart in My Mouth 191

CHAPTER 41
Black Heart 193

CHAPTER 42
Balancing my Heart 202

CHAPTER 43
The Heart of Revenge 210

Important Note to all readers 216

About the Author 217

CHAPTER 1

Heartburns & in-Deceptions
by: Leelia Lexings

Like seriously, it all began out of REVENGE. And the problem was all because the door wasn't shut. As in, it was pushed closed but the lock wasn't secured. It wasn't safe. I could've and should've latched it but I didn't, and it wasn't that I was too caught up here either, just wasn't sure I was really going to go through with this or not. It's summer, June 11, and lord did I need this three months break from UWI. I was so charged up about it until I threw myself into this situation I'm in right now. I planned it, but sitting here face to face with it right now, I'm not sure how I should feel inside or what I was feeling. My age? Nineteen. Just turned nineteen in April, and believe it or not, today is probably the biggest day I'll ever have in my life already. And for sure the most important day in my brother, Vance's, life. I nervously looked towards the lock on the plain white door. Don't judge me, - BUT – today, this was happening in the bathroom.

"Hey, take our picture. Just like we are now."

I instructed him, while sitting in his lap. My arms hugged around his neck, both of us were dressed in formal clothes and sitting in the bathroom. My breasts were outside the cups of my strapless satin dress, and my nipples still wet from just slipping out his mouth.

"Of the two of us?" he asked tilting his head, shocked and puzzled, looking straight into my eyes. His pants zipper half-way open. It made no sense to him, but to me I knew exactly why I wanted him to do it.

I barely mouthed, "Yeah sweets." Raised my bosom up, and brushed my nipples against his face, my nipple rubbed above his opened mouth, grazing it. "You don't have to make your face show in the pics." I freed one of my arms from around his neck and quickly glanced back at the lock, turned back around and lightly petted the side of his cheek. "I don't want you to get in any trouble boo, but make sure my face is showing ...

Pretty please...," I lowered my face close to his as I said 'pretty please' and continued to speak with my lips almost touching his cheek and close to his ear, "And show exactly what we're doing. OK?"

He girthed around my slim waist with both hands and eased me off him a bit. "Like this!" He panicked. He knew if a word of this ever got out and this shit ever hit the fan, it would be a very nasty tailspin. His eyes were searching all over my face, trying to see if I was sure. He asked, "Half-naked? You serious?"

I was. As serious as a heart surgery on Obama.

"Yeah. Email me them." I pampered my hand seductively down the chest of his white long sleeve shirt, rubbing with pressure, so I could feel the sexual raise of his huge erected nipple through his shirt.

"Ping me when you send them off boo." My palm was pressing over the roundness of his nipple, I slithered my hand down his muscular chest and back up to his nipple, twinged it between my thumb and index finger, pinching and pulling it hard. Rolled it between my fingers and he licked his lips, licked them again, slowly, his teeth biting on the underside of his lower-lip. I clawed his nipple playfully with my manicured nails. His penis twitched upward.

His face changed; a hint of anger painted his eyes. He grabbed my hand, held it steady. "Mad woman, suppose Qwan see them?" He was looking in my eyes as if I were a person on some cheap, wholesale crack.

I became aware of where I was; anyone could walk in on us at any minute. Lord knows I wouldn't want that. With no smile on my face, I answered him in a hushed tone,

"Don't you worry about it, umm ... Nate. It's Nate right?" he bobbed his head agreeing and said,

"Nathan."

" OK. Don't worry Nathan, Qwan won't find them ..." I saw a rush of relief filled him, the fright slowly leaving from his eyes and somehow it seemed like his pupils changed, maybe it was the size of his pupils changing with his mood, growing bigger and fuller as he regained a calm, a peaceful composure in our bizarre situation. His face relaxed, about to smile. I finished my sentence, hardening my jaw as I gritted the words, "I'm going to show them to him."

His eyes slammed open, the formation of his smile reversed, his mouth opened, fright flying back into his eyes. He flashed my hand down with a sharp thrust, it slapped into my lap. He held it there. I wrung my hand out his grip, asked,

"Is what? Eehm? You intimidated by Qwan?"

"N-no...No .. but .. bu-ut .. you righted?"

"If mi righted?" I looked away to the bathroom mirror in front of us. "Mi want it burn him." The bitter hurt I felt from it all lastnight began to swell, bubble and explode in my chest. "It's my damn revenge."

Nathan and I snapped several very provocative photos. Despite him being fully clothed, wearing his tall sleeve white shirt, black pants and a cakesoap blue tie, his erect penis was standing outside his zipper in some of the pictures, in some it was sticking in me, and in some I placed it in my mouth, posing for the camera. We didn't have sex, we only posed.

I still wasn't satisfied with just the pictures. It wasn't a big enough get back. So torn by thoughts of lastnight, so hurt, I had sex with Nathan right there. Nathan's body jolted with a four hundred volt of electricity when he orgasmed, spewing his cum out of control and creaming everywhere he didn't want to. Some even caught on the tail of my white gown.

We went a second round. I didn't want to keep my panty on anymore, it was making me too hot and bothered. But if someone walked in, it would be a dead giveaway once I had my panty off. The tight elastic around the rim of the legs were squeezing me and I didn't like the feel. He slid the crotches of my white panty to the side to get himself into my pink hole. I lifted my white gown, pushed both my thumbs down both sides of the thin elastic waist of my underwear, swiftly dragged it from underneath my long dress and it came off in a rolly twist from around my ankles as I stepped out of it, exposing my naked ass, clean skin, long legs.

I tossed my panty over the shower rod. It had a blue shower curtain with pictures of yellow rubber ducky all over . Hopefully I could get back in my undies fast enough if anyone should bust in on us. My skin was a smooth color of creamy Milo as I bent over and cocked up my ass to take his Godzilla size into me, doggystyled position, my love-hole jumped, wanting his warm cock between my pussy, now. My walls seeping wet with my goo. I peeped between my legs from my arched-back. Waiting on his stiffness to be forced through my fleshy hole. He hoggishly hoisted the

The Heart of Revenge

tail of my dress over my petite round buttocks, the tail bunched scraggly on my back. Roughing up my gown as if he forgot that today is a very special day for me, my biggest day. A feint worry about my brother's situation slid across my mind. It's a big decision. A difficult one. I'll just do what Mommy encouraged me to do, we already came this far with the plan, I can't turn back now. Can I? After so many years.

I slapped my hand on to the rail of the white bath tub, fingers latched. I bent and peered at him from between my legs, my breasts bouncing from my bending over. His cannon camera hung down by its black strap from his shoulder, swung awkwardly back and forth like his balls were swinging back and forth. The tiny split in the center of his fleshy purple penis-head was damp; he aimed it right at the opening of my vagina, my entire body anticipated his cock being worked into me so sweetly, so divine, parting my flesh, stroking in me. Deep. Sensually. Fucking me. He braced his hips forward, my shoulder blades squeezed itself together, I felt the tip of his swollen head pressed against my hole. It felt warm, smooth. Chills danced on the back of my neck. His entire penis jerked, it sprang up and down slightly after the jump, like an aftershock. I felt it and my hole throbbed, my spine tightened. The smooth warm head touched the tip of my pussy-lips, just barely touching them. My arm reached between my legs and grabbed hold of his cock. My small hand could not wrap completely around his kong, it was too thick, too fat. It felt like a ten pound giant sausage in my hand, as thick as a plaintain but black. It had a fat broad head. My body jittered. Gosh! I want to feel all of it inside me. My urges were taking over. I tried to take a grip of myself. I shouldn't enjoy this so much, but .. but my body, it's too aroused, ready, wanting, roaring.

I ran my fingers down his full length, the pad of my fingertips stroked over the smooth yet sharp zig-zags that his lightning veins forked from the root and sides all the way to the tip. The straight and long main vein running smoothly up the side, like a thick rope, it made the biggest bulge of all the veins. The softness of the thin skin that wrapped his penis will let me feel the swell of the veins for sure as it rubs up and down in me, but with a smooth feel, a textured feel when my juices lather it. I couldn't wait to have this juicy cock in me, feel it in me, feel it. A feeling ran through my body. Hot, excited, wanting. So wanting. My belly jerked quietly, like an hiccup of horniness, it nudged my heart rate, my heart speeding and I could feel each beat pounding against my breasts. I couldn't control my body's reaction. I wiped my thumb midway his cock, side to side. God! I wanted this. My pussy clasped itself shut and then released. I shouldn't have another contraction till couple more seconds. But I was so horny my clit jumped again in seconds, one right after the other, pulling my clit inward. I bit my lip. Squeezed the middle of his flesh. Clit jumped again. What's happening? And again. Jumped again. I squeezed my fingers around it, at the root, close to his balls, stroking it up and down, jerking him, jerking it, jerking his big fat cock. I felt it growing even stiffer in my hand, swelling thicker, solid, heavy. It rose higher, lifting my hand, horniness ravishing through its veins. He desperately wanted to push his cock into the sweetest place on earth. Inside me. He looked down at my arched back, pushed his hip forward, wanting to fuck me, fuck me till my titties fall off. I wanted to feel him inside. I didn't see his face, I heard his desperate moans,

"Leee...Leee..." dragging his words and begging,

"Let mi push it inside you, pleeeaase."

My slender fingers held his cock firm, squeezed it, aimed it to the center of my slit, cringed my face to feel his entry, released his kong and left it standing stiff in the air behind me for him to delve into my wetness. He entered me slow. The swollen head pierced its way through. I uttered a silent, 'Ouch!'. A sweet pain. I felt a tearing pain of his big hood parting my pussy lips. He shoved himself far into me, fucked so far down inside me, a Digicel phone could not pick up signal. I grunted and breathed hard, a loud sexual breath of satisfaction, a delicious pain. I felt his hugeness filling me up, filling me up in places I had no idea a man could reach with a penis. It felt insanely good, the pleasure it made me feel inside doesn't stay steady, it ran from my belly to my spine, to the tip of my fingers, to my toes and exploded with an earthshaking blast ontop of my glistening clitoris. Can't say everyone describes the feeling the same, the sensation you feel every time you reminisce on the greatest sex you ever had. The orgasmic feeling it brought into your body. A feeling so strong you can feel it in your body literally whenever you think of it. A feeling so powerful you seem to re-live it everytime you get horny. I don't know your word for it but I know it feels fucking good, the best feeling you can ever have bolting through your body, like a ping pong ball, hitting one pleasure spot then rolling down to the next, twisting your legs, twisting your face, curling your toes, even if you don't want to act a fool, you still do, you have no control. Pleasure takes over your body, you remember grapping the sheets, screaming his name, pulling him in deeper, kissing him hard, him biting your neck, licking you with passion, fucking you so deep, so good, you bite the pillow, moaning in your pillow, wanting it hard, harder, harder, more, thinking how good fuck feels, never wanting the feeling to end. Just remembering that feeling makes you breathe deeper, you get aware of your breathing, aware of your heart beating faster, you get aware of your body reacting to that feeling, your nipples get hard, your vagina reacting, getting wet. He sunk it deep and stroked his loin smoothly into me, his hugeness fucking me hard. Fucking me deep. Kept going in and out. Ohh, that feeling. Speeding up his strokes, grabbing me tighter, grabbing around my waist, fingers gripping into my waist, pulling me back as he pushes himself forward, fucking me harder, groaning, his thighs muscling, slapping into me, the feeling, the feeling, the feeling taking me over. I shut my eyes tighter, forced my body backward to meet his lengthy strides, damn that feels good, sliding down his thick warm cock, oh damn. I bit my lips, I'm not just wet, my pussy must have took a dive in the pool because it was fucking soaked. The smooth feel of his veins running against the inside of my flesh, the feeling of having someone inside, someone this big, this good. Oh God! I'm in heav... Halleluyah! Praise God! DAMN! I felt a ferocious belly cramp, a pang of pain echoing at the bottom of my belly, I felt my period coming down. Damn, he's big! The feeling built up. I didn't want him to stop stroking but I couldn't bend low anymore it's too much pain, I wanted to stop. I didn't want to get caught doing this in the bathroom, I lifted my back somewhat and like a hoola-hoop the haunting thought of my brother was coming back around in my head again. I couldn't do this. I tried straightening myself up, my wedding gown fell off my back. Yes, my wedding gown. My long white wedding gown fell to the floor.

CHAPTER 2

God in her Heart
by: Leelia Lexings

I looked at the bathroom door, my heart raced and worry enveloped my mind tight. I was having a change of heart, I don't want to do this, Oh my God, I shouldn't be doing this. I would die if my mother caught me. She's in the livingroom, just down the corridor. Of all the family in the house, it would be Mommy knowing about this that I couldn't live with. I had to make her proud, this certainly wasn't something to make her face spread a proud grin about, is it? Maybe she would die if she caught me like this, then again, maybe not, but I didn't want her catching me like this. She gave up too much for this. Mommy was determined to make things better for us, the family, I remembered how hard she tried, how much she sacrificed. A woman of God. One particular day to church stood out clearer than any other day, it was this one, six years ago.

The big ball of fire in the sky was red hot that Sunday morning. The wind blew my pink frock I wore to church most Sundays, it swept a cloud of dust on my skin and into my face. I stopped and covered my face with both hands, Mommy tugged on my bony arm,

"Walk up nuh Lee."

She stepped off brisk, wrung her ankle, broke off one of her heels and her hands dilly-dally in the air trying to balance. She almost fell flat on her face. Bending, she picked up the broken heel out of the dry dirt, she prayed to God,

"God mi fed up of mi life, mi wish you would just take mi life and done."

Most people in Mommy's case would just commit suicide rather than wait on the help of God to wipe them off the face of the earth.

"We turning back honey."

She was tip-toeing awkwardly in her one and a half shoes. I zipped my gray handbag open, took out a ball of Vaseline wrapped in a piece of clear plastic bag, sank one finger into the soft dab, then wiped my finger on my cracked lips to hide that we had not eaten breakfast this morning, nor eaten anything yesterday. Luckily, the day before yesterday, my big brother Vance got a finger of banana, two cornmeal flour dumplings and some red herring and ackee from our next door neighbour, Ms. Merl. He shared it among me, my bigger sister, Pinky, Mommy and himself. Mommy said we must not leave any for our worthless father, because he deserved to eat just pure air with nothing pie for dinner, for the rest of his life. I could not agree more. We didn't leave him even a small scrapings of the red herring bone.

I wanted to go inside the church. I didn't want to go back home because we walked almost two miles in the sun since Mommy could not afford to take a taxi and refused to go to the church in our ghetto community.

"Mommy mi tired, we can't just go to church go sit down for a little beside the fan?" I was sweaty. I wanted to get some of the free artificial breeze blowing in my face. Breeze off little. I put on my best sorry-for face as I spoke, "Mi want take some of the cool breeze first."

Like a loaf of bread in the oven, the sun was baking my forehead. I wiped off some of the sweat and dust from my face. Mommy looked at me for a few clock ticks. She didn't reply. She put the broken off heel in my handbag, took off both shoes and was trying to stuff both of them down into my handbag. Mommy's parents were rich, according to her, she had it all. Since she met Dad her life had made a drastic turn, and it was downhill from then on. Now Mommy didn't even own a bag for herself, apart from a few black bags at home that we called scandal bags and a few bags under her stressed out eyes. On Sundays when she wore black or gray to church she'd take my little gray handbag.

"Mommy pleaseee." I whined in my squeaky, thirteen year old voice. Mommy still didn't answer as she finally force-fit both shoes in, but had to keep the piece of heel in her hand to make the shoes fit into the tiny bag. "Pleeease Mommy, the sun is pelting mi."

Mommy was fighting with the mouth of the handbag, pulling the zippers close together so she could zip it shut. Sister Wilkins pulled up at the sidewalk in her silver Starlet. She rolled down her window and I felt the cool a/c breeze escaping the car, her wrinkled hand adjusted her glasses above her wide nose and her voice was shaky but polite,

"Good Morning Sister Aubrea, you need a lift dear?" Mommy immediately responded

"No." Almost with a snap in her tone, "Mi just turning to go back home for something now."

"What?" Mrs. Wilkins squinted her eyes and pushed up the broad rim of her matching white hat to see in Mommy's face as the bright sun hazed her vision.

"I left my phone at the yard and I'm getting an important call today." Mommy twanged and held the unclosed handbag behind her.

"No problem deary, I'll help you out man, I can just take you quick and come back."

Mommy stuttered,

"No... no... That's alright, we taking a taxi 'cause I have to make a stop about some money business that haven't reached my U.S. account, you can just go on to church leave mi." Mrs. Wilkins looked down at Mommy's feet - no shoes – no stockings – no lotion – two dry poppy-poppy foot.

"Heh Heya! ... Ok Sister Aubrea, God bless you dear."

"What that mean Sister Wilkins?"

"Nothing, nothing."

Mrs. Wilkins rolled up her window. The hot pavement seemed as if it had silvery water in the far distance as Mrs. Wilkins silver car drove down the road to church. As the car got smaller and smaller in distance Mommy muttered to herself,

"All of you just love show-off your dirty self, like people frighten for car and a/c and damn cellular phone." Her pride was bruised, maybe her grudge even ripened, she puffed out a breath of I-can't-stand-her.

Mommy was use to car, she had a car once before I was born and Daddy set it on fire one day. She didn't have any U.S. bank account, Mom didn't have any taxi-fare and Mom didn't own a house phone much less a cellphone. She carried the handbag back to the front of her and hackled the zip.

"Hold down the shoes make mi zip up the bag Lee."

Mommy's dry lips needed some of the Vaseline. My hand crammed down the shoes while Mommy angrily yanked at the zip and dragged it up in frustration, bursting off the zipper-head in her hand. She threw the zipper-head, the shoes heel and my one deggeh deggeh handbag in the dirt, threw her hands in the air and walked off saying,

"Mi fed up of this here life enuh! Mi fed up! Mi fed up! Mi fed up!" Mommy wasn't crying but her eyes were watery. "Mi don't know what to do again, God know." Praying, she turned her head to the sky and eye-water filled-up her eyes.

"God you see and know what mi going through, help mi God, please... Help mi." She shook her head as she spoke and the tears thickened on her eyelashes. A feeling of giving up burst inside her. She tried to hold back the eye-water.

"God take the case and give mi the pillow." She cried. A long tear slid down her disheartened face, the water lengthening from her eye to her chin. Mommy didn't look sad. She looked suicidal.

That Sunday evening Mommy cooked dinner. She prepared dumplings with cooking oil and we poured cold water in plastic cups to help wash down our Sunday dinner.

That was my last time ever eating poor squalor for a Sunday's dinner. God didn't have much credit on his phone to chit-chat with Mommy, but he still answered one of Mommy's prayer.

A week after that, Mommy began doing some work with Mr. Micheal Douglas. She took money to deposit at the bank for all his hardware, supermarket, security company and landscaping company, and she also ran other petty errands for his businesses. Mommy was earning OK pay and told everyone she was Mr. Micheal Douglas's Personal Assistant, not his "Bearer".

Though Mommy was earning some dough it didn't come close to what she desperately needed. She needed money for the huge doctor bill that she worried so much about. She was worrying so much that the poor lady thinned down to skin and bones and her eyeballs sank deep down into two holes. Mawga like brother dog. No matter what she did she couldn't come up with the money. It drove her to make one of the most difficult decisions a mother could make and it led to my wedding. This wedding day. I was fourteen when she had to make the heart-wrenching decision. This is how it went down.

CHAPTER 3

It Started When I Was Fourteen
by: Leelia Lexings

At fourteen years young, my flat chest was rounding into breasts. Mommy thought it would be best if she remained in the ghetto but moved me out the braka-tat-tat warzone. She sent me to live on my own with my boyfriend uptown. Well actually, he wasn't my boyfriend yet, but Mommy knew what she had to do from the get go.

Blue. Dark-blue it was on that bleaky morning before I left. Mommy explained everything to me the best way she knew how. Lassy barked ecstatically outside as Mr. Micheal Douglas' Pajero pulled up at our zinc fence. He killed the purring engine and left only one noise standing in the morning's lightlessness, Lassy's meagre echoing bark.

Mommy stooped down before me, her hands busy buttoning up my yellow blouse, it had frills running down both sides of the buttons. The livingroom was not bright enough for me to see her face clearly through the thick darkness of the wee morning. The chokingly unbearable scent of the cheap red carbolic-soap that bathed my skin smelled harshly acidic in my nose and aggravated my allergies. I sneezed. It rushed my eyes into squinting. I used both hands to cover my nose and mouth. Sneezed again. Wiped. Sniffled.

Mommy spoke with a resentful cry in her voice,

"Lee, what I'm asking you to do is for a good cause, you hear mi? A good cause." She used her shoulder to wipe her running nose, then wiped mine. She sniffled but I didn't think it was from allergies. I think it was from how overwhelm her heart was, the big cry inside there. Her voice became throaty. "You understand mi honey?" Morning dryness in my eyes and inside my mouth minty with the taste of Colgate - no tea this morning. I nodded yes, though I didn't quite understood why she was crying. We were doing this for a good, things would be better. I was going to miss my mother.

The sun was still dead, not yet risen and no moon nor clouds were in the motionless sky, only the sorrowful emptiness and Mom's lonely voice shaking.

"Remember what the pastor said, you remember? ... Sometimes doing the good will hurt. It's not an easy road, ok?" She ran both hands down my blouse then lightly rested both palms on my chest.

Mr. Douglas tried opening the our zinc gate. The gatet had black rubber hinges made from square cuts of car tyres. The noisy rattling on the zinc gate was added to the sound of Mom's voice. The rubbery hinges gave the gate an automatic slam-shut that sounded like God clapped his hands in the quiet. Mom and I snapped our head around at the sound of the zinc slamming. She knew he was coming. This was it. Her lips trembled and she spoke faster,

"Look this way honey, others going to judge you bad baby." She placed one palm on my cheek turning me around, "Look this way, look ... they'll say bad things, but honey, they don't know, they don't know, lord knows they don't know." I listened as my nose grabbed a lungful of the cool atmosphere, the clean morning air tunnelled through my nose and into my mouth; it tasted unpolluted and filled with nature's fresh morning-dew, the light smell of blossoms, rivers and the perfumy essence of flowers. Mommy's face looked like crucifixion.

"You see, doing the good sometimes is doing the lesser evil. And it hurts, every strand of my hair and every muscle in my body pains me." The tears came in two streams down her face. Lassy barked as Mr. Douglas stepped on to our raw-concrete doorstep. She pulled me into her bosom and wrapped her hands around my head, rocking with me and protecting me.

"Listen Lee and never forget." Both her open palms clasped my cheeks and she firmed her eyes into mine. "No matter what others say, never let it stop you from doing the good, no matter how difficult the good is. Pride is as invisible as the words of gossip and it will hurt you deep." Her palms pressingly shook my cheeks with passion, "But only when **YOU** let them hurt you Lee ..." Her heart hoped that I understood at only fourteen. My slender fingers squeezed on my gray handbag.

She was counselling herself too as she sent off her girl child. Her eyes penetrated deep beyond my child's eyes and her words aimed at the goodness of my soul. "But only when you let them WIN Lee ... Only when you let them WIN! O.K? You understand mi. Right?" Mommy quieted. The morning became a listening silence. I answered,

"Yes Mommy."

A chilly wind blew through the window, swayed Mom's black slip, and all her tears broke loose from her eyes. My small hands brushed away her tears. I would not let her down.

The heavy scent of Mr. Douglas' cologne climbed through the faulty joinings of our board house, spread into the livingroom, and forced itself up my irritated nose. There was a knock-knock at the door and a husky voice in a formal tone called,

"Mrs. Lexings... Mrs. Lexings."

Knock! Knock! Knock!

"Mrs. Lexings!"

Mommy waited forty days and forty nights before she answered.

"Coming."

She kissed my forehead, ran one hand down my blouse one last time, breathing out forcibly, and then stood to her feet. Beside her small feet were all my packed belongings, in three black scandal bags.

Less than an hour later, emergency. Asthma. Mom was rushing with Pinky to the hospital, with the only money she had left. The dinner money.

I took my eyes off the bathroom door. Nathan hoisted back my gown over my bent ass.

CHAPTER 4

Heart Forgives but After I Revenge
by: Leelia Lexings

I can't afford anyone hearing us, I quietly yelp to him,
"Take your time with it babes ... It's not running away."
Wincing my face in an ugly plea, eyes rolls to the sky but pussy wet and drooling with delight, almost dripping. He slows down, driving his cock into me from behind with slow thrusts, with nursing care, then shoves his gigantic penis the furthest I've ever felt a fucking cock in my life. I flash-dash my hand over my mouth, gagging myself, squirm. I want to yell at the top of my voice but I can't, my family is in the livingroom. I'm through fucking; his cock is cervical-cancer big. I can't take it anymore. I stand up straight so his cock would slip out my cunt, but the head of it is still in me. I yawp out desperately
"Oh my Godmother! Please stop Nathan, PLEEAASSEE."
He didn't even open his shut eyes to look into my pleading face. I put my hand behind me, flagging it frantically for him to stop. Useless. I want to curl up in a corner on the floor like a mosquito destroyer, grab my belly and cry.
"Nathan! You hate mi!" And finally he stops.
The short-man wraps his arms around my wire waist, drags me to the other side of the bathroom and forces my back down, bending me over the face-basin, the pink of my pussy exposed to him. I stare in the mirror at him standing behind me as he slings the hampering camera off his shoulders and rests it on the face-basin. Grabs my two ass cheeks. Squeezes, then spreads them apart. He kisses one of my ass cheeks, suckingly. Moaning as he sucks it. Bites. Sucks hard, devouring it with wild kisses, all over my round little romp. My eyes roll over as his big warm mouth caresses and tongues my quivering ass, sending a titillating pleasure erupting through my entire body, up my spine and curling my toes senselessly. I bite my lips from the sweet heavenly pleasures, his oral softness on my sensitive zone, my nerves swells so huge as his soft wet

tongue pulls on the flesh of my ass and licks the round creasing underside, long licks, slow licks. He sloppily dines lower, his wet tongue licking against the lowest tip of my pussy cheeks from behind. I shut my eyes and gape my mouth wide open as I feel the play of his sharp teeth on my sacred flesh, making naughty hungry sex bites, while his naked tongue passionately stimulates the skin of my tender flesh underneath me.

He spanks one of my ass cheeks while biting his lips, my firm flesh gently bouncing up and down to his taps on my other ass cheek. He slaps it twice. He bites the nape of my neck, deep-sucks there with a broad motioning tongue, floating smoothly over and into the bothered nerves of my neck, the tip of my ears twitches with excitement, his hot breath tingling the nerves in my neck as much as his skilful tongue drives insane pleasure at my neck, through my neck.

"Oh God Nate, Don't stop sucking."

He lowers his head back down to my ass, his big mouth clasps over my entire pussy that is shaking and drizzling juice. He impartially sucks my drenching pussy lips sloppily into the back of his mouth. He spots a wet trail my pussy sputum made when its juice dribbled formlessly down my legs, he stretches out his soft pliable tongue and curves the tip to lick clean every ounce of sweet vaginal spittle off my leg. He plunges his thick tongue deep into my sticky pink wetness, licking out my sweet melted icings, his adam's apple sinks down then quickly rises back up as he greedily quaffs down the sugary taste of my succulencies, right down his horny throat. My eyes fluttering, as I lose my fucking mind, my body shaking awkwardly, sexual nimbleness high in my bones, my knees wobble helplessly at the way a single talented tongue could suck me into cumming a thousand times into his mouth.

His lips pulls on my pussy-lips as he tries to suckle the milk out of them, he gathers both of my cheeks together, feeding both of them into his professional pussy-sucking mouth, some of my flesh rests on the roofing palette of his mouth while the remnant sits on top of his wavy motioning tongue, he works his tongue like a slave inside my pussyhole and feasts his face full of my marinating liquids, flicking his warm tongue deep down in every crevice of my pulsing hole, licking the tip of my womb. His nose so close to my skin, his hot breathing sends thrills through me. He releases my lips, his lips smack sloppily, loud, rising my body heat as he feasts on my pussy. Such a greedy boy. Such a freak. Eat me up. Eat my pussy. Eat every ounce of my pussy please.

He runs his stiff tongue from the very top of my hole to the end, his tongue lingers under my clit, then licks with a slow audible melody, 'SCLIP, SCLIP, SCLIP'. The sound of him eating makes me drip more juice in his mouth. I want to ride his face, hard, real ... fucking... hard, wipe my pussy in his mouth. Wipe my pussy on his tongue, just fucking wipe my pussy all over his fucking face. Sit in his face and smear my pussy juices all over, glaze all fucking over his face.

His sharp teeth salaciously bites the crevice of my inner thigh, he sucks up some of my thigh into his mouth pulls on it and my heartbeat races through my breast, my breathing heavy as I try to catch my breath. He bends over my back, reaching for a fistful of my breast, kneading my breast, swiping his tongue on my nimble earlobe, flicking his moist tongue in the hollow of my ear, ran his tongue slow on the outside rim of my ear, kiss the back of my ear, flicks his tongue in the hollow of my ear again, again, again and again. Every atom in my body awakes, gets so intensely sensitive that if his tongue touches me one more time I'll spring into the air like a frightened cat. He slowly, slowly - real slowly, licks in the hollow of my ear again. My knees buckle, quake uncontrollably, my nerves race wildly beneath my skin. I feel my pussy squinting, him painting his dick up and down, up and down my slit, desperately trying to find his way into my hole. The head of his cock feels too swollen, too stiff, too big to make it into my steaming cunt. He paints it up and down my slit again trying to enter, I can feel the heat his cock emanates, I feel it rubbing on my pussy, the head feels smooth, shine, he slides it down the mouth of my vagina and up again, down and up, up and down, his smooth flesh is above body heat, its pleasuring. I slowly close my eyes at the sweet erotic feel, enjoying the pleasures of his warm solidness rubbing on the most sensitive flesh between my legs, my pussy. I know it is warm and I can almost feel it already in me, like the entire length is in my vaginal canal, I'm feeling it. I'm feeling it there. I'm feeling it inside, I'm feeling his steel cock being pushed into my pink supple passage. My inside jumps, anticipating the pain, the pleasure of him grinding my pussy, wanting him to sink and lose his cock far inside me. Brace his cock deep and hard, with every muscle of his body. Fuck me out of my mind.

The Heart of Revenge

He stops squeezing my breast, lets go, spits on his fingers. I already feel tender. He rubs his spitty fingers up and down in my cunt, dipping two fingers into my wet hole, trying to help his horny self find his way in. I know my pussy is about to be crucified. But I think about my revenge and tense for the pain. I pout up my ass, close my eyes tight, bite my lips and hope this will feel like a more satisfying revenge. Maybe I shouldn't feel this terrible about this. I've never done anything like this before in my life. Today, the best day of my life is the worst day of my life, I'm dying inside as I listen the low chatting in the distance. It was Mommy's voice I heard the clearest.

He spreads both lips apart with two fingers, rest his stiffness right at the mouth of my hole. I felt his warm and sticky pre-cum from the tip of his dick mingling with the juices of my flood. He paints small teasing circles around my waiting vagina. His cock gently makes a smooth pressing feeling, circling round and around the rim of pussy, teasing me, my clit jumps. The circles he makes are a wet mix of both our juices, mostly mine, on the outside skin of my pussy and it sends the coldest shivers up my spine, he slaps his stiff shaft to the top of my pink then slides it down the center of the slit, my pussy jumps, tightens, walls squeezing together and collapses as he slowly centers and shoves his pelvis forward, sinking the head of his cock to enter me and it feels like the head of a child crowning out of a vagina, opening my tiny hole with a stretching pain that burns, I love it.

He pushes his huge head into me and my mouth gapes. He pulls it back, half-way out, I frightenly suck in a swift deep breath again, my belly went flat, my pussy and asshole flinching shut at the same time, a sudden contracting spasm skating through my whole body. He withdraws his purple head out my hole, and my pussy lips feels like it was lit by fiery lava, and my lips slowly re-shrink to a closed slit. But when he is deep between my flesh, the pain doesn't matter, just the pleasure. But what's more, is the revenge.

I want him to fuck me hard, fuck the life out of me till my pussy is soft and creamy. He slowly shoves his hugeness back into me and grinds his hip slowly down my flustered pussy. I gush air out my nostrils heavily, you can hear my loud, deep breathing over and over again. I cover my mouth with one hand, rest the other on the face-basin, my naked shaved body helplessly bend over to his cock, he works it in and out of my hole, the feeling let me lick my lip and clench tighter on the basin, he grinds steady into me and I feel my juices running already, oh God he feels so fucking good, so good, I don't want him to stop, just keep going, keep fucking me, right there, right fucking there, keep fucking my pussy. I see the door rattle. About to open. I stop moving. My heart drops into my belly.

I stare at the door. Where's my panty? I keep listening very carefully. Listen to who it was. Listen for the voice. No one.

I still don't make a move. Keep looking at the door.

Ok, I'm certain now, there's no one there.

I slowly rock my ass back to meet his strokes, still eyeing the door. I resume to the heat of the moment, rocking back more ravishingly, satisfying my heat, my horny hole, sliding my pussy along the thick length of his hard cock, satisfying myself with each push I push back down his veiny length, savouring in the unbelievably good feeling of it parting me, rubbing inside my pussy walls with unending care of anything around, just feeding my horny pussy with his cock, he is hitting deep beyond my walls and it vibrates a sensation to my swollen clit, making me into the River Nile, my pussy wet out of control, my teeth grits tight together, fist grabbing hard into the basin. I breathe heavier, louder, bite my lips hard. I push back harder faster on his dick, my tits bouncing, my flesh splashing into his groin and it turns me on even more, I want to scream from the unbearable pleasure, scream loud, let loose, scream his name out, but I can't. I'm in the bathroom, I press my hand harder over my mouth, bounce harder against his stiff hard cock, sliding back and forth on his pole, in and out. I want the all of it inside me, everything, all of it in me, my hand still grabbing my mouth, I screamed in a gagged voice filled with tiny orgasms,

"Oh FUCK! Oh Fuck! OHHH FUCK!" made a sound, an animal cry for his mercy, "Mmm! Aaarr!" Bite my lips hard. Push back harder on his dick, pushing back with brute force, biting my lips and shutting my eyes tight as I sink down all my weight and flesh into him, him deep into me, making sure my pussy crash hard against his groin and ram his entire cock the farthest it can into me. I bounce him one step back and he tenses himself, firm his stance, fingers dig into my round ass cheek, pulling the rosy flesh upward and my pussy feels pulled backward slightly, he grips my other ass cheek tight, turns it upward, I hear a noise in the hallway getting closer, I plunge down mindlessly on his cock. Two more strokes. The voice getting closer.

The sweet agony of fucking. He holds my waist, takes control, strokes slow, painful, unbelievably pleasurable with every thrust. Warm blood courses through my pussy, charges into my clit, my clit swollen as big as a butterfly as I feel the length of his thickness sliding up my quivering hole, filling it, stretching it, pleasing me. I want to ride off his cock, God I want to sit on it, ride it so hard I break it all off into my hole.

I look at the lock, let go my mouth and stretched my hand behind me, touching his rippled abs to make sure he fucked me quiet, slow, smooth but hard, fuck me hard. My other hand reaches behind me, he works his waistline sensually inside me, it hurts. And I pull him deeper into me, savagely; I want him far inside my hole, loving the feel of his warm cylinder of pleasure buried into my flesh. My face in the face-basin, my two hands pulling and pushing his waist into me hard and loud. His pants rubbing against my naked skin, his size doesn't matter anymore, I'm dripping wet, I want it deeper inside me, all of it. ALL OF IT. Everything. My feelings turn me into an animal, ecstasy brimming in me, I command him,

"FUCK ME! FUCK ME NATHAN! Good God! Fuck me!" He unbuckles his belt, drops his pants. He starts cannoning his cock at the speed of light, elated from the pleasures that he's ripping through my body, my body feels limp on the face-basin, eyes roll over, I feel every single nerve in my body opening up, he plunders my pussy, just like I want it, a sweet revengeful fuck. I'm swampy, soaking his black cock with my creamy fluids, all over it. The jingle of his buckle getting louder at his ankles, sweat running down is legs, his blue tie swinging from his rigorous thrusts behind me, pumping into me. I nab my mouth, stifling my whimpering as he hits that perfect spot, that spot, that sweet spot, good Lord, aaarrhh, I began spilling out my naughty desires, shouting low at him,

"FUCK IT NATHAN! FUCK! YES BABY! FUCK IT, FUCK IT! DON'T STO..." and a distant shout frightened the hell out of me,

"Leelia! Leelia! Which part you at gal!" I wanted to collapse.

CHAPTER 5

Busted Or Not?
by: Leelia Lexings

Jesus Christ! To hell if I was getting caught today. Hell to the no. The voice sounded like my big-loud mouth sister, Pinky. That would be the worst thing to ever happen right now. She couldn't hold down her voice no matter what. She was just always boisterous and brawling and BOTOO! I hoped it wasn't her. Please.

"Leeeee!"

The sound of Pinky's second shout terrified me like an alarm going off in a building and I'm the thief. My heart was thundering through my breast. Not now, this was not my intention, not to disgrace the Lexings name. Please God, no, everyone was here. Though Mommy would be the most understanding of the family, she would be the most hurt. I'm the youngest one, the wash-belly who should sort out this problem for the family, take care of my bigger brother according to the plan. Not be caught fucking in my Mom's bathroom on my wedding day. Without thinking about my pain and in a sudden rush, I tried to scamper to get my panty off the shower curtain rod quickly, but a sharp pain hit me, slowed me down, my knees bend. I limped. I fell to the white tile floor. The pain was at my leg, my shin bone, it still hurts.

Nathan was big and no doubt painful, but was nowhere close to the pain that returned to my shin. I was already used to the beating in my belly; which was where Qwan would always fist me, so luckily no one would see the bruises and scars the beatings left. I had a second fracture to my rib but never had he strike me anywhere else, it was always my belly he plundered. But lastnight he got in an uncontrollable rage.

Lastnight I couldn't move, I was too shocked, as he cannoned a new tin of condense milk at my face. I was in the living room and he sailed it from out the kitchen. As the tin sailed, flipped and spun through the air towards my face, it hit into the lowly hung chandelier, ricocheted, and smashed brutally into my slim shin bone. The unopened tin dented when it connected in my shin bone, chipping off my skin, bursting the flesh, swelling my shin instantly. I was happy the sailing tin of milk didn't hit me in the face; I imagined what it would have felt like. A brilliant degree of pain that wouldn't cool blasted in my shin; I lose my feet, collapse to the floor hard, tears instantly sliding down my face. I felt something warm running down my shin, I couldn't touch my shin but with watery eyes I saw red, my blood beginning to puddle on the floor.

All that pain, times two, wasn't hurting me half as much as what I felt when I caught Qwan doing the worst thing ever earlier that night. I could just die. Just fucking die.

Maybe if I don't answer Pinky she won't come inside the bathroom, or maybe if I shout *'I will be out in a minute'* she'd return to the living room where the rest of the family was. Fat chance! Pinky had not even a crumb of respect for privacy. No matter what, she'll be barging through this door any second. I glanced around at Nathan, pain still firing in my shin, whispering,

"Quick! ... Go inside the shower, quick."

Nathan hastened, pulling his pants up, stuffing down the tail of his white shirt down his pants in a panicky rush. Pulled up his zipper.

"Make haste Nathan, Make haste. Quick." I urged him.

The brisk steps of Pinky's heel thudding down the hallway sounded louder and louder as she came closer to bursting through the bathroom door. The sound 'clum... Clum ...CLUM!" got more terrifying, I could almost feel the door swinging open. Me getting caught. The beat of my heart was mighty. What the hell would I say? Caught by Pinky made it twelve times worse. Pinky hated my guts for getting the chance to live with Qwan Douglas in luxury, Stony Hills, uptown, while she starved in the ghetto, Tivoli, downtown. My heart was skipping beats like a scratch record, I knew how nasty this was going to be. No, I didn't hated Pinky, but she definitely hated me.

The calling was right at the bathroom door,

"Leeeee! You inside the bathroom?" Pinky was right infront the bathroom door, she raucously continued ontop of her big-mouth "You nervous till you can't stop pee-pee eeh gal." She burst out in a big mampy-sized laugh, "Or is constipated you constipated in there? ... PEPTO-BISMOLLL!!"

Pinky tested the lock, it was open. I saw the handle turning.

Fuck! My heart galloped. I pushed Nathan towards the shower, "Quick Nathan." Poor Nathan got confused, heading towards the face-basin. I pushed him the right way towards the shower. He tried to speak but stumbled over his words,

"But...bu-but –bu..." As he disappeared behind the shower curtain, from the help of me pushing. I dragged the shower curtain, hiding him.

'Boow!'

The bathroom's door blasted open, no knock, no finesse, no respect for privacy, the typical Pinky, what if I were on the toilet seat?

"Puss eye gal, what you inside here doing so? You never hear mi calling you?" I ignored her and tried to look calm. "How you look so nervous, like you belly taking you, you have running belly?"

My dress was a little twisted; I twisted it in place casually, not looking at Pinky, as if I weren't tormented by her barging intrusion, but obviously she was seeing some fluster on my face, at least that was what my guilty heart was pounding in my ears.

"Is you mi a talk to enuh Lee, you never hear mi a call you, you think a dog calling you?" She took one step closer to me, "You couldn't answer mi?" She was towering over me with her Eiffel-tower height. Her colourful tattooed hand akimboed waiting on a reply. I looked up, but not at her, to the mirror, examining my makeup,

"Yeah, but I was---"

"But what?" she asked sharply, without even waiting for me to finish, her long black false-eyelashes not even blinking.

"Was just wondering about this marriage, I don't know if I ---"

"Listen mi little ... spoil gal, a fifteen grand mi pay Ms. Merl to make mi dress and is not mi getting married ... You need to cut out you fuckery. You hear mi?"

What was she bickering about? Fifteen grand? My original ivory satin Chanel wedding dress costed two thousand five hundred US that's almost two hundred and fifteen thousand in Jamaican money. She continued to bicker

"You think money grow on tree?"

"But Pink ... I ..." As the pain stirred in my shin I could not speak straight, my face grimaced.

"Shut up enuh gal, you a get marri---" She stopped talking and popped her eyes open at an object on the face-basin.

"But wait! ... Is what this? ... Is the cameraman camera that?" her stare now piercing, eyelashes unblinking. I tried to hide my guilt, made a limpish turn facing her, looking into her questioning eyes,

"Yeah." I didn't realise that Nathan was trying to pick up his camera when I was shoving him to hide behind the curtain.

"What you doing with the camera?"

"I borrowed it."

"For what?"

"What you mean sis? What else? To take pictures?"

Pictures were there on the camera alright, but definitely not for my big mouth sister to see, no way, not Pinky at all.

"Show mi them."

I didn't move. She looked at me intensely, grabbed the camera off the basin, started pressing every button. My heart skipped ten beats with every button she pressed. She kept on pressing, determined to see the pictures.

"How mi turn on this?" She asked while her fingers busily experimented with pressing things on the camera that couldn't even be pressed. They not even buttons. Immediately I said,

"The batteries died on me ... That's why I stopped." She looked up from the screen of the camera, looked at me in concentration then as she seemed to find what she was looking for in my eyes she began pressing more buttons faster than a BB texter, and said,

"Is lie you telling, mi don't believe you." My heart raced up to my neck as I saw a green light blinked twice at the side of the camera. I yelled.

"Put it down! Because it more expensive than your dress, you can pay for it if you mash it up?"

She knew me well. She could sense I was lying, something I was hiding. The money bothered her, she put down the camera from whence it came.

"Mi hope you never fuck the picture man on your wedding day enuh gal."

"What you take mi for Pinky? Seriously. Mi can't believe you said that."

Even though she was right, I wanted her to feel guilty for jumping to a dirty presumption like that. I raised my voice to seem really hurt about it.

She looked back at the camera, grabbed it up. I yelled,

"Put down the frigging camera nuh!"

"Mi see one button that mi never try yet."

"Put it down!"

"How you getting so vex?"

She pressed the button. Nothing happened, pressed again, a red light blinked. Pressed again, nothing, continued, pressed again.

"Pinky put down the camera nuh! My God you persistent. Mash it up, mash it up, 'cause is that you want do."

She put back the camera down once more. I shook my head in disgust and vented,

"Sometimes I wonder if you really are my sister."

"If me and you a sister? You trying to say that you better than mi Lee? You think you better than people through you go College and live on hillside?"

Something turned inside me. Although I was sick and tired of this same argument, I was used to it because no matter what we talked about it always ended up here. Nothing new.

"No Pinky, why you always bring uptown into everything? Why you would even think that sluttish thing about your OWN sister?"

She didn't seem a bit perturbed about her presumptions. She answered with no emotions towards my feelings,

"'Cause that is how uptown gal stay... Think any of you easy?"

"Hug and kiss my ass Pinky! Just get the hell out the bathroom and don't let the damn door knob hit you on your way out. Hsst. You getting mi seriously upset with your stereotype thinking. The typical botoo behaviour, I can't expect anything better from you." I was pointing her to the door. "Not because I am getting married and you have two different baby father and none of them stayed, you jealous like ..."

"You don't hurt up your head 'bout mi an my babyfather, we is quite alright, ooh. What you must worry 'bout is your nasty dirty life you living. You and Aubrea is the same thing." It was as if Pinky was unloading some bad feelings from off her chest. "Mi can jealous of you? After you not better than me." She stepped closer as if she could just fist me right in my mouth and said,

"You only marrying Qwan for his money, sell you selling yourself, at least any man mi sleep with mi did love them ... not their MONEY."

I wasn't pissed. Pinky knew there was much more to the story, but her mind was bent one way and it made no sense even trying to teach her anything if Mom couldn't. Pinky thought I had a choice not to do it. I, on the other hand, knew I had to do it, Mommy knew and told me I had to do it and my brother life literally depended on it. I must marry today.

"So why you have a man if him can't help you in life? I prefer do what I have to than breed and suffer for some careless man that can't even find food for themself much less buy a pack of Huggies for the baby."

Since Pinky wasn't leaving, I stormed out the bathroom with a slight limp in my step trying not to let Pinky notice my bruised shin. Flashes of sex with Nathan brought back sensations in my belly, I wore a small smile, No one will know what had happened behind that bathroom door that swung to a close as Pinky trailed behind me like a chaperon. I pretended to be angry at her, you know, making it seem real, as if I cared what she said,

"It's my wedding day, can you at least be happy for me, at least once in your life?"

I marched briskly down the narrow baby blue corridor, the bedroom doors painted in white with gold doorknobs, then it flashed in my head, Oh Shit! I didn't take Nathan's BB pin.

Pinky's shout from behind frightened me out of my thoughts, "Sis! Sis! Stop! Wait, wait!" She had a shock sprawled out in her voice.

I turned a deaf ear to her. Kept bolting down towards the living-room where the rest of the family was chatting up an excitement over the wedding. I could barely feel the pain in my shin as I strode hurriedly. Pinky hastened her steps behind me, trying to catch up, caught up, she snatched my arm and tugged me to stop. I had no choice, she was bigger and stronger. I stopped in the corridor almost reaching the crowded living-room. It was so surprising, Pinky was whispering, very unlike her,

"Sis, what's that on your dress?" she was looking at the tail of my dress.

"I don't know. What you see?" I was worried for some strange reason but what the hell could she have seen? Pinky was trying to figure out what she saw, she spoke in a low tone,

"How that look like cum so much sis?"

Shit! I didn't wipe Nathan's cum off my gown. I baffled for the appropriate lie to tell,

"Huh? ... Nooo. What you talking 'bout?"

"Come here, make mi show you."

Pinky's strong hands pulled me closer, I pushed her hard, she grabbed me, I pushed her harder, she grabbed me tight, I could not move, she lifted the tail of my gown, I grabbed my gown out her hands and cursed at her,

"Why you don't just leave mi alone Pinky?" While I flashed my body in temper. I slightly slipped from her hand. She snatched high up on my arm, just below my arm-pit, got a more steady grip of me, rough and powerful, hauled me closer, squeezing my arm so tight it hurts, "It's none of your business, leave mi alone!"

"Leave mi bloodclawt."

"Is mi nose naught." That was the best lie I could come up with on the spot. She wasn't buying it.

Determined, she stuck her index finger in the substance, and with a swoop of her finger wiped some of the creamy substance on the pad of her finger tip. She rubbed the sticky substance between her index finger and her thumb, testing to find out if it's the real thing. She sniffed it, pulled it away from her face, wrinkled her face, questioning, smelled her fingers again. Her eyes widened and her mouth opened as if trying to swallow a football whole,

"Bloodclawt!..." I yanked the tail of my dress out of her hand, "Is cum this! ... How you say you never fuck the cameraman?" She gave a mix-up smile and burst out,

"Mi have to go call Raga 'bout this one here to rass!"

CHAPTER 6

Jacket Or Abortion
by: Leelia Lexings

I remained silent, still looking at the ground, pulling my gown out Pinky's hand. Mad at her, ashamed of myself, I wanted to bury myself under the earth out of shame. My tears about to mess up my makeup. My lips were trembling, hands were shaking, I was about to have a breakdown on my wedding day. Oh God please, don't let this happen to me, please. I was wrong and stupid, please, please forgive me. I know I was stupid, but I was so angry too, it just got the best of me. I really wanted to hurt back Qwan and I know how jealous he was. I know jealousy was the deepest hurt I could cause him and that's what I wanted, revenge. To hurt him back the worst way I knew how. But God, what I did was so stupid. So stupid. The tears trickled out my eyes and unto my face. I stood there silent, crying, wishing I hadn't. I could not answer sis, nor could I look at her. She will desecrate me with her vandalising mouth, cast an unending spectacle and shame.

Pinky whispered,

"Come sis, make we go clean it off before nobody see it."

Not what I expected from her. I budged, then stopped, stood still in my tracks. I didn't want to go back into the bathroom where Nathan was. I didn't want to make situations more uncomfortable with the three of us in the bathroom, and there's no telling what Pinky might do in there to Nathan. She's so unpredictable. But I had nowhere else to go. Everywhere else was too lively with family. We hurried back to the bathroom, she held my hand, we reached the door.

"Leelia! Leelia! Lee!" Mommy's voice strained from the livingroom and echoed down the corridor to us. I stopped, turned towards the livingroom.

"She soon come!" Pinky replied for me, pushing me forward towards the bathroom door. We both pushed the door open, walked through it. I was greeted by a hint of sex smelling in the air. Or, maybe, I was only too conscious that I just had sex in here. There was no Nathan. He must have snuck out. Pinky still insisted to look around, peeping under the sink as she called out,

"Pictureman! Pictureman!" walking and searching. She pulled away the blue and yellow shower curtain as if she expected him to be hiding somewhere in the bathroom.

Pinky's eyes grew pattoo-wide, her jawbones dropped and she blurted out,

"Cocka-clawt! Jesus Christ Pictureman, what a rass hood BIG!" She couldn't take her lusting eyes off his penis, "No sir, Almighty, you bless." Nathan got uncomfortable in his skin. Pinky continued to lust, "God know, you bless."

Nathan remained standing in the shower, one hand behind his leg, trying to hide the piece of tissue he was using to wipe off the head of his penis. Pinky suddenly spoke from an angry place.

"Hope you never cum in mi sister enuh pictureman!"

Nathan looked at me before raising his voice at Pinky

"Stop call mi pictureman! Mi is not no pictureman!" His voice got sterner, "Pictureman take picture on mall and sidewalk. Is mall this?" He asked Pinky with his eyebrows muscled up "Mi a photographer. A professional photographer."

Pinky walked up to him, her fluffy bosom in his forehead, she looked at his dick, mouth almost watering, grabbed it and tugged it, almost pulling it down to his knee, asking Nathan

"You love fuck people wife?" The sex look roaring in Pinky's eyes, "You suck pussy, pictureman?" and she dipped her hand under her skirt to take off her panty. Nathan's eyes were lusting at Pinky's curvaceous shape as he nodded his head yes, up and down, mouth near drooling as if he were frightened for Pinky's brown skin or to eat brown skin vajay-jay. Her brown skin didn't make hers any better than mine. I folded my hand, watching Pinky.

Pinky stepped out her white panty. My eyes got pregnant with disbelief. O.M.G. My sister about to have sex with the man I just had sex with minutes ago, right infront of me, on my wedding day, in the bathroom, with Mommy in the livingroom. Like seriously? What a shock. What an eventful day. I mean, this was so not like Pinky. She wasn't even a cheater; she just not the type. I had no idea a cock could turn on someone that much. Was that even possible? Evidently it was.

She held her panty up in the air above her head and Nathan gazed at it held high in her hand. She swung her panty down mightily. Slapping him right in his face almost blinding the short man. She lashed him in his face three more times powerfully as she instructed him,

"Go suck your woman then and leave mi little sister! Big hood pictureman!"

Nathan stuffed his dick in his pants, tucked his camera under his arm and scrammed through the bathroom door like a coward mongrel, without looking behind him, tail between his legs.

"Watch the little coward." She smiled. I chuckled too. She turned to me and said "You good still enuh Lee, you so mawga, how you take that big thing?" A ridiculing smile curved the corner of her lips, "No, mi rate you little gal."

I was still a tiddy bit embarrassed. I looked groundward, staring at Pinky's leg. Her dress was the shortest of everyone in the bridal party, I stared at the green, red and yellow tattoo on her leg. It was big enough to hide an awful scar she had got when she was a baby. She was still embarrassed when anyone stared at her scar, even though the tattoo was hiding it. She walked towards me,

"Come let mi help wipe off your dress." I waltzed over to the facebasin and lifted up the tail of my gown. Pinky went to the toilet bowl and reeled tissue around and around her four fingers as if wrapping a sprain injury re-enforcingly with bandage. She placed her other hand on the tissue to stop it from spinning in the holder, the amount of tissue around her four fingers looked like half of the roll. She popped the reel and shoved the bulk of tissue from around her four fingers, then squeezed it into a ball in her palm. My eyes were shouting, I asked,

"Where you going with so much tissue?"

"Nuh must to wipe off the cum, mi don't want none of that touch mi hand."

Pinky waddled over to the face basin where I was, her big round bumper rolling to a beat. She barely turned the knob of the pipe so the water only leaked from the pipe's mouth. She placed the white ball of tissue under the dripping pipe. She didn't let it stay there a second before she pulled it back from under the pipe. She turned the knob till the water stopped running, she continued to turn the knob, more than tight, almost breaking off the thingy. I asked her,

"You gone spoil the pipe?"

"With what?'

"Why you turning it so much for? You never needed to wet the tissue enuh."

"Is cum stain, not because it white now, if you just wipe it off alone and don't wet it, it will leave one brown stain round the edge when it dry up. You never know that?"

I had no idea that would happen. It's not like they taught you these essential chemical reactions in chemistry class - what would happen if cum dried up on your white clothes. They may need to add it to the syllabus I joked to myself before answering,

"Yeah. Of course I knew that, my mind just wasn't thinking about that now."

"You mind never a think none at all today, is like you turn idiot."

"Which idiot?"

"You never 'fraid you catch one pretty little disease name AIDS?" She eyed me with a weenie bit of temper and a huge hunk of how-can-you-be-so stupid-gal, "You never use a condom sis, is carelessness that enuh, suppose you all end up breed for the pictureman?"

"Why you have to think the worst? Nothing can't happen because I still have two safe days."

Pinky held her palm upturned and opened with the gown spread over her palm. Biting her bottom lip as she rubbed the tissue in small circles on the cum-spot. She released her lip,

"Then what if you get pregnant still? That can happen. What you would do?" She turned her eyeball at me, "Give Qwan the child that is not his own? Give Qwan a *jacket*?"

I looked at my reflection in the mirror. Brushed a few strands of my hair neatly back in place from off my forehead. I stuck my thump in my mouth. Pinky's look hardened at me,

"Take your nasty finger out of your mouth and answer mi. You just done fuck and you just throw your dirty finger in your mouth like is nothing. Take it out man." I took out my thumb.

"Wouldn't give him any jacket. Mi wouldn't give him the baby."

Pinky ceased rubbing and with a bewildered gaze asked,

"You cold eeh man? After you married, you'd really tell him you breeding for a next man? What would happen to our brother?"

Pinky was smart and usually caught on to things quickly. I thought she would've read between the lines already. I tried to avoid the argument 'cause she just wouldn't understand my point anyway.

"My face needs a little touch up, a little face powder, don't?" I angled my face in the mirror, "You can apply some for me sis?"

"You mean, you taking contraceptive then? Pearl or injection?" Pinky was chatting casually, I should have just agreed and said, 'yes pearl'. Or even the injection, any of them, but instead I stepped on thin ice and said

"No, those things bloat mi up and let mi put on too much weight."

The green veins in Pinky's hand rose as she muscled to crack back the pipe knob she had tightened. She wet the tissue again, then rubbed circles in a new spot on the gown close to the first one. I said to myself. 'Is so much juice Nathan let go. Damn! It doesn't look like he wasn't getting any chunny.' Pinky replied to my earlier comment,

"Me too. Alright, you remember when mi did start put on a whole heap a weight after mi did have Dushawn?"

"Mhmm."

"Is because mi did start take the pearl contraceptive and it was swelling mi up like bull cow. Mi did a look too awful , so mi just done with the contraceptive thing. So ..." She took a second to ponder, then continued, "What you would do if you breed for the pictureman then?"

I looked through my reflection in the mirror for a moment and contemplated before I spoke the truth,

"I wouldn't carry it."

Pinky stopped the rubbing, looked at me with a perplexed forehead above her cringed eyes. I kept my head straight, looking pass my reflection in the mirror and looking at Pinky's befuddled expression in the mirror as she studied my words.

"You would dash away the belly? Abortion?" Pinky spat in the sink and turned on the pipe to wash it down. Maybe she was disgusted at me, I don't know, or maybe ....

"Pinky don't tell me you pregnant again! How you can spit so much?"

My gaze darted to her tummy. It wasn't high, it seemed normal. She wasn't pregnant. Was she? Then again, if Pinky really pregnant again. At this point of her life. For a third baby father. She doesn't have any ambition. Why carry the child and spoil her life? She should've aborted her pregnancy from the first time she got pregnant. Like seriously, what Pinky needed to do right now is try to get back on her feet, before she goes back to breeding. Pinky too damn fertile.

"You too inquisitive. And what wrong if mi breeding?" She took a second to consider what to say to me, her next sentence came out slow, "No mi not breeding. Answer mi question. You would do abortion?"

"Then what else you expect mi to do? Mi not even finish college yet. How can I go have a child now?"

"Carry the baby! ... After is not the baby tell you to go take man and go breed." Her brows knitted tighter, "So how you turn 'round want to kill the little baby for your mistake?"

"Mi not spoiling my life to have baby, that can wait. I have a plan for my life and I'm not making through pregnancy I end up being somewhere in life I never planned for... Not when I can do something 'bout it." I remembered Mom's advice and repeated it to Pinky, "Sometimes doing something good is doing the lesser evil."

"The baby is your life. What spoil life you talking 'bout? Anyway your life turn out with the baby, is same so God write your life. You can plan your route in life but God decide your destination." She got harsh, "God wouldn't make you breed if him never plan it."

I snapped around sharply to face her, my motion dragged the hem of the gown, it slid over her palm and right out her hand.

"God wouldn't let me abort it if he didn't plan it! My voice was louder than hers."Mi plan my life and mi not making what happen to YOU come and happen to ME."

"Mi proud of my two youth them. Mi don't shame."

"What about stretch marks?"

"After mi don't have none, look how mi belly still pretty. And even if mi did have, that is nothing to be ashamed about. That natural."

"Still think you have them too early. What if you did stick to your plan to be a lawyer and never make baby spoil the picture, is not like you did dunce at school. If you did give your life a shot at education I'm sure you would find away to hustle the money for college. Right now you would be a lawyer. But instead, look how your life hard now." Pinky was thinking deeply, near meditating, she knew I was speaking the truth, as I mouthed to her, "Things could be better Pinky, trust mi. Just with one surgery."

"Your brain must be spoiling inside your head. You mad my girl? Mi can't imagine my life without Perry and Dushawn. Is mi heartbeat them. Mi couldn't have the heart to do that. Look how much woman have abortion and can't breed after. Them sorry. Mi not running them risk to come condemn my womb. Look how mi two son them sweet."

"Well, if you waited till after college you babies would still look sweet. Look how you brown."

"You love talk 'bout brown eeh. You prejudice?" Pinky looked in the mirror and straightened the bosom of her dress. Of course I would love my baby to have pretty hair and pretty brown complexion, but I couldn't have said that to Pinky. She would've said I was too prejudice. Not saying I wouldn't want a black baby, if so be the case then fine, I would love him just the same. But if I had a choice, I would pick the pretty hair, just like Mommy picked Dad. Pinky was still chatting, "At least no gal can't call mi belly cemetery, or call mi skull in a belly." She looked away from the mirror, I remembered Mom saying, 'Gossip are words of wind and can only hurt you if you let it.' I couldn't care less what others may say. Pinky's hand froze at her bosom, her unmoving face asked, "You ever do it yet?"

There was a short delay before I returned an answer.

"No sis. But if Nathan get mi pregnant mi not carrying it at all. Nathan not even have nothing. Look how you a suffer because you breed for men that have nothing. Sorry, I don't want that life, mi love myself too much for that."

"Mi will badger-badger with them. If Father God never want mi have no youth, him wouldn't bless mi with them." The air of contention between us was stiff. She'd not let go her dumb point. Always hard-headed, stubborn and persistent. I got fed up, blew a small fuse.

"That's STUPID! Hsst. You responsible for your actions in life, not God, and first of all God don't even support sex before marriage, so why him would plan to have you breed two time outside marriage? Eeh?" Pinky couldn't answer my question, she just blankly stared, like a dumb cow. "We are all accountable for where our life go based on our decisions and actions, we are responsible to correct our wrongs. If it's a mistake like with Nathan. I would deal with it. Plain and simple."

"Who you calling stupid? You go church more than mi, don't you know it's a sin? Thou shall not kill! And if there was a eleventh commandment it would be, Thou shall not dash away belly. Cause it wrong."

"Well, if you get pregnant again. Now. In this hard stage of your life and carry the baby you not stupid, you is a frigging IDIOT! .... What you want in life? Better? Or Bitter? Pick."

Silence. Pinky's mouth came to a rare standstill and desisted from speaking, briefly. She fell back into deep thoughts, reflecting perhaps, or absorbing what I had said, finally getting it through to her tough skull. Pinky choose her words carefully as she spoke unusually slow and weak,

"Aubrea did have it hard." She paused for a breath, her voice soft as a lover's voice across from you on the next pillow, she looked into my eyes, her eyes filled with genuine emotions and asked,

"What if Aubrea did abort you?"

We both went silent. I could hear Pinky's breathing. The dripping of the water from the pipe sounded like God's clock ticking. Drip ... drip ... drip.

Pinky slowly took the tail of my gown and softly brushed away the rolly remains of the wet tissue off the gown. Drip ... drip ... drip.

"Lee! Lee!" the shout was coming from the living room. I felt like I lost control of my bodily functions because I am sure as tax, Pinky gonna make this extra when she's informing to Mom.

Drip ... drip ... drip.

CHAPTER 7

Daddy Wishes Son Dirt
by: Qwan Douglas

"A Limo at the gate Mr. Douglas." Our security, Mr. Willie, said over the inter-com. Dad replied.

"Let him in Willie."

Willie did, and my best-man, Carl, walked from beside me, heading out of the downstairs' hall we were in and to the Limo driver outside. I was in full white with a pink tie, nervous but ready, my pants the exact length it should be. I never thought I would ever have a woman propose to me, but Leelia loved me so much that she did. She knelt on one knee and proposed to me in front of everyone in the crowd. Dad stood at one end of the elongate-shaped table and I stood at the other end. He had to lift his voice in order to reach my ears because of the distance that we stood apart from each other.

"Qwan, you sure you want to go through with this, huh?"

"How many times you gonna ask mi the same question Dad?"

It took Carl two hefty pulls to open the entry door. It was a heavy Honduran custom-made door carved from mahogany wood. It was stained in cherry to compliment the emerald tinted, decorative glass panels in the center, accented with gold strips all the way around. Carl pulled with too much strength the second try and the door swung wide open. The white stretch Limo was just pulling up by our semi-circular layered steps. The white marble column to the left blocked my view of the driver's door, I could only see the middle portion. The windows were tinted jet black and even the tyres were glistening. I walked off from the table to the door, after about twenty steps I had reached the other end of the table where Dad was standing. He grabbed my hand and pulled it, shifting my jacket sleeve out of place and squeezing my watch. He had a dead serious stare and he kept his stare dead into my eyes.

"Put it this way then Qwan, you must NOT marry that girl."

I yanked my hand out of his.

"If you don't have anything good to say then just don't. Why you not happy for me?"

"You just think about what you doing before you make this big mistake, I'm telling you. What about Shamelle huh? She's a nice girl. She loves ya." I began straightening the sleeve of my Jacket,

"Made up my mind, love it or hate it, I'm marrying Lee. She's the one for me."

"Shamelle is a better girl, listen to your father, mi know things."

Carl came back through the door to ask me,

"You ready Q?"

"Not yet, just give mi a minute." Carl pulled out the white rag he has been pat-drying my sweat with, he flagged it out and looked as if he wanted to come over to see if I needed it. He budged forward but stopped, stared, recognised an unpleasant tension between father and son and said,

"Cool, cool, hurry though, is soon time and you suppose to reach before the bride remember." Carl went back out, glanced over his shoulder with a doubtful expression.

"I can't understand what's the big deal. Why you acting so strange since I told you I'm marrying Lee? Look, it doesn't change anything. We basically married anyway, look how long we living together, why it's a problem all of a sudden if we get married?"

"You don't know the half, just take mi foolish advice and don't marry that girl if you know what's good for you."

"I love her. She's the one I love, she never cheated and despite the games you played lastnight to have her not marry me, she still wants to marry me. How many women would still stick by their man's side after lastnight? How many women would turn around and still marry me the next day. How many?" My neck began to perspire and I needed Carl with the rag.

"Get this straight Qwan, she don't wants you, you hear mi?"

"She's marrying me Dad, me. Are you jealous? Is that it, I see the way you look at her, you think I don't know what you are up to, you think everything's a secret? It'll will never happen, NEVER! Not while I still have breath."

"Watch your fucking tongue boy. You think mi and you's size."

"Watch your tongue old man."

"So you think you're a big shot now huh? Can't hear, then you must feel, remember mi did warn you."

"Why now? Why you didn't have a problem from six years ago when you took her to the house? Why now?"

"Listen, I'm your father. You think I want anything bad to happen to you? You don't know what happened why Leelia stayed at our house. You marrying her was not a part of the plan."

"Plan? What plan?"

"Her mother is a little ..., she ripped me off, the deal was to --- "

Carl barged through the door and interrupted.

"Yow, wrap that up nuh, time going enuh, you have to leave out now."

I shot back at Carl.

"What's the damn problem? You deaf? You don't hear mi say mi soon come?"

Carl held his head down like a shame puppy and walked back through the door.

"Just listen to mi son. I know her mother good, and she's just like her mother. No different. She is nothing but a whoring ghetto slut. She's all about your money, not you. They are thieves and they'll do anything for money."

What if... Hold on, I have been giving Leelia a lot of money recently, but ... then again, I am her man, her fiancé right? Who else she should have turned to for help? And if I can help her, why not? She's my other half. It's not like she spending the money doing crap, she going school, even though I suggested paying her school fee, so that don't even count, but Dad have a point that ... Hsst ... something's in something.

"I'll give her anything I damn well please, anything she wants. That's love. You wouldn't understand that now, would you? And just so you know, I know what you did with Shamelle, and I know you must have tried it with Lee and it didn't work why you hate her so much and telling all manner of lies on my wife."

"I swear, I've never made a move at Lee and just so YOU know, Shamelle's the one who came on to me."

"Either way, she is a bitch. And you want me to marry her? You disgust mi."

"If you marry that slut then you'll see disgust."

"I'm marrying Leelia and nothing in this world will change that."

"Then you'll have to get out my house."

"I'll pack tomorrow."

I turned my back. Walked off.

"SON!" I stopped stepping, turned around. "Listen, you can stay here, but I'm telling you, she's real bad news. Crosses ontop of crosses ontop of of crosses. Don't marry that little slut."

"She's no SLUT! She's my woman, my wife, try to understand that. She'll be the mother of my kids, take it or leave it, nothing's going to change that. Now, you don't have to come to my wedding now, do you?"

Silence.

"How's it going to look if I don't go to my son's wedding ... It's going to look too bad."

"Don't worry about what people say, they already saying much worse things about you."

"Like what?"

"Whatever you gave them to say."

"It's Ok, it's Ok, I'll be there. Can't say mi never warn you. It's her mother setting her up to run all kind of game on you. For your money."

"BYE!"

I didn't look back. The happiest day of my life, worst morning ever. Dad just stood still, he was statued because it's my first time talking back at him so hard, not backing down and disregarding blatantly what he ordered me to do. And it's all over one girl. Lee. I slammed the heavy door behind me. Carl swung open the limousine's back door. Can't help but to think that there's something more to this puzzle, something I'm missing, what if Dad's right? What if I shouldn't marry Lee? What if it's a huge mistake? But deep down in me, my gut feeling tells me it's something personal, some vendetta or something, maybe something personal between him and Lee's mother, or is it jealousy? I bent my head down, put one hand down on the cushiony white leather seat as I climbed into the limo. Sat. Tugged on the lapels of my jacket, Carl stared at me but didn't ask any questions. It was obvious I was furious and chit chat wasn't particularly timely now. I looked away from him. The limo drove by the fountain, I stared at the running water sprouting up from the mouth of the fish statue in the middle of the fountain and thought, a deal gone sour maybe?

Jealousy, deal, vendetta? I pondered them all as I signalled back a hail to Mr. Willie. We drove through the wide iron gate. Which one could it be, One? Or two? All?

Jealousy? A deal? Vendetta?

What plan was dad talking about by the way?

CHAPTER 8

Death, His Final Supper, Served As a Hearty Breakfast
by: Leelia Lexings

Breakfast. Mommy was through frying up some saltfish frittas with the eskellion and blackpepper in it, alongside some frankfurters, some boiled green bananas and liver and she also made some peppermint tea.

"Who's going to take the pictures?" Mommy was waving the silver camera in the air, anticipating a stampede from us to snatch the camera out her slim feminine fingers. No one budged. No one did as much as even shift the black of their eyes to the camera.

She looked both sides, turned, her eyes searched behind her, not seeing who she wanted she gave out,

"Vance .... Vance .... Where's Vance?"

Ms. Merl full-eyed little baby girl, Loriel, zoomed by me. I could've swore I saw a pink wind tailing off her little white dress at the speed she ran by. The pink high-waistband was untied and blowing behind the bubbly little doll as she zig-zagged between everyone and around the furniture in the livingroom. She was giggling at the playful Lassy chasing right behind her. Lassy's fluffy black tail and long-furred ears was blowing and his tongue out to the side as he chased her. Jason, Qwan's little cousin, was the third in line, chasing behind Lassy. Loriel would be the flowers girl, she was like family. We told everyone she was our little cousin because she spent most of her time over by our house, mostly with Vance.

Pinky answered Mommy.

"Him must still be over the old woman yard."

"Ms. Merl still? But everybody ready, what's wrong with that boy, him not getting ready?"

"Mi you asking?" Pinky sounded dry and rhetorical. Mommy turned her mouth towards the window, bellowed,

"Vaaance! Vaaance!"

"Yes Mom! Coming." came sounding from the distance next door.

The Heart of Revenge

" Come get ready now."

"Coming Mom."

"Stop the coming and come."

Vance jogged through the door within the next blink, no shirt, broad flat chest, sweat running over his dark nipples onto his light brown skin. His hands so big, they looked like two claws detached from plough tractors and attached to his shoulders. Both his hands caked with mud up to his wrist, looking like the ugliest pair of gloves, something only Mr. Death would wear when taking your life too early. Death was on his hands.

Pinky burst out laughing,

"Is farm work you doing now Pops?"

"No, mi just helping Ms. Merl with her flowers."

'Again? That can't wait?" Mommy interrupted, "You forget today is your sister wedding?"

"Yeah mi remember but mi just helping her with the new garden fence, since mi done did promise her already."

Mommy's phone rang and the vibration made a humming 'bbbbrrr' sound on the wooden table top as it danced.

(((Rrring. Rrring.)))

(((Rrring. Rrring.)))

She quickly snatched up her phone to catch the call, in too much haste, shifting and crumpling the burgundy tablecloth. She looked at the caller ID, thought twice. With her eyes fixed on the phone screen, her thumb crept slowly to rejecting the call. She carefully placed the phone back on the table, looked up, switching looks at me, Daddy and then Pinky without moving her head, only shifted her eyes side to side then looked away from everyone, avoiding eye contact, lowered back her head down to the table, kept it there, her face looked lost, her thoughts way out of this timezone. Worried perhaps.

Loriel zoomed from around the corner, giggling, one of her dolly-like hand holding the tail of her dress. She heard Vance's voice and made an instant U-turn in the middle of the livingroom, she is slightly tilted forward while running towards Vance, looking as if she's about to stumble forward on her face. She was chuckling, Lassy chasing close behind her, Jason behind Lassy. In her baby talk she said 'Uncle Vance' but it came out as,

"Hunko Vance, Hunko Vance." She charged towards Vance with his mud covered hands, in her pretty white dress.

Her baby smile brought smile to everyone's face, her tiny arms wide open to hug around Vance's long legs, her chubby cheeks squashing against his knees, eyes closed, giggling

"Hunko, hunko" squeezing his legs tight and wouldn't let go.

Vance bent to lift her up. Mom phone rang again, she grabbed up the phone and yelled at Vance

"No! No Vance, your hands." He froze half-way bending to pick up Loriel then straightened back up. Mom put her phone under the table, looked at the caller Id. Rejected the call.

"Hey Lorie baby," Vance said looking down on her flowy hair which would be dancing at her shoulders if it weren't bunched up in a bun today and tied with a pink ribbon. The ribbon matched the high waistband around her white dress. Lassy was in a playful mood and wouldn't leave from behind her, he snuffed and nudged at her back, panting impatiently, kind of signalling, *'Hey let's go, let go of his leg and let's go play, come on, come on, run'*. She paid Lassy no mind, giggling and baby-talking to Vance,

"Wif mi up Hunko, wif mi up, tehehe."

"Can't lift you up now baby, mi hands dirty." Lassy urged her to run and play with a single bark, that caused Mom to jerk. She looked suspiciously around. Lassy nudged Loriel with his wet nose. She slapped Lassy on top of his head and shoots off, giggling in a high pitched voice. Lassy sprang off in a happy chase behind her. Jason followed Lassy grabbing at his shiny black tail. Mom's phone rang again.

(((Rrring. Rrring.)))

(((Rrring. Rrring.)))

Mommy stared at Pinky. Pinky wasn't looking at her, she was looking at Vance. Mommy looked back at her phone, rejected the call. Planted the phone in between her lap under the table and began typing a text. Pinky laughed out as she watched Vance and Loriel in adulation,

"No man! Sure that little girl not yours? Is how she love you so much man?"

It sounded like a compliment. Children seemed to just love Vance, Loriel was one of them, but obviously by the dirty eyes and the tension in Vance's hardened look at Pinky, you could tell Vance took it as an offense. He assumed she was throwing an insult at him, by saying he'd sleep with the old woman, Ms. Merl, next-door. Which to me, by the way, would still be better than him being a twenty-one year old virgin. I waltzed over to take a chair beside Mommy, her phone dinged as a text came in to reply to hers. She read it and was replying to it while she replied to Pinky also,

"I don't know why every little children round the place love him off so much."

Pinky wasn't talking to Mommy. She rolled her eye at Mom, turned her back and walked straight out of the room while Mommy was talking to her. Mommy turned her head to Pinky walking out and called out to her,

"Pinky, remember we taking some picture now, don't leave yet."

Pinky didn't stop walking nor did she looked back at Mom, but she did look back at me and with a mischievous laugh she replied,

"Mi don't want take not a picture .. ask the one beside you, 'cause it look like she love take picture." She did her mix-up laugh, a big deep belly laugh "Wooii," and trailed off adding, "Mi gone pee-pee."

Loriel's giggling could be heard in the distance. Vance looked at me with a scrunched forehead, I could see his brain muscling, trying to figure out what Pinky meant by that. He knew Pinky meant something more from her laugh and gesture. Mommy turned and she too knitted her forehead at me. She knew I hated pictures. So what was Pinky talking about? Mommy put her phone down on the table. I looked away from everyone and gazed at my black shadow that was on the table. The light from Mom's phone was fading to black, fading, fading until the light disappeared and her phone returned to black. The light in my shame also went out.

I felt squeezed, the room felt tight around me, Mommy asked.

"When since you love take picture?"

The outside roof of my nose tip was spotted with tiny round sweats and my palms were getting wetter. I answered.

"Me?... Me? ... I. I don't."

"So what Pinky talking 'bout?"

"I'm clueless. Pinky just love chat." Pinky's voice excitedly bellowed from all the way down the hallway.

"Mi body! RAAAEE!!"

Mommy turned both eyebrows inward at me. Afterward, she relaxed her face, gently placed one hand over mine, her other hand wiping the sweat off my nose,

"You really nervous eeh honey?"

"Yeah. Today is really big."

"You know you have to pull through with this right? You know this is the only way."

"Don't worry Mom." I took a short thought about things, then comforted her. "I know. You stop worry. Ok?"

"I'm not worrying. Just remember you doing the right thing, OK?" She squeezed my hand and looked toward Vance. I knew how important it was to Vance. I had the urge to wipe my sweating palms on the side of my gown but I didn't want to wrinkle it, I wanted my dress to remain looking neat. Vance used one muddy finger to scratch at the liverspot on his shoulder and Mom said,

"Vance everyday you helping this lady with garden, you can't be working out yourself so much for people like an idiot enuh. She paying you?"

"No. But she's old Mom. What's wrong with helping her?"

Mommy would do anything in the world to help her children, herself and whoever she cared about, but everyone else she didn't give jack-shit about. She hated to see any of us giving away anything. That's the only thing about Mommy that irritated me. I butted in,

"Nothing's wrong with him helping out the little old lady, leave him alone."

"Is something she looking from a young boy. From her husband dead she just take a set on Vance so, is like every damn day she have work giving him to do."

Vance stared at Mommy with some amazement at how cold her comment was. Mommy wasn't fazed by his glare at her, continued in a nonchalant tone,

"You can stay there looking at mi. You better mind you give her what she looking for. She so old you might give her heart attack same time too."

Immediately, Vance face saddened, as if a ghost had drained all the joy out his face. He heard the word heart attack and it triggered an alarm button in him about his terminal heart condition. He would probably die soon. He looked away from his mother, bowed his head down and used one muddy hand to slowly wipe the other muddy hand.

I felt sorry for him. I felt my eyes quivering in their sockets. I wanted to cry. If I could give him my heart I would in the blink of an eye. I would do anything to save his life. In February when he got his worst attack ever, I had to pay Dr. Reid four thousand U.S. Dollars that I didn't have, well actually it was Qwan's money but whichever way you looked at it, it's still a lot of money, especially since Qwan had just paid my tuition and in the next two months my tuition is due again for the new school year again.

Its eating me alive to know that after marrying him, I have to ask him not for an additional four thousand U.S. for Vance's medication next year., but for forty thousand US for Vance's surgery. I felt like I was using him, just an opportunist and I didn't want to use anyone, especially since Qwan had been there for me since I was fourteen. I'm marrying him for the wrong reason. I didn't want to marry for the sake of getting his money. I didn't want to use him. But I needed to get forty thousand US for Vance. I had no choice. I looked at Vance and my eyes got wet, I tried to steady my voice and liven up Vance,

"Vance come on man, you're living, you OK, you not gonna die, stop acting like you dead already. Cheer up man."

The pain wasn't well hidden underneath my awkward smile that I tried to fake. Vance could see the pain, the worry, the uncertainty of living. He was looking at me but not seeing me. He was in a deep and reflective zone.

"How mi must smile? I'm dying in less than a year." His tone went down. "How you would feel?" His muddy hands, with palm stretched to me, begging me to answer, "How? Put yourself in my shoes, how?" An ugly dropping of mud fell from his hand to the floor. Mom, Vance and I stared at the brown splat that fell. No smile. Just stared. In pain. Hurting.

My heart moved, the tears came running down my face. The silence in the room seemed to stand there for a year. I finally broke the silence.

"Everything's gonna be OK after today," Stifling my cry, I stumbled over the word, I. "I...I ...I" deep inhale, gathered myself "I talk with ... with Dr. Reid. Arranged everything already .... Everything's gonna be OK. I'm certain." I promised him.

Lying. I was lying. I wasn't certain things were going to be OK. I felt a heavy weight on my shoulders. I had to marry Qwan for my brother, but I wasn't certain how things would work out, I just wasn't.

Vance's reply was unexpected. It came as a humungous shock to me and probably to everyone else too.

CHAPTER 9

Vance Has A Big Heart
by: Leelia Lexings

When Vance was twelve he was a lively twelve year old. In the month of March, when Vance had turned twelve, he didn't get the royal blue and white BMX bicycle that he wanted for his birthday. But, he did get a bright-yellow and black, handheld textris videogame. He'd never put down his birthday game even if the house was alighted on fire and he was trapped in the middle of the blaze. He'd play with his bright-yellow game all day and even late at nights we would still hear the videogame sounds after Mom shouted,

"Put down the game and go to your bed nuh little boy!"

His face would be stuck in the game in total concentration playing to beat his last highest score all the way till the small hours of the morning. He had the proudest smile that shone on a young child's face whenever he made a new high score – *his joy – his complete happiness*. Also that March, Mom found out that he had a heart that would kill him. He would be dead before he was thirty-six. She cried so much tears, she soaked the bosom of her blouse straight through. You could wring her eye water out of her blouse. She held the news, contemplated for seven days if she should say it to Vance or not. He was the happiest child on earth. She had a hard time getting enough strength and courage to tell her twelve year old son his heart was going to kill him. She cried while telling him and later that evening she cursed Dad for two hours straight. She was crying her eyes out while she cursed him for turning up the TV too loud. Vance didn't cry when he got the news and he didn't smile either. He never played his game that night, the day after nor ever *again – his joy – his complete mourn*.

What's happening with his heart was that his heart muscles were overgrown. It's growing too fast, getting bigger than it should normally be and if he didn't get a surgery to cut away the excess muscle-growth from his heart then the upper and lower ventricles would grow too big and completely cut off his blood circulation to and from his heart. His heart condition is known as cardiomyopia but Vance simply called it an overgrown heart or the red hearse in his chest.

Dr. Reid quoted the cost of his surgery in U.S. dollars. It was nineteen thousand U.S. dollars and he needed to get an ICD (Implantable Cardioverter Defibrillator) which would help to regulate his heartbeat. The ICD would use electrical shocks to slows down his heart when it went too fast and speeded it up when it went too slow. Basically, keeping it at a normal pace and preventing sudden cardio attacks that persons with his heart condition were prone to having. But more importantly, the sooner he got one of these ICD implanted the longer he may live. The cost to have the ICD surgically placed in his chest, was twelve thousand U.S. dollars. A total of thirty-one thousand U.S. dollars. Mom didn't have ten thousand Jamaican dollars in her account and her U.S account was closed with a small balance that was on the minus side after the bank deducted its maintenance charges. Dad had less money than Mom.

Vance's heart was big in other ways too. Despite the fact that he would be dying the same age as Jesus Christ, but without the resurrection, he always smiled. Whether it was to hide his pain and concern from everyone or it was genuine, only he could tell.

Vance spent most of his time on non-strenuous activities such as at the Help the Youths Club (H.Y.C.), and in the garden next door that Ms. Merl had. He seemed to get a sense of relief being with nature and just nurturing it. He wanted to start a garden at home for himself but our yard didn't have the space. Ms. Merl's garden had sunflowers, daffodils, poinsettias, roses and more. It was a beautiful array of colors and Vance played a huge part in keeping it beautiful.

No one at HYC or even Ms. Merl knew he had a fatal heart condition. Vance hid his terminal condition from everyone, not wanting to burden anyone and too proud to take a crumb of pity from a soul.

His favorite channel was GOLTV, he'd watch football till his eyes bled a football-field but when his friends passing by the house kicking a soccer ball to each other, dressed in jersey shorts, tightly laced football boots and old sneakers, his brethren, Patrick, was always the one to stop by our gate and holler,

"Yow! Sissy Vance, you not kicking some ball?"

The Heart of Revenge

Vance would snatch up the remote, aimed it at the tv and hold down the volume button till it was close to mute. This was his way of hurriedly shoving the sound of the football match he was watching on tv and hiding it behind silence. He always seemed to look at his black and red football boots he had bought four years ago before he answered Patrick. His boots were ontop of the shoe-box it came in and still he had never worn it before. It was still brand new and house dust was in his boots more often than his feet were. His reply would often be,

"No. Mi have to go help out with something by the club," and by the club he meant by HYC. His friends all knew it was a lie and knew that was always the answer he gave. They purposely stopped and asked every time they were going to play football just to shout back at him saying,

"Yow, you a gal! Sissy! Sissy Vance! Mi never see you play no sports yet. You a big sissy! Hahaha."

When they were gone, Vance would leave the house and go into the old lady's next door garden. Even if Ms. Merl wasn't outside he'd still go into the garden by himself, all alone, just him and the flowers. It was true though. He didn't play any physical sport and he couldn't, because it's a life and death situation with his heart if he ever tried to get too physical. If his heart worked too fast, it may lead to his death, a heart attack.

And that was how Vance earned the name **_Sissy Vance_**. On Saturdays when Mom was at the market and the healthy footballers were passing by, knowing Mom wasn't there, they would not call him Sissy Vance. They would call him by the name they called him more freely in the streets, Battyboy-Vance.

But even with that, Vance would not let anyone know the real reason he could not kick ball with them, nor play any other sport. He remained silent and took all the degrading names, insults and shame.

In the streets, Vance always wore his navy blue New York cap low to his brows, hiding his eyes. He didn't walk with his chin up either. He kept his eyes on the ground, hoping he would not hear any of his nicknames Sissy-Vance or Battyboy-Vance.

He had only one close friend and that was Beanie-Boy. Beanie was not like the others. Apart from the fact that he loved fashion and he was hype nuh pussjook, he had never called Vance a sissy. Or a battyboy, even though Beanie wasn't aware of his heart condition. Vance had no problem lending Beanie his stuff, mostly clothes . I had bought a black leather band watch for Vance for his fourteenth birthday that he really loved, but three weeks after he didn't have it anymore. Beanie had borrowed it and still hadn't return it. Vance didn't have much clothes but Beanie still borrowed Vance's shoes, shirts. He got in a squabble with Vance when he wanted to borrow Vance's blue New York cap and Vance told him no.

On the contrary, because Vance stayed away from parties and going out, he had never borrowed clothes from Beanie. On a couple of occasions when Beanie really wanted stuff from Vance and he refused to lend, him he resorted to calling him a big gal, a bigger gal than Cecile and Angel together, and so. Vance took it, smiled and didn't let it get the best of him and up till that point Beanie still didn't bring back Vance's black watch.

One thing that never failed to put a smile on Vance's face during these rough times was his HYC meetings. On Sunday nights, after the meetings, he'd be so perky and happy. Only once I saw a gloom on Vance's face after he came from one of his meetings. It was when he was sixteen; he was sitting in the sofa. I put down the ice tray I was filling with water by the kitchen sink, turned off the pipe, walked over to him and had a seat beside him. It had to be something really terrible that happened to get his spirit down after a meeting. I had to find out what it was. I touched him on his knee and asked,

"Why the sad face?"

CHAPTER 10

Vance Has A Good Friend
by: Leelia Lexings

"Nothing." He shrugged his shoulder but he didn't look up from the floor he was looking at.

"Come on, I know you better than that, what's wrong Vance?"

"I just don't understand people, it's like they think you are obligated to them and if you say no, they hold it against you, like they gave you anything to put down or ....?"

"Hold on, hold on ... slow down." I shuffled over closer to him and rested my other hand on his knee. "Now, who you say is it?"

"Is Beanie. Mi and him friendship cut off for good!"

"Why?... But he is the only friend you have."

"Him is not a true friend."

"He called you gay like the others?" He looked around at me and looked back at the floor. I felt bad and wished I hadn't mentioned that.

"No. Is something else."

"What?" He didn't responded immediately, fisted both hands and sunk his knuckles in the mustard color cushions of the sofa to ease himself out and stand. I covered both his knee caps with my palms and applied some force to them, suggesting 'don't get up as yet, I am talking to you.' He took his hands off the cushions, remained seated and plaited his fingers between each other. Bobbed his head from side to side in deep consideration while talking,

"The man borrowing mi things to go beach and mi tell him no." He stopped talking. Stared blankly. I asked,

"So?"

"And him vex with mi over mi own things." He began pulling the buckle of his black leather band watch from his wrist. I hadn't seen that watch in almost a year. Seemed like the friendship cut off for real, and Vance got back his belongings. But who else would Vance have as a hortical friend? - no one. I guessed he would be even more lonely now.

"So why you didn't just lend him and done? That wouldn't be better than to end the friendship?"

"You mad! Mi not lending no man mi brief to wear go no beach. No man can't wear mi brief. Mi not into them things with no man. You must be mad. If him want vex and thing, make him vex. But mi not lending him mi brief to go sporting on beach."

I wanted to keel over with laughter. I tried holding it back. But the laughter was too much. It just burst right out of me. I couldn't believe I was laughing so brawling. Vance got angry and braced himself up out of the sofa. He turned to me and said in frustration,

"You taking serious things make joke!" I was breathing and taking deep gasps in between, trying to catch my breath as I answered

"No Vance," I gasped for air, "No." Gasped again, "But that's funny still ... Mi can't believe that hype boy like Beanie want borrow your brief to wear go beach. Is which one of your brief him want borrow?"

Vance hissed his teeth and walked off to his room. I was dying with laughter. What a dirty friend! Oh my godmother, Pinky would say 'a dutty friend behaviour that.' Oh boy.

The next day, Monday, Dr. Reid told Vance that the age of his death had moved from the age of thirty-six to thirty-two. Vance needed to be on medication. Dr. Reid had prescribed lanoxin, metoprolol and catopril. He told us that if he took these drugs it may help him to live longer and avoid his heart getting any worse. The cost of the medication for the year totalled roughly two thousand U.S. Mom wanted to help Vance and soon after she put her pride aside and got a job with her friend Micheal Douglas, a job that she'd normally frown on and rather stay home than doing. It wasn't much but Mom had saved some money towards Vance's medical bill. With all her efforts, it still wasn't even close enough but 'at least it was a start,' she would say. She began working some overtime, coming in late just to get that extra dollar towards the bill but time was against her, as Vance was getting worse faster than she was saving her little dollar, dollars.

Pinky's asthma took her again. Mommy had to spend all her savings to take care of it. Mom was left dead broke and back at square one while Vance wasn't getting any better. She nor Dad could afford the medicine

The Heart of Revenge

and Vance had no choice but to do without. Vance had some horrible chest pain that year but he still managed to smile a lot with everyone.

At seventeen, Dr. Reid told Mom that Vance's heart was growing faster and getting worse than before because he wasn't getting the medications he needed, and if he didn't get the medications every year it would only get worse and worse till death. The rapid growth had stolen two years from how soon he would die. He told Mom that Vance would now die at thirty. It was that year Mom made the difficult decision to send me to live with Michael Douglas and Qwan. She needed the money.

However, it wasn't until Vance was eighteen that I successfully got some help for him with his medication. I got the money to help him from Qwan, two thousand U.S. that Qwan's father, Micheal Douglas was questioning. He wasn't happy about it, to say the least.

The medication had helped to retard the growth of his heart and slowed down its unusual growth drastically. By the grace of God, Vance's heart didn't grow much that year, but Dr. Reid told him he had developed a severe left ventricular dysfunction and one of his heart's valves needed to be replaced. He added Vasotec to his prescription which, by itself, cost about another two thousand U.S. making his medication bill for the year just below four thousand U.S. dollars. Dr. Reid said that he'd die at twenty-six. Vance now had only eight years to live. From that moment Vance tried not to get attached to anyone. He had no girlfriends and the nickname calling got a lot worse.

Now it was rumoured, better yet taken as a given, that he was gay. And he had to be gay. In the ghetto at eighteen, no girlfriends and played no physical sport. He must be gay. Everyone now more prevalently called him Battyboy-Vance. Once coming from school he was clamoured in his back with a river stone. He didn't see who threw it but he heard a voice that sounded like a grown man shouted,

"Battyboy-Vance! You must dead! Leave the place battyboy!"

Another stone was pelted into his thigh with a bigger rupture of pain than the one before . He ducked, cover his head and began running. He felt another river-stone shot into his side. He managed to ducked the one that was blasting directly to his head. Ever since that, Vance got scared of going on the road. He hated the road. Hating to go to school. Hating the unfair world. Hating life. The world hated him. He wanted to die.

Vance turned nineteen without having a girlfriend. He spent even more time in Ms. Merl's garden than ever before. He spoke less and he spent more time organising and doing projects for the HYC. It wasn't easy but I got the four thousand dollars from Qwan for his medication. Qwan had to let it be a secret from his father because he didn't approve of the idea. Micheal Douglas would say it was not his responsibility. That I wasn't his wife, he should not be stupid and give me that large amount of money, but I convinced Qwan to do it anyway but under the quiet. Dr. Reid told Mom Vance would die at twenty-four, only five years to live. After that news, Mom's blood pressure went through the clouds.

Things finally began to look up, at twenty, Vance was taking his medication and it was his best year since he was twelve. His heartbeat didn't fluctuate beyond normal, no mild heart attacks, no dizziness, no complaints about chest pains. A couple of times well, he got out of the house, laced up his black and red football boots and played some Salad-A-Kick with Patrick. He and Beanie were friends again and his life was getting to what we wanted it to be - normal. Vance was fit and kicking and Mom's high blood pressure went down. He was skilful with the football and earned his respect on the football field. The other boys always wanted to pick him first on their side. Even before Patrick, who was the top footballer amongst them. Though Patrick was skill with the ball he was even more selfish with it. Patrick began to carry feelings against Vance for that. No one wanted to pick Beanie on their team. No one. Beanie was too slight. And when he ran too hard his knock knees always plunged him into the ground. Poor thing.

February, the 13th of this year, when Vance was one month from his twenty-first birthday he laced up his black and red boots and headed out to play some football with Patrick and the other boys. Before they had even shouted for him by the gate, he was ready and waiting. Mom had got used to the fact now that Vance played football every evening. She'd call me almost every evening when Vance went to play football just to say,

"Lee, Vance gone play football today!"

And she'd never get tired of calling me and repeating that to me. She always sounded so happy every single time that she was on the phone telling me. She'd go on and on with much chirp in her voice to say,

"God is on our side. I can't believe he has stopped wearing his cap! People not calling him those dirty names anymore. It's like God answered all my prayers Lee. What a blessing."

It was more than a rainbow, I was seeing a thousand bright colors in Mommy's voice. I knew very soon he'd have a girlfriend before it even happened because even his swag had turned up. It was just really awesome seeing him getting back to a normal life and having fun. He got a heart attack on the football field that day. He was hospitalized. Induced into a coma for six days. Strung up to a drip for twelve. He lost two week's memory. But he told us he remembered clearly the big fist he got in his chest and that he would get his revenge on the person who did it. He didn't want to call the name of who it was. We insisted on him telling us who it was.

"You sure is someone thump you Vance? You sure?" Mom asked.

"Yes, mi sure. After mi not a baboon Mom, mi remember everything good."

"But remember you lost two week's memory, so how can you remember that?"

"I don't know, I just do." Vance's voice was slow and weak. He looked away to the ceiling.

"Tell us is who." Mom face looked as if it was falling apart. She didn't look as if she really wanted to know who it was for revenge, she was just insisting to know more out of curiosity, just an automation to her questions and insistence. Surely, she looked too filled with sorrow to be angry. I had an idea who it was. He was always number one on the football field and now that Vance was getting more respect than he, he resorted to playing him dirty. I didn't think he knew this would be the outcome though, because he didn't know about Vance's heart problem. So I asked,

"It's Patrick, don't?"

"No."

"It's not Patrick?"

"No."

Mom touched Vance on his shoulder, tugged him a bit.

"Look on mi, is who then?"

"Everything cool Mom."

Pinky's voice sound as if she wanted to retaliate at who it was when she urged him,

"Vance just call the name nuh, please."

"Just cool nuh, mi have my plans, everything good."

"Vance is who?" Mom's loud voice caught the attention of several persons in the ward. Vance looked to Mom, paused in silence for a while staring in her watery eyes and slowly muttered his answer.

"It's Beanie." His closest and only friend.

On visits after that, Vance would spend most of the time apologising to Mom for what he was putting her through. Over the six days that Vance was in the coma, Dr. Reid had put Mom on catopril too but it was for her high blood pressure. Dr. Reid suggested that we take Mom to therapy, because the whole ordeal had terribly traumatized her. We could not afford her the therapy. Mom had to do without.

It was Thursday afternoon when the four of us, me, Mom, Dad and Pinky gathered around Dr. Reid in a semi-circle. Pinky was at the end of the semi-circle furthest away from the bed avoiding to touch the bed or anything to do with hospital. Pinky always felt nauseous every time she had to step foot into a hospital and scorned everything in there. For some reason she just hated hospital. Dr. Reid stuck a black pen in the top of a clipboard that he had in his hand, took off his colorless latex glove and dumped them into the big square pocket of his white doctor jacket. Dad spoke to Dr. Reid,

"So how things look Doc?"

Everyone was listening and watching out for Dr. Reid's news. It could be something bad as Vance seemed to be deteriorating more and more every year, but since steady taking of his medication, we had all witnessed his progress and hoped things had either stabilised. Or would get even better over time, maybe add a couple more years to his life, moving it up from twenty-four. Though we all were brimmed with worry, we still had that gut feeling that things were going to get better, it's something we could feel.

Dr. Reid breathed out, looked down, adjusted his stethoscope around his neck and mouthed.

"Well ..." he used both hands to adjust his stethoscope once more and in a small continuous motion, rocking his head both sides, as if shaking a slow no with his head as he responded, "Vance ain't doing so good."

"What you mean?"

Mom asked before he could utter another word, her hand instinctively went to holding on to Dr. Reid's hand as if pleading with him to tell her that it is not so; things weren't worse. It wasn't getting any worse; it couldn't be. Her fingers clung to his wrist, Dr. Reid took a moment to sort out the best way to say what he had to say. Mom tugged on his wrist and Dr. Reid could see the emotion in her eyes, felt how disturbingly tense she was in her grip, she could have a breakdown, right there, right now. She asked again but in a more hollow and terrified voice, as if she was unsure she wanted to hear or not.

"What you mean?"

"Well.." He rubbed the back of his neck then squeezed on it. "How do I put this? Your son has suffered some mild brain damage, there's a chance he may not be able to perform some daily activities. I've a neurological therapist I can recommend you to."

Where would we get the money? I thought. I went on to ask Dr. Reid, "How much will that cost?" he directed his eyes to my face.

"I can't say, you'll have to call Ms. Winters about that." He shifted his eyes and steadied them into Mom's, "If your son suffers a next attack... well ... he won't make it." Mom's eyes got feeble and she was blinking a lot as if she were trying to clear cloudy tears that were forming around the ball of her eyes. My tears were already raining. "But if he gets the ICD implanted, it can reduce the risk of him having another attack, he is really lucky this time, less than five percent of people survive a SCA, I mean a Sudden Cardio Attack, but his heart is growing so fast that, ..." He looked over to Vance's bed, then at the bag of drip then lowered his voice, "That if he doesn't get his heart reduced soon, he's going to .... you know... He won't make it ... And because his heart has gotten so bad with the heart valve needing to be replaced, the cost for his surgery and ICD, we now looking at a new cost." I didn't have any control over the words that jumped out my mouth, they just did

"Jesus! How much more again?"

"Well, an additional nine thousand."

"Forty thousand that in all?" I was calculating aloud in my head and Dr. Reid nodded his head confirming my calculations.

"How soon is soon?" I asked, while I slowly pulled Mom's sorrow-filled hand off Dr. Reid's wrist. My hand supportively hugged around her fingers, curled them into a soft fist wrapped by mine.

"Maybe next six months ... I don't think he will make it for this Christmas without a surgery."

No one replied, Dr. Reid fidgeted with his stethoscope, making it long to one end then pulling it back around his neck to make it long at the opposite end. He was looking at Mom when he asked

"Can't you get the money anywhere at all for the surgery? A loan, anything?"

Mom had a breakdown. Her crying went to a louder cry, then to a bawling then to hollering, then to falling on the floor. Dad tried to pick her up; she pushed him away. I lifted her from the floor, her arm around my shoulder, hugged her to me tight and wrapped my hand tighter around her fist I had formed. Placed it up on my shoulder. Pinky cried on Dad's shoulder. Mommy's monstrous noise woke a lot of sleeping patients and drew a lot of the nurses' eyes over to us. She also woke Vance. He sat up, saw the whole family crying. He ripped out the drip from his veins.Rran out the hospital in his plain blue pyjamas with the needles still plugged into his arms. No shoes on. Ran.

The following Sunday I knelt on one knee, held Qwan's hand and proposed to Qwan on the stairs of Sovereign Cineplex. The busy crowd took time out to watch a woman proposing to a man, on one knee, instead of the other way around.

Vance wasn't a man of much words but that Sunday he was even more silent than regular. Mom was talking to him but he wasn't hearing her most of the time. His mind was in a different place. By the fall of evening, Vance got ready and left for HYC or so we all thought. No one knew he sneaked out with the kitchen knife in the waist of his pants. No one knew he was heading for Beanie's house. No one knew he was pushed over the edge. No one knew if he would stab Beanie to death.. No one knew.

CHAPTER 11

Ice cream for Pinky?
by: Leelia Lexings

I just honestly didn't expect Vance to say that; his response was,

"Mi don't really want nothing from Qwan enuh. Mi don't chat up to him, and mi prefer if him avoid mi."

Was madness a side-effect of cardiomyophia? 'Cause Vance must be losing it. Whose money was buying his medication since he was eighteen? Maybe Vance was tired of fighting and now was embracing death, accepting it, hating life. I tried calculating where was this coming from but I couldn't finish the thought,

"You realise that the only person who can help you right now with that forty thousand U.S. is Qwan, right?"

"If you married him, it doesn't mean him must pay for it either, 'cause him know mi don't like him."

"What you have against Qwan? I can't understand. Because you and him seldom ever talk, so how you hate him so much now?"

"Mi just don't trust him."

Trust? I wondered, why would he even need to trust Qwan, I mean, if anything, it should be Qwan not trusting him. Qwan was the one with the money. Vance had nothing to lose and life to gain.

"What you mean by trust?"

"Is alright man, mi just don't like the brother, leave it at that."

"What him do you?" Vance didn't answer, "VANCE?"

"What? ... Mi just don't like the brother, him move ..." Vance swallowed the tail of his words. I was a bit agitated.

"WHAT HIM DO?" I'm not usually loud.

Everyone was tensed, me waiting on Vance to answer was like waiting on him to empty the water out the sea with a teaspoon. It took forever.

"WHAT HIM DO?" I repeated, breaking the still silence. Dad's question came right behind mine

"Is what him do Vance?" Vance turned facing Dad instead of me,

"You don't notice anything about the brother?" Dad shook his head while saying,

"No, is what?"

"Well mi don't like how him look on mi then ... Like ..."

"Like how?" Daddy asked

"Like mi a woman."

I reflected on my wedding, getting married, what I was going through for Vance and if he really appreciated it or not. Was I doing the wrong thing? Should I go through with the marriage? What about what had happened lastnight? So many questions running through my head. I replied to Vance,

"What's wrong with you? You paranoid little boy?"

"Lee mi older than you. And mi telling you, him not going to help mi, him not doing it, mi just know."

"Answer mi this, you want the help or not?" He answered by slowly nodding yes, I was trying to decipher if the slow nod. Was a reluctance or uncertainty? Or was it a big boldface lie? My mind was in a limbo about what to think of it. What would anyone make of that?

"Don't worry about me getting the money, don't I got it from him to help you out for three years now?"

"Yeah,... but ---"

"Just stop worry. I promise you, once we married, I'll get the money, stop fret."

But honestly, deep down inside I knew this was not a certainty, good God, we are talking about forty thousand U.S. that his father would have to know about. I just didn't see this happening as smooth as I was trying to make it seem to Vance, but I just didn't want him to worry. If he had a short time left to live, at least he shouldn't be spending it worrying.

Mom said nothing. She placed her thumb over one of her eye and the following four fingers over her other eye, trying to fight the tears. I began sucking on my thumb without realising that I was. Mom may lose her only begotten son soon. She tried pulling herself together.

"For heaven's sake man Leelia! Is ulcer stomach you want catch like me? Take out your finger out your mouth. You twenty now."

Still sucking on my only comfort, I replied,

"Not this argument again Mommy please ... and I'm not twenty yet."

"Qwan know you still sucking finger?"

"Of course, but what him can do 'bout it? It's not like him can stop it."

Though I was sucking my thumb the taste of Nathan's dick was stronger in my mouth. I wondered if I had it on my breath, I wondered about kissing Qwan after I said 'I do', wondered if he would taste another man's cock on my breath. Christ lord! What have I done? Heck! I was so stupid to ever thought that's was the best way to get my revenge at Qwan. What the hell drive me to do something so horrible? I was angry at what Qwan did lastnight but what I did in the bathroom didn't recover anything and it didn't make anything better. I didn't even feel better. I thought I would feel better hurting him back with jealousy. My revenge when I showed Qwan the pictures. Hurt him for what he did lastnight, but honestly, all I felt now was guilt, all I felt was remorse, all I felt was shame. I made a mistake. All I felt was worse.

You know what, I got to go and brush my teeth. I looked if there were any dinner mints on the table. None was ever there. What was I thinking, this was not Qwan's house.

"Qwan need to put his foot down in the relationship and stop make you rule him." Mom said while I puffed a breath out trying to smell it. I inhaled. Only the scent of the fry frittas and liver for breakfast in the air. I replied to Mom's statement,

"Really now?"

"So what him say about your drinking?"

I put my elbows on the table leaned my forehead in my hands, squeezing it, and did not answer Mom's interrogation.

"Ahh sah, the one thing you take from your worthless father, is the worst thing, him drinking."

My eyes were changing. My gray eyes were getting red.

"Nothing's wrong with a little vodka … At least it's always there to wash away my problems."

"Same thing, you sound just like him too, same thing him would say."

My voice had aggression inside it when I said,

"I'm nothing like Dad!"

And would never be. I'm like my beautiful Mom.

"Qwan need to start bust your ass when you doing foolishness, like drinking, him too soft."

Dad was ignoring the argument or at least it looked like he was trying to. Mom had a playful tone in her voice about Qwan busting my ass. My face had a horrible frown under my hand. I blew my breath upward to my nose again. Tested my breath. Mom continued,

"Vance wash your hands and come take some picture for mi please."

"Alright Mom." Vance was gazing at the sofa. He narrowed his eyes in concentration, then asked aloud,

"Is who trouble mi bag mi left in the settee?" Everyone looked towards the sofa.

"Why?" Mom curiously asked.

"Mi have some things in it for the club ... And mi hope nobody don't trouble them nor the ice cream mi left in the fridge that mi buy for the little youths."

HYC, that's all Vance seemed to talk about. As the Vice President for the club, and from what I saw, he probably put in four times as much as anyone in the club and ten times more than their lazy president, whom Vance did everything for.

"What things?" Mom was curious as to what was in the bag. We all knew she wasn't particularly fond of Vance always spending his money, sometimes all his money on the youths in the youth club.

"Mi buy some notebooks and do twelve HYC cap to give away at meeting Sunday."

"You deaf to stop use your little money on that club. All of them little thieving boys and force-ripe little gal that mi see going to meeting not turning out to nothing good." That was the loudest Mom's soft voice spoke all day. Vance walked over to the fridge, opened the freezer door, looked at the box of ice cream, opened it and instantly asked in shock, at the top of his voice,

"Is who eat out the ice cream so?"

He looked into the ice-cream box again, then said with unbending certainty, "Is Pinky!"

"Why everything everybody love blame Pinky?" Daddy asked. "Pinky don't trouble nothing man. If a pin move in here everybody jump on the girl name."

Vance's muddy hand snatched the box out the fridge in one brisk haul, opened it wide and tilted it to Daddy, so he could see into it.

The Heart of Revenge

"Daddy look, look here, who else in the house would've do the ice-cream so awful? Look how she walla-walla inna it like she's a hog. Kill mi dead, is gwabaliscious Pinky do it."

"Can be anybody else," Daddy re-adjusted in the chair, scratched his knee, pulling the leg of his pants up and down to expose his cream and blue diamond socks. "Good gracious man! You acting like nobody else don't have mouth and belly in the house."

"Daddy you seeing what mi showing you?"

"Of course mi seeing, after mi not Ray Charles."

"You see how the hole them deep that dig down in the ice-cream? Is Pinky alone deal with ice-cream like so, so bad ... Everybody else just skim the top and scoop it up, but when she go in it, mi don't know why she have to massa-claw and dig-dig it up so much for. Look how the ice-cream look sawka-sawka." Vance was one slow to anger but obviously his frustration was swelling into it. He continued, "A bet that if mi pee-pee in one soda bottle now and leave it to cool in the fridge Pinky drink it off before daylight. Bet?"

Mom fanned her hand at Vance and said,

"Lock up the box and put back the cream in the fridge man. What you gone do, send Pinky go prison for it? You never see her go in there, so you can't blame her." She stopped talking, turned her back to him then added, "What if somebody in the house eat little of the ice-cream? Hsst."

"Is little that?" Wide-eyed, Vance had a look of complete and utter shock. His expression changed to one of ah-ah!-I-figured-it-out, as he asked, "So is you eat it out then Mommy, and you playing genial?"

"Lord, you must be Frighten-Friday for the little children them and they not going nowhere in life. Hsst."

"How you can say that? You don't even know one of them and you judging the youths."

"Mi don't have to know none of them. All of them is criminal, all the smallest one wearing Clarks, you know in my time police use to harass street boys wearing Clarks, or natty dread."

"Times change. Fashion is not a crime now."

"Hsst. You wasting your time and your money with all them board-head children and you don't have anything for yourself yet. Help yourself. That's what you must do with your money."

"Mi suppose to die Christmas, What mi need to have? ... House?"

Mom went as silent as a gray wall.

Vance looked down the hallway, marched towards Pinky's room, hands still muddy, angered. He chewed on his lips and grumbled from a place in his heart where hurtful words come first, foolish action second and regret comes after.

"Watch mi and the one Pinky!"

CHAPTER 12

Before I Touch it
by: Vybz

I had her open in the warehouse. Her scent best described as - sexified. "You smell so good. I could just ... could just ... Just ... Eat you."
And I would. Nastily. Sloppily. Wet and noisy. You like that?
Her soft peachy color panty tightly squeezed her fleshy vagina into a mouth-watering plump. Her panty was made of a see-through sheer material. At the front was a peach mesh and running up the front was a thin white lace. Victoria Secret written in white straight around in the thin elastic waistband. From the manner in which her panty was straining and buffed high, it looked as if she had stuffed Blue Mountain in her panty. I could see her luscious chocolate mountain of flesh clearly through her peach mesh and lace. No hair. My face alighted. A clean, well-shaved pussy. The tip of my cock was wet. It was steel stiff, hard enough to be used as a bat and break someone's leg. Her luring scent lingered and flavoured between her crotch with a pure irresistible eroticism that kept pulling my face and tongue closer, and closer, down into her captivating crotch, between her legs, my face, so close, my nose, so close, if I barely breathe, she will feel the tingles in my breath, breathing on her trembling inner thighs, sending shivers through her whole body. I took a long, deep, satisfying inhale, the whiff, perfectly fresh, mouth-wateringly suckable, my pink tongue muscled up and stiff, ready, dying to taste her well-kept pussy. Slide my wet tongue inside her warm waiting slit. Lick her, lick her in-between. Kiss on it. Suck on her sweet sugary pussy till she cums in my mouth.

It had no smell of sweat – yet. Intoxicated by the ambience of her lovely scent, I noisily sniffed in her scent again, greedily pushing my nose against her, held my breath, trying to keep her marvellousness inside me, breathed out harshly, pouring my hot breath out like a dragon. It steamed out my nose and pattered insensitively against her legs, she quivered, just slightly quivered. I lightly blew a soft breath on her, between her thighs. She quivered hard. I stretched the head of my pink, stiff, pointed, tongue towards her, towards her thigh, licked the spot, the spot just below the foot of her panty, on the inner side of her thigh, flicked it fluidly, slithered it freely on her thigh, my lips clasped around the flesh of her thigh, just barely licking and sucking so close to her sweetest spot. She went fucking mad, the feeling of me passionately sucking close to her pussy was sending her up the wall. She grabbed my head. Both hands. Terrified, can't withstand to ever having me touch her right now. She's too aroused. Too turned on. Too horny. Wanting me to touch her, suck her, but can't stand it, her legs can't stand straight, she can't stand another touch. I had to touch her, I had to suck. I squeezed her breasts, wholesomely sucked up the flesh of her thigh into my gifted mouth. Wetting the light baby hair on her inner thigh with my sloppy mouth. The wet spot became more sensitive than the rest of her thigh, she could feel where it was wet, it felt cooler, more tingly, more sensitive, making her legs jitter. Imagine the feeling she must be feeling if her whole body is shaking, so hard, so hard, whenever my breath blows onto the wet spot on her thigh. She tried not to shake, but she can't, she feels my every breath on the wet spot of her sensitive inner thigh, she shook like crazy. The baby hair on her leg stood stiff, I sucked up her thigh again, wetting her thigh. My warm mouth, wetting the light baby hair on her skin. Blew on it softly. My mouth went closer to her pussy, sucked her thigh up in my mouth, all the way up, midway my tongue, the brim of my lip curled backward, bracing against the elastic of her panty's leg, lightly touching the crevice of her thigh and sacred flesh, deep-sucking her, so suckingly, my cheeks sunk into two deep dimples, my tongue working smoothly, making flowy waves over her skin as I tongue kissed her thigh, closing my eyes, humming in horny delight into her flesh, the vibration of my base voice humming into her thigh sent thrills up her pussy and twisted her spine. She rose her hips, held my head steady and tried to feed her pussy into my face, my mouth, force her pussy down on my warm lengthy tongue, sit on it, ride it. Her juices drizzled down, seeping to the edges of her horny orifice, wetting the walls of her soft pink lips.

Imagine the feeling.

And then I realised I hadn't even touched her pussy yet.

CHAPTER 13

A Clean Heart, Muddy Hands and Who Breed
by: Vance Lexings

You ever hear 'bout vex? Jah know, is because you don't know how it hurt mi bad. Just burning mi and eating up mi brain, if mi don't tackle Pinky 'bout how she dig-up the ice-cream, mi can't cool off. And how she one manage to eat off almost half of the three gallon cream? Her belly must cut her today. Mi mind can't settle down. Not even wash mi don't wash off mi hands, is straight to Pinky room mi march, elbowed her door three times, three loud bangs, 'BOOP! BOOP! BOOP!' like mi a landlord and she owe mi seven months' rent. A little of the mud flashed from my hand, splashed onto her white door. She didn't open the door quickly. I couldn't wait, before it was opened I yelled through the closed door,

"WANGA GUT Pinky! You awful eeh gal! ..." Mommy hates when I use the Patois word, 'nyam' instead of the English word, 'eat', as if it is not just a Jamaican word for eat, or as if it is a badword, but to how mi head on fire, is that word mi use to tell Pinky mi mind, 'nyam'. Mi keep on cursing, "You one sit down and nyam off nearly gallon and a half of the cream, mi hope is so-so fart you fart up yourself in the wedding later. Pure fart." Mi don't like wish bad on people, but Pinky really got on the tip of mi nerves, God know. Mi continue to tell her anything that came to my mouth, "Mi hope you don't stop fart till you batty bust! SPLIT UP INNA TWO! You too craven man!"

The door still wasn't opened and I could swear I heard her laughing away inside. I elbowed the door again, one knock, 'BOOP!' pure mud fly on the door. Mi start to curse again, "You love your belly too much. You not going to stop nyam out people things out the fridge till you nyam poison. Watch if mi not going to set rat poison with icing ontop inside there for you. Make it bang your rass belly." I loved Pinky but right now I just had to tell her what was on my mind and how I felt. It really hurt mi star, because mi done plan everything for the youth club and Pinky not even look like is taste she taste little of the ice-cream is wad she wad her rass belly with the cream. I continued to fume, "A bet once mi pretty up the rat poison you thief it out. And nyam it off. Watch if you not going to swell up and stretch out."

Pinky didn't sound peaceful when she yelled back from inside her room,

"You! You mustn't call nobody craven, who craven like you? And when you going to any little party or nine night you walk with your pickle-pepper in your back-pocket for the people them free food."

"CRAVEN GAL! You too craven for gal."

It's not wicked mi wicked why mi calling mi sister craven, but anybody who swallow down one small nail in their food when they eating, don't deserve to pass it out easy, they deserve to pee-pee it out and have pure problem to pee-pee it out, because is just raw-chaw cravenness that. Pinky never chewing her food properly yet, just cut and swallow. Yes, Pinky swallow one small nail in her food already.

"You see when mi nyam out nothing?" She swung the door open, looked at me, spoke slower and dipped her voice a little lower, asking "You not getting ready? ... You come to mi room with your mud-up hands and beating down people door like the house burning down. The house a burn down?" A smirk stretched her lips towards her ears. I could sense that she was guilty. She almost wanted to laugh, I could see the muscles flinching at the corner of her lips in her big red face, fighting to hold back her giggles, she smiled while saying, "Mi can nyam all the ice-cream mi feel like, mi not farting down nowhere, after mi not lactose-intolerant or have weak bowels." It sounded funny, but mi never laugh. Mi vex till mi want bust. She couldn't hold down the laugh anymore, she burst out into a big hell of a down-town laugh, with one hand patting her thigh. From that gesture, nobody can't tell me is not Pinky nyam out the ice cream, all if God come off the cross today and tell mi is not Pinky, mi still won't believe. She too terrible man, mi eyes beaming anger into hers, red like blood and she still laughing and said. "And even if mi belly take mi today, whole heap a toilet tissue in the bathroom, so what? Mi not afraid of running belly."

"Is you nyam out the rass cream enuh. Playing like you innocent. YOU! You same one nyam it out." Pinky patted her bosom slowly, one time, while dragging out her reply,

"Miiii? ... Mi? Poor mi ... Lightning strike mi right here so, mi don't touch a thing darling dear. Check again." She turned her back and walked off leave mi fuming, rolling her ass to her bed,

"Is you! Who else would've dig, dig-up the ice-cream so? Eeeh?" The culprit sucked her teeth disregarding my accusation. It didn't seem to get to her one bit. It was then I realised maybe it really wasn't she. Who then? Mommy? Pinky didn't reach her bed yet,

"Hsst. Listen to mi nuh little boy, don't draw mi tongue, you hear mi. Is that you really come bother mi peace 'bout? Before you go bathe." She reached her bed and before sitting said, "So what you gone do if is mi eat it? Beat mi? ... Is that you come in here to do? See mi here. Come beat." She touched into her chest showing me where she is then began bending to sit on the bed. "Who you suppose to fight you not fighting. Why you never stab up Beanie when you take out the kitchen knife and go look for him? Is mi you have strength for?" She sat beside a small pile of colourful clothes cluttered on the bed, dragged a batty-rider jeans shorts from under her legs that squeezed her under her thigh. She winced, and wrinkled her face like a raisin while dragging it out, tossed it close to the messy pile. I glared, pressed my fingers in my palm, sunk them pretending I was squeezing Pinky's neck for eating out the youths' ice-cream. My fingers felt a bit stiff from the mud beginning to dry and harden around them. Her face got lighter and boastfully bragged,

"Ice cream can't hold mi, that little toops of ice-cream would've just drop one-side in one well in mi belly." She began to turn her head of false hair towards me. "If mi did ever walk through your cream lastnight you would've stay anywhere you at and feel it, 'cause is the whole box of cream mi would've brush off clean and lick out the plastic bag." She looked right in my eyes and blinked once and the whole demeanour on her face changed to a jovial one. "You can stay there, is a empty box you would've come see lock up back well neat in the fridge like it don't touch yet." She spanned the wiry smirk on her face. "You must thank God mi never go in the freezer, hsst ...you lucky yaah." I was just standing at her open door, glaring at her in disgust, she fanned me off and said, "Go bathe your skin and move from mi door with your dirty hands them..." The pupil of her eyes went to the brown mud spots on her white door, mi never want she spot them enuh. "Look how you dirty up mi door ... You going to shine it off back with piece of wet cloth, you know that."

I didn't move. She continued to run me from infront her doorway,

"Think is school this that you always don't want go. Is your sister wedding. Go bathe and make sure you wash out your arm pit them good." I still didn't move. She longed out her neck towards me and asked "Is what? Stop act like a mawma-man and a murmur-murmur over the little drop of cream and ..." Then her voice deepened into a base tone, lips visibly pronounced every word, eyebrows went to the top of her forehead as she bawled out "GO BATHEEE!"

"You talking like is mi never want go school."

"Stop take me for bighead bird, mi head might big yes but mi not fool-fool, mi know is plenty time you use your heart make excuse to don't go no school."

Pinky turned her back to me. I slowly released the squeeze of my hands, a flake of mud crust fell from my hand to Pinky's burgundy carpet, I simmered my words in a gravy of thoughts before parting my teeth,

"Maybe ... Its ..." I added more thought, "Maybe I was depressed. Depression. Sometimes mi heart, mi mean, like inside is just ... I can't describe it. But I know when I wake up to my heart's beating and it feels like a bad thing..." I looked to the fluffy carpet and the brown flakes of mud that fell there, "Mi not happy. I don't want to hear my heart beating." I quietly bent and picked the flake of mud from the carpet, held it in my muddy hand, gazed at it. "Well maybe scared, maybe mi scared, you know."

"Scared of what?"

"Dying."

Pinky turned to face me, the scent of her room was clearer now; it was a chemical, the raw acidic scent of her yellow bleaching cream. She rubbed up with it every morning as she wake up. My body lost its anger and so too, lost its liveliness. The same feeling began to wrap me that I had most mornings, the mornings when I told Mom I didn't want to go to school. The feeling to be alive but dead. Inside had no life. Inside has an overgrown red hearse. I hated to feel it pumping blood.

I wanted to block out all I had heard. I hated that Dr. Reid played God, telling me when I would die. How much longer mi have to live. Mi wish mi never know anything, let mi live without this worry 'bout dying haunting me, menacing me and killing me before I go. I wake up every morning thinking of it. And with all the expensive drugs I took, I was getting worse and worse and worse. What Dr. Reid predicted as age thirty-six was now age twenty one, months away, six months away, just in time for Merry Christmas. I wished Christmas never comes, but everyday it' was racing closer, the distance of my death getting shorter, driving up closer to me, getting bigger and realer as the distance shortened and came up closer to me, it's bigger in my vision of reality and I could see its face pulling closer as the days went by, it's ugly. It's scary. It's death.

Leelia getting forty thousand U.S. out of Qwan in itself was a next issue. Even though mi don't really agree to Mom sending Leelia at fourteen and courting Lee over the years into seducing a big old twenty-one year old Qwan. The truth was, if she never do it, mi would've been dead from three years ago. Qwan was twenty-three and Leelia, the unconsented age of seventeen, when he yielded to Leelia's being a little temptress with grown seductions. Mr. Micheal Douglas' interference hindered it from happening much sooner. He didn't want his son to be with Leelia from the vibes I saw him giving off. Maybe he hated Leelia or something.

My sister was underage when Qwan had sex with her. I hated him with all my heart for that. Later that year, he gave Leelia two thousand dollars to buy a year's worth of the medication I needed to live, and the year after that four thousand. I wanted to bow and kiss Qwan's feet for that.

Qwan had been giving Leelia the money for my medication for three years now. The last amount was four thousand but now I needed ten times that, forty thousand and I knew that wasn't the easiest thing for Leelia to do, plus I knew the reason why he wouldn't. I didn't even really want him to do it, if it wasn't for her. For her. So now I prayed to God that he did. For her.

For the feeling I had, depressed was the wrong word I used before. Scared was wrong too. Hopeless and helpless nailed it closer to home. Hopeless. And helpless. That's what you become. That was how I felt.

There was this dark hollowness I felt, laying all alone in bed, in the quietest times of dawn, listening to the haunting beats of my heart. I would wake up to a death drum beating, the reminder of my death. To fight this feeling of helplessness, I helped all I could with my hours. It's the only medication that truly helped, me helping others. It made me feel helpful instead of helpless, purposeful instead of no purpose, worthwhile on this earth instead of worthless. And that's all I desired, all that mattered, not fucking one million beautiful women, no expensive food, no driving around in fast and expensive cars. I just wanted to help others. That's all I wanted. That sedated me.

And I didn't want anybody being sorry for me. I was not a pity case. Everyone has to die someday. I didn't need to burden anyone with mine. I didn't want Qwan's money to feel like a parasite pesting him and his father's bank account. But if I should open my heart and speak, I did need his money, not for me, but because staying alive was being there to father my child, the person that will need me the most, needed my support, needed a father, needed me to be alive and be here, my baby, not Mom, nor any family, my baby. I wanted to stand by my baby in the hardest times, I want to take my child to school. I didn't want to die, I was scared, not for me, for my child.

My shoulders slouched low. I lumbered over to Pinky's bed, my mind still in thought, sat beside her on her floral sheet, some of it dragged off the bed, the slanted end hung untidily, swaying slightly back and forth right above the furry fluff of the carpet.

"You not going to dead, stop talking like Dr. Reid is God. Him can blow breath and shine sun? Him can make big stone? Him can make mango tree? Him don't know when you or nobody gone dead, him trying to do God's work," I wanted to believe what Pinky said, I thought the same thing, but Dr. Reid studied medicine and heart for years. Pinky studied weed. And if we talking about God, Pinky didn't go to church in God's know how long. And the only Bible she owned was the one Mom bought from her booklist in grade seven. Mi doubt Pinky know it's Genesis start the bible not Psalms. But Pinky never stopped. She went on to knowledgeably preach about the Bible and Christianity, "Anything God planned for you, that's what going to happen. God won't let you die. You a good youth. You is a bigger virgin than Mary. Just trust in father God."

Looking in outer-space, eyes too focused to blink, I replied,

"Is not miself mi worrying 'bout." Pinky went ahead of me and wrongly assumed it was Mom I was worried about.

The Heart of Revenge

"Aubrea live her life already, stop worry 'bout the old foot."

I stretched my hand to turn on the fan, but my hands were depressingly muddy, somehow to me it looked like doctors placed my hands in casts made from mud. My hand fell back to my side without an ounce of life in it, and from my very low tone you could tell my mind was still far away as I replied,

"Not Aubrea .... My baby."

"What?" Pinky clapped her hands together and bowed forward "Watch here now! You have woman?"

My eyes swung up at Pinky. My mind morphed back to earth, and I crash-landed back into reality. I said too much. I should cover this up. But ... You could hear my deep exhale through my nose, I answered without any urgency,

"Yeah."

"How mi never see you with her yet? What she name? Which part she live? Talk the things."

"Just chill nuh." I realised she took my baby to mean a girlfriend I had and not my child. I wiggled my ass on the mattress to find a more comfortable sit on the bed. "Don't worry 'bout that," You could hear my puffy exhale again and almost see the puff of wind that jetted through my nose. "Mi just feel it for her and mi feel it for ---"

Pinky broke off a piece of my sentence when she gently wrapped my muddy wrist with her clean hands. I stopped talking, looked down at her hand holding mine. Her fingers firmed into the underside of my wrist as she got ready to say what she was thinking,

"Mi can imagine how bad that feel bro. Jah know. All she must have it hard when you tell her that things gone to less than a year."

My mind was dazing off back into thoughts, outer-space.

"Mi don't tell her yet."

"Jeesam!" her hand jerked and fingers clamped tighter into my wrist, "So she don't know yet? ... You must tell her man. Is what? You 'fraid?" She had sincerity in her voice, mix-up and vulgarity was absent from her soft tone, just a kind concern as she advised, "Oh God! You must tell her. Mi would prefer to know if mi was your girlfriend." Her hand tugged mine closer to hers, "Big man thing Vance, tell her."

I lifted her hand off mine.

"You nastying up your hand." She grabbed on back to my wrist, and with her feisty attitude her words pounced out her quiet demeanour at me,

"Water take off mud!" Her voice descended back or more like transcended to being angelic soft, she leaned her head down and to me, trying to look into the eyes of my bowed head,

"You gone tell her right?" Her index finger hooked under my chin and pulled it up into her stare, "Vance. Tell her ... She deserve to know if you care about the girl."

"Mi don't want it burden her down especially with the baby."

"Which baby?" Her hands flew off mine, tilted her entire body away from me, her eyelids crumpled.

Inside me felt different, more than panicky, there was an inner body effect happening in me. It wasn't good. My heart was racing, needles sticking, twitches in my heart, my heart tightening and every thud my heart made jerked my chest outside my body. Heart Attack. Stiffness. Heart wringing on needles. Heart slowly failing. Fighting. My muddy hand grabbed my brown naked chest, wishing I could shove my hand through my chest and squeeze my heart to stop the ache, squeeze it to stop the stabs, the twitches. I utter a soft,

"Uh." The beat slowed down,

'Bo-dum ... Bo-dum.'

'Bo-dum.'

I glanced up at Pinky, the skin of my face contorted in a twist of agony. Her hand dashed around my shoulder, she pulled me closer, her hands were not steady, shaking, trembling.

"Vance is what? You alright?" My heart was returning to normal heartbeats,

'Bo-dum, bo-dum, bo-dum.'

I swallowed, looked up, spoke cheerily,

"Yeah man, mi good, is not nothing."

"You sure?"

"Yeah man. Mi gone bathe and go get ready now."

Mi get up from the bed and walked to the door. This strange, the mud splashes on the door looked a lot more now than when I was standing there. The scent of the yellow-green bleaching cream was always in the room but now its returning to my consciousness. My heart still a little tight and sticking, sticking, sticking me. Pins. Needles. Chest pain. I was use to the feeling. Hated it.

"Vance you can breed nobody though?" I stopped walking; my belly squirmed. I remembered all I ate since morning was the Julie mango and June plum Ms. Merl gave me. The Julie mango was so sweet, mi eat the seed till it turn white, white, white before mi throw it away. I still hadn't ate my breakfast yet,

"She pregnant?" My hearted jumped. Pinky's question was adding more tension to the tight strings in my heart. I increased the pace of my walk to the door, answering Pinky with nothing but silence.

"Vance! Little boy, answer mi nuh. She pregnant?"

I kept walking, my head spinning like a CD on repeat, dizzy. I replied,

"Mi gone get ready. Mi late." I exited through the door, closed her mud-splashed door and turned down the long baby blue corridor, no shirt and muddy hands. I heard Pinky's shout,

"Is pregnant she pregnant Vance? ... Who you breed?"

CHAPTER 14

I'm Building a Mansion On Quicksand
by: Leelia Lexings

The sky was a wide sea of blue, sprinkled with swirling strips of white cotton candy. The wooden door to enter the church must have been made that big to let through a Mack truck. Both sides of the door were wide open welcomingly, letting in the bright afternoon light. The gigantic windows were letting in square packages of sunlight into the church. I have this beautiful, clean, serene feeling when I am in a church. And today I felt like a filthy gutter.

The wooden cross above the window reminded me that God is here with me, I could feel his presence in the cool breeze blowing. The wind seeped through the huge willow tree outside with a hollow 'wooooeee' sound into the church.

The front row of chairs was seated with close friends and family all smiling and antsy with anticipation. The anxiety in the church was weird, it's not like the regular ones at most weddings where the guests were happy anticipating a joyous matrimonial union. It was more a type of wonder, wondering if this marriage would go through or not. Would he say yes? Would I say no? Qwan had long decided, and I was on the border of yes. No. Yes. No. My mind in total anarchy.

Our neighbour, Ms. Merl, arrived late. She was a little bit wobbly coming through the second side door. She tried not to disrupt the wedding, walking with quiet, apologetic steps against the white walls and long rows of chairs. She found her way into the third row upfront, wrapping her orange, wide-skirted dress around her legs as she slipped down by seated guests to midway the row, right behind Munchy and Vance. The stocky pastor's shiny cheeks sunk into a dimple, deep enough to catch a paint pan of water from when he greeted Ms. Merl with a smile. He dipped his head with a small bow approvingly at Ms. Merl taking her seat. I looked above his low-cut gray hair to the brown wooden clock on the wall, studied the time. I felt my stomach twisted instantly. Only minutes away. I felt the sharp blade of a knife twisting both directions in my stomach.

Pastor Ellis looked through his gold frame glasses reading from Corinthians fourteen in his black Bible. My mind's in strides. I wanted to grab my belly bottom, suck my finger. I fidgeted with my fingers and looked over at Vance. My heart was collapsing.

Pastor Ellis stood so close by me and Qwan on the wooden step that led to the empty pulpit, that as he read, I smelt his hot breath. It wasn't a bad odour, but I could smell that he had ackee and salt-fish for breakfast or someone's saltfish for his breakfast.

Wow. Qwan was just gorgeous, cladded in his full white Armani suit and powder pink tie. His taste in fashion had never been slighted, always on point. Except for today. Not that I am picky or anything, but I wished his pants were two inch closer to the ground, and I had said it to him when he tried on the suit, but I remembered his baritone voice saying with much chirp to it,

"It's perfect. Nothing's wrong with it, it's the exact length I wanted. It's an Italian fit boo. This is the length it's supposed to have. Not long down and sweeping the floor."

I didn't want it to actually be touching the floor or sweeping it, but two inches more wouldn't hurt either. It was close to showing his socks when he walked. But that's how he wore all his clothes exact, close-fitted to his muscular sculpted body and bow legs.

He had been smiling like a pleased chimpanzee as he tried on the suit, showing his two sharp and pointed teeth at either side of his mouth that made his smile stand out. He turned and wheeled around in the full length mirror. Checking out his suit at different angles. I imagined it was Ajrien in the suit. That it was Ajrien I was marrying.

"Perfect." He smiled, he spun his back to the mirror, holding the lapels of the white jacket, head turned behind him, smile widening.

"This is perfect boo." I walked out the room. It disrupted the smile on his face.

"Where you going?"

"To get something."

"What?" I reached by the long bladed knife in the kitchenette.

"Something."

"What?"

"Our favourite. Just wait."

I returned with some Grey Goose Vodka, two liquor glasses and no ice.

"Lee?"

"What? Stop acting like a girl."

"Lee!"

"What?" I shrugged.

"That's your favourite, not mine. You know I turn into an idiot when I drink."

"Qwan, we celebrating. What's better to celebrate, than with Vodka."

"Leeee." His expression got stern. "I don't want to drink no vodka."

"Baby please, you got to, we celebrating our marriage. You gonna be my husband in the next three weeks. Aren't you happy?"

"Not happy enough to beat and abuse you."

"Don't worry. I can take it." I poured out two full glasses, gulped down one in one heads-up and refilled mine.

"Lee, I hate when I hit you, and you know that's what the drinking does to me. I'm never drinking with you again. I'm serious this time. You not making me. This shit is tearing me apart."

"Hear me complaining?" He folded his forehead and squinted his eyes.

"This shit needs to stop! I'm not drinking any Vodka and you need to STOP." I went straight ahead and took a shot, drank half glass, one swallow.

"This the only thing that makes me happy. Why you want to ruin me? Why won't you make me happy?" I motioned the glass forward, "Drink."

"Stop being an ass Lee. Making you happy or hurting the only woman I love? Our marriage will be hopeless if you don't kick that habit. Make any sense to you?"

"Relax honey, just drink with me man. Let's get ontop of the world. Whenever you do it with me, I'm on top of the world. Just the two of us in our crazy little world." He smiled with disbelief, shook his head at my pressing determination. I wanted him to share the moment with me, live a little, be on the edge a little, be a bit more stern and aggressive with me, be like Ajrien.

"You're a nut case, you know that?" The look in his eyes sounded as if he was tired of this, "You're damn crazy."

"We crazy boo. It's our world, me and you, just me and you. Our crazy world." I handed him the glass. He gently pushed it back to me with the back of his hand,

"I can't live with myself hurting you, I don't want to." I drank my glass empty and poured some more, thinking he is so soft sometimes; such a bitch. I wish he'd harden up, be a man. Drink.

"Qwan please, just until we get married. I promise I won't force you to drink with me after we are married."

"No ..." He stopped. Thought for the small time between two seconds. "Well, I will but..." his eyes were soft as he gazed into mine. "Promise me you will stop this drinking too." He looked far into my eyes. "Please." I didn't answer, "Please Lee." It sounded like forcing more than asking.

"I promise." I knew that promise was out of my league, but I lied. "I PROMISE Qwan." He kept his gaze into my eyes, took the glass from me, drank a sip and walked into the kitchenette.

I heard ransacking and rattles in the kitchen. What the hell?

"What in the world you doing inside there Qwan?"

"Keeping our promise." Contrarily to the ransacking I heard, his voice sounded calm and level-headed.

Things got louder. I heard glasses being smashed. 'Spa-shenk! Spa-shenk! Spa-shenk!' I hurled into the kitchenette. Damn. He got so violent when he drinks. It's like he morphed into being a raging machine.

"Already? You drunk!" He flung the last of the six bottles of Vodka into the wall. Broken Grey Goose bottles on the floor mixed with froths and bubbles. 'Spa-shenk!'

"You getting mad Qwan! Stop it, stop it!"

"Only three weeks left. What the hell we gonna do with all this Vodka? Keep them here just to tempt you to pick up back drinking. A deal is a deal. No drinking after we are married?"

I stomped over to him, my hand smite him right across his cheek, 'CLACK!' his face slashed around, his teeth seemed to clatter.

"You! ... Wasteful!... Inconsiderate! ... Arrghh!" I searched for words. "Little ... fucker!"

"That's all?" He asked smiling, with his sexy side teeth surprisingly still in place. He grabbed me by the arm, pulled me in, the front of my body leaning on his white suit, belly to belly, I could feel his hard chest. I wiggled myself in an anger tantrum. He overpowered me to a calm. Looked into my eyes. I held my head down, not wanting to look back in his. He placed his finger under my chin, pulling my face skyward to his, kissed me, pressing his lips firmly into mine, his eyes closed. He spoke with his mouth so close to mine. His breath, so seductive.

"I can't wait to be your husband." I rested my head into his chest with love, wrapped my arms around his obliques. Looked floorward. Sighed. A little more than a sigh, it was a longer exhale that travelled from below my heart. I felt as if I were building a mansion on quicksand. I wasn't sure what to reply. I didn't want to lie. I replied in a very simple tone,

"I know."

I kept on building my mansion on the quicksand.

CHAPTER 15

Picture-woman Munchy
by: Leelia Lexings

Pinky's friend, Munchy, the devil, would not have the decency in her to squat her ass down and stop taking pictures while Pastor Ellis is reading from the Bible. Pinky did zit to discourage it.

The rotund Munchy, posed, leaning to her left, one hand on her knee holding her weight while the other hand akimbo. Pinky snapped the picture. Everyone in the church stoned them, dog rotten, with their hard stares of incredulity. That was exactly what the disruptive Siamese twins wanted- attention. Before Munchy could even tweet the picture, Pinky posed, pushing her elephantine bumper to Munchy's BB phone.

"Take mi picture. Catch this one Munchy."

The church was blessed with three bright flashes as Munchy snapped away in fantastic paparazzi style, spinning her BB flat, then tall, fitting Pinky in the screen, cross-way, - snapped, then longitudinally, – snapped.

"Ladies!" Pastor Ellis eyes toad-out, his obese nose-hole widened, nose hairs sticking out of his two dark caves.

"Take your seats!" His body jerked, his harsh voice rumbled in the church as if he had yelled through a mic.

"This is not WEDDY WEDDY WEDNESDAY!"

At the sound of the thundering command, Munchy froze, her face knitted and her eyes feistily piercing the pastor. Her bulgy ass reluctantly went downward to her seat, fingers pressing buttons on her BB as she jeered Pastor Ellis loud enough for the entire church to hear,

"See you damn face look like bullfrog back. Bout take seats, hsst." She plopped down her hind meat in the seat and stuck out her broad tongue, zipped it back in then rocked her head side to side, teasing,

"ABAY make you ugly. You don't cute! ABAAYYY!"

The pastor resumed. Munchy snapped Pastor Ellis' pic and tweeted. I could just imagine the caption under his handsome picture.

"Will you take this woman to be your lawful wedded wife?" The pastor looked to Qwan.

CHAPTER 16

An Heartfelt I Do
by: Leelia Lexings

Within an eye-beat Qwan answered firm and loud.
"I DO!" And immediately sentimental water build up in my eyes.
A burst of joy on Qwan's face when he saw how overwhelmed and schmaltzy I was. He was mistaking my tears for tears of joy. He gazed deeper into my water-puddled eyes; he saw the truth. The joy crawled out his face and left it pale and his eyes weak. The water grew higher over my gray eyes. Qwan felt the hesitant shakes in my left hand he held on to.
"And do you ..." Pastor Ellis turned to me, "take this man to be your lawful wedded husband?" Pastor Ellis smiled. Qwan's hand that held mine shook, a slight twitch. I gazed. My heart racing, beads of sweat on my nose, my armpits felt clustered with the hot sweat forming. It made me feel even more uneasy. The sweat trickled down my underarm unto my strapless gown. I swallowed my spit, racing my thought. YES. No. Yes. What about lastnight? I shouldn't marry him. He loves me but ... What about Vance? Maybe I'm marrying for the wrong reasons or do I really love Qwan... Maybe I can live with him forever without regretting this decision. I do love him. I am certain I do, but ... Well, it doesn't matter, does it? All that matters is saving Vance. I'm his only hope. YES is my only option.
I pressed my arm against my sticky hicky armpit trying to stop the sweat from running down without embarrassingly wiping under my arm. Heartbeats passed in silence, the agitation inside the church felt unnerving on my skin. I felt the eyes. They were all staring at my lips. Pure and complete silence. A silence so quiet, it seemed even the clocks stop ticking and were listening for an answer too because not even the clock ticking could be heard. No sound whatsoever. My heels all of a sudden felt uncomfortable. My legs straining to stand still. The silence spread so wide I could hear the softest wind blowing outside. Not just my foot, my whole body was uncomfortable and mind in disarray.

The Heart of Revenge

I couldn't get the words "I DO" out because of the throbbing bile in my throat. My throat was dry, better yet parched.

Qwan touched his pink tie, jerked it a nudge. His adam's apple went down then up and he had tiny globules of sweat forming a thin line across his upper lip. The church as silent as emptiness. A long hollow pause went by and persons shuffled their bottoms in their hard wooden seats.

Qwan's Dad, Micheal Douglas bald head flushed with sweat. I wasn't sure if he actually wanted this wedding to go through. He had not smiled all day. He looked at me with some fire, some threat of a sort, couldn't quite make out what those eyes meant but they were the same look he gave to Qwan when he was pissed off about something he did. Or maybe he's fretting about what he had done and held under the wraps. He had to be, it was too scandalous. Terribly.

Maybe he was wondering if that's causing me not to say "I DO". Trust me, it was more than enough reason to not say "I DO" to Qwan. Yes. I wasn't talking about the rumours of him in his community of paying all the young girls who just begun to grow hair over their vaginas, to get a taste of it, a sample. And In return he'd offer them money and trips to foreign countries. Rumours had it that he couldn't perform sex for over five minutes, but when it came to oral sex, he could suck a woman until she came enough times to make her whole body dry. I heard that some girls even asked him as a favour to have that tongual experience. I thought if Mr. Douglas was the last man on earth, I still wouldn't let him do me, not in a million years. He was too disgusting and he gave me the creeps.

It was only a rumour though. Micheal Douglas didn't need to buy vagina and he wasn't that type of person. He basically built the community I was from. He was the backbone; he had so many businesses there. He never forgot his roots and still gave charity handouts to many of the youths and unfortunates from the community and provided employment for many, including Mom. He took me in as his own when I was fourteen. He was a good man who could've easily became the Member of Parliament (M.P.) for our community, but he hated politics. In my eyes, Mr. Douglas was a respectable man, innocent until proven otherwise.

What I caught him doing may've been a mistake or not. I wasn't the type to stick my face in other people's business but this secret I had for him was valuable and worth protecting. As bad as the rumours were, this was definitely more terrible than the rumours of him buying green vaginas as delicacies. It was much worse. Much worse. I swear.

The awkward pause would not end. As a jockey, riding his horse for victory, with both reigns in hand jerks the reigns for the horse to giddy-up faster, so was the jerk Qwan gave my left hand. Sweat beginning to form small crystal balls on his forehead in the cool church. Persons were tossing in their seats watching my lips in immaculate silence. I spoke so low the pastor had to strain his ear to catch what I said.

"I don't know."

A gawk of disbelief from Qwan. His firm grip widened and went loose from around my lifeless hand. A surprised "Huhhh!" escaped from the startled crowd in unison. Their loud gasp swept across the silent church with a hollow echo ringing through the tense air of the church. Their frightening shrill made my knees less strong, they felt like porridge, weak. I tried to keep standing and keep in my urine.

Dad fidgeted with the sleeve of his oversized jacket, shoved his hand down his pocket and glanced over at the bridal party. They all had unblinking eyes and perspiration was building up on their foreheads.

Pastor Ellis stopped looking through his glasses, instead he looked over them at me. He pulled his head back with a short neck movement as he tried to decipher the foreign language I had just spoken. Mom shouted. It was sharp and piercing through the pounding silence of the church. It was almost as if I could hear my ears beating, not like a drum but exactly like a heart would. Bo-dum! ...silence Bo-dum! Complete silence ... Bo-dum! Terrifying. Mom's voice rang in my ears.

"LEEE! Jesus Christ. Mi did dream 'bout this lastnight enuh!" I knew Mom was obliterated. I knew she was thinking of Vance. I knew me not saying yes was stabbing her in her heart with a cutlass. Killing her. I could hear it in the shakiness of her yell.

Qwan's neck went soft. He could barely keep his head up high. Too ashamed to look at the congregation, too ashamed to look at his family, too ashamed to look anywhere else but in the gray watery pupil of my eyes. His lips trembled, his blood too cold to speak. Pastor Ellis adjusted his gold frames on his nose, trying to clarify what he had heard, he asked,

"What?.. What you mean?"

The Heart of Revenge

The shame and embarrassment in Qwan motioned his anger. He made a powerful swift tug on my hand. Squeezed it with a hurt-filled and pitiful heart. I felt disgusted at what I was doing, it was difficult. I could either lie to Qwan and rob him of his money to save my brother, or tell him the truth, rip his heart to pieces and watch my brother die. In his eyes were earnest sincerity and desire to be my husband. His eyes went narrow, half shut and so intense it seemed as if they were screaming at me. I felt his confusion, his rage, his hot blood. Munchy snapped a picture.

My brain pleated in contemplation. Should I forgive Qwan? But Vance? All these thoughts were flying through my head in less than two seconds. I couldn't even process Pastor Ellis' question the way I was confused and lost in my own tug –of-war decision. What the pastor had asked me before? ... I heard his words, but they just didn't stick to my senses. The flurry of emotions in my chest rose in a rough tidal wave choking the windpipe in my neck. If I tried to speak it would sound crackly. I looked in the crowd. I wasn't willing to let go my tears; a single one slipped from the corner of my eye. No yes, no, yes, speeding through my head. The air started to smell of perfume and old clothes mixed with perspiration, as if everyone was sweating and I was certain somebody in the crowd didn't bathe, because there was a stench of moldy arm, I wasn't saying that water didn't touch their skin, but that person definitely didn't bathe, maybe just a quick wipe up or tidy. The frowsy scent was really close. I think it's the pastor. Pastor Ellis didn't bathe.

The air in the church felt hotter. My neck sweating. The silence was blank and the congregation was all staring at me. I made up my mind. What I decided scared me. My heart's swirling around in the bottom of my belly. I wanted to use the toilet.

I breathed out, looked at the time on the wooden clock. My voice rickety almost clickety clack rather than a confident tone as I answered louder than I did before.

"I.. I...I" I stuttered, "I don't know."

My left hand that Qwan held was like a rattle snake. I tried my best to keep it steady, tried my best to keep my eyes out of his. My heart felt the biggest I had ever felt it, as if it was swollen. My heavy heart crashing in my ribcage with every heavy thud it made, 'bo-dum, bo-dum, bo-dum'. Over and over again. The congregation all together swept another gasp at my answer sounding like they all sucked in their breaths at once, a big loud and definitely frightened "Huuhhh!"

But this time they didn't remain silent after the gasp, instead a sheet of gossiping spread over the stunned congregation. Everyone was turning their heads around to suss with whoever they could. I felt embarrassed. The whispering blather from everyone summed up to a loud scandalous chatter. Shock and disbelief stood stiff in everyone's eyes. Mom desperately tried for me not to screw up everything. She pelted out at the tip of her voice, almost bursting her lungs,

"LEELIA!"

The tip of Mommy's Chanel heels must have been real sturdy how loud it sounded each time her heel hit on the hard floor running over to me.

She snagged my arm above my elbow with the brute force of a Pinky. Thoughts racing through her head, she whispered in my ears, and tears came down my eyes, dripping spots of water slightly brown from the makeup it rolled over and washed away. It fell on the breast of my white wedding dress. Mom asked,

"What about your brother eeh? Vance? You going make him dead?"

The pink cushion with the ring fell from out Loriel's tiny hand. The solid white gold made a soft metallic dingle when it hit the tile. 'Bing'...bounced... 'bing-bing'. Rolled, fell flat 'bingy-lingy-ling'. Stopped just by Qwan's white shoes. Another loud shout came. From the sound of it, it sounded like Pinky,

Hey BOM---!" Yes, it was Pinky." Hey mad gal Leelia, stop act like a frigging infidel! You a novice or what?"

Pastor Ellis' saltfish breath was urging me to answer with a roughness "YES or NO ... CHILDDDD!" The tip of his tongue hit the pink ceiling of his mouth and he held it still as he prolonged the pronunciation of his last word, "CHILDDDD!"

Munchy snapped a picture.

CHAPTER 17

My White Gold Wedding Ring
by: Leelia Lexings

Before I could answer Pastor Ellis, Vance shot straight up out of his seat. He jumped up so wild and so much out of control of what he was doing that his hip clashed into the front row infront of him, bumping it forward and caused the people in the front row to make some slight commotion. He made a spectacle as he dug pass everyone sitting in the row to get out. Everyone in the front row flashed their heads around to see what was the matter. Why was he so shaken by the whole ordeal? His eyes avoided eye contact with everyone and he looked over their heads, keeping his eyes focused on the second door, the same wooden door Ms. Merl had come through.

He walked brisk, then hurried, ran, then went into a sprinting dash through the door. The church all wondered why, but Mom knew. I knew. Mom's eyes flooded as she watched her dying son's back bolted through the door, ran pass the willow tree and through the church gate.

It was his escape. Too proud to let the entire church see him crying. He never looked back.

Qwan bent to pick up the ring at the side of his shoe, but as he did so, he went down slow, as if he was unsure, his mind telling him let it stay there, thinking, this wedding made no sense now, already embarrassed, too embarrassed to go on with the wedding. He stood straight, both hands at the side of his white pants, none of his hands having the ring. Empty hands. The ring was there on the tile and we both stared down at it, the entire church did too. The church was a shuffle when Vance sped through the door but now, now it's, it's silent, so silent. I heard the wind blowing through the big willow tree, 'wooeee ... wooeee .... wooeee' and I didn't know why, but I took it as an omen, as a sign of warning, calamity ahead – WOE. I knew worse was yet to come.

In some sort of way Loriel seemed to feel what was going on, though she was so young. Somehow she could feel the tension in the entire church, read everyone's face, no one was smiling. The skippiness vanished from her face, her little princess dress was still pretty but her face was not. It wasn't that her face wasn't pretty. No, not that. It was worried, like everyone's face in the church was, as if the worry was a contagious disease and it infected the child. In a hesitant and careful motion, her small jejune fingers picked up the ring from whence it had fallen and remained. Mom brutishly snatched the ring from out Loriel's hand and stretched her arm at me, the ring in the middle of the bald hairless portion of hand. The ring had grains of dust clung around the white gold. It wasn't glistening much anymore, maybe it too had a sad-face or a face of worry of what's to come next. Mom spoke,

"Here."

She grabbed my wrist and forced the ring into my hand. She stared at me stern, penetrated my eyes. Her jaws tensed and it was as if Mom was sending me a silent message, or stronger, a silent threat. Of course she was. She had carefully devised this plan six years ago and today I was on the verge of wrecking it. Tearing away all her hopes from her chest of saving her only begotten son.

I looked away from her fiery stare, opened my hand and looked at the ring. There was no dust on it anymore. It was glistening, a sign of hope perhaps. More tears came to my eyes as I realised that my whimpish actions would not only kill Vance, but I was killing Mom at the same time too. I had to do what I had to do. Inside, I forgave Qwan for everything he had done. A tear fell in my hand, and another fell. It made a tiny splash on the ring. The pastor spoke,

"Ms. Lexings ..." He then paused a beat.

I slowly turned my head up from the ring in my palm, looked at the pastor, my vision blurry with tears. I rubbed my wrist across both my eyes, rubbing back and forth as if dust had blown in my eyes.

A voice broke off the Pastor before he spoke again,

"Lee, stop behave like mascot nuh!" Everyone looked at Pinky's loud mouth, her lips covered in bright red. The pastor continued his question,

"Will you take him Ms. Lexings?" This time Pastor Ellis spoke calm and patient, he waited on my reply as he sensed my battle inside. He saw the bloom of my love for Qwan conquering all else, waited on my internal turmoil to stop boiling, simmer, reach to a calm, a solid decision. He stood there lay-waiting my answer. The entire church did, all waiting in silence. Munchy tweeted. The yes may have come a long time sooner if it were Ajrien.

Qwan saw the positive vibe that was returning to me. His eyes revitalised. Everyone eye's were staring at me so intensely that their stares felt like pointed needles sticking all over and into my skin, even though it was my lips they were all staring at for my response. As I tried to make my answer come through my parted lips, my knees felt totally useless and my lungs were beating like a heart so bad I couldn't talk. Not speaking, too anguished to find a voice in my throat, I shook my head, nodding in approval, yes. I do.

I cleared my choked throat with a "Ahem-em" and mustered up all the power in my voice to say 'I do' aloud this time, so all the church could hear. I opened by mouth and a brawling commotion at the church door interrupted. What the hell was going on?

It was an onslaught of attacking badwords spleening violently. In a church? At my wedding? The biggest day of my life? Who the hell was this? I spun to the direction of the door. The girl had a teenage-mutant-ninja-turtle shape, Donatello. She was charging into the church, pointing directly at Qwan. A hot fever took me over as I sensed the cataclysmic mayhem and debacle that's about to take place in less than thirty seconds. I grew cross, angry, miserable, gnashed my teeth. I couldn't believe the choice of a scalawag Qwan was cheating with. This definitely didn't look good on me. She was nowhere close to my class, not by a long shot. How could Qwan stoop so low? She was a jessibel.

My body flustered with trepidation and stirred with discomfiture. And only if Judas was an hypocrite, then so was I. Because buried inside, I felt a quenching burst of glee, a cheer, to know Qwan was wrong to have been cheating, it was like I had recovered from my hesitancy of saying 'I do', and now all the blame was on him. One question was in constant rotation in my mind. Who is this bitch? Who is this bitch? Who the hell is this bitch?

After what Qwan did lastnight, now this? How much can I take? To live in a lifelong marriage with all this? All of this? This is a huge exchange to save my brother's life. Because I was basically handing over my life to live in a lifetime of frustration and disrespect as far as I could see. Look at this trashy bitch. Who is she? But you know what, Qwan had handed me a packet of power over him. Gave me the upper-hand in the situation. I didn't felt guilty any more. I stood straight.

I looked at Qwan with disgust in my eyes and Qwan returned the stare. He looked more surprise than I was. He asked me,

"Who is that dirty old ghetto whore?"

I looked down the isle at her. I realised she wasn't pointing at Qwan. She was pointing at me. Me? My heart plummeted, shot down into the pit of my belly. Who the hell was she? I regained maximum strength in my legs. Rocketed out of the church, heels cantering away. My ankle twisted. I collapsed under the willow tree in its cool shadow. Got back up, quickly. Sprinted even faster down the flank. I knew who she was. God damn! This was one big dirty scandal and eruption. I fled the scene.

I looked behind me just in time to see Qwan collapsing, head slamming on the floor, connecting at the exact spot the ring fell. The willow tree made an even louder 'wooeee! .... WOOEE!'

Munchy snapped close-up pictures of Qwan knocked out cold on the church floor, I heard Munchy cried out,

"WOOIIIEE!! A yahso nice! MIX-UPPP!!"

I didn't look back. I kept running and the uproar in the church got ten times louder as Pinky gnashed her teeth an pelted like a gladiator at war towards the girl. Things were spiralling out of control and Pinky wasn't trying to cool it down. Pinky was about to create the greatest mayhem ever to occur inside a church; right now.

CHAPTER 18

Braveheart, I Won't Run
by: Pinky

I don't 'fraid of no man. No gal. Nowhere.

Mi short of breath take mi the instance mi set mi eyes on the three color face gal that zooped through the church's door. She come through the door with some long dirty badwords in her mouth and calling up Leelia name. Mi head get hot, blood start boil, eye start fry. Mi don't know why Leelia run gone from the hippopotamus, all mi know is that if she don't shut her rass mouth, mi smashing in every single one of her thirty-two Chiffon butter teeth. Mi heated and couldn't control mi tongue, as the concubine step through the door, mi start daub her up.

"Hey little stinking swarthy gal, what you know 'bout mi sister?"

Everyone was shuffling away from her. Mi charge towards her. Weave pass the crowd that clustered around Qwan. They were fanning him, trying to revive him and Micheal Douglas shouted,

"Somebody call the doctor!" then in a snort-like grunt added "Huh, huh!" He was kneeling over his unconscious son, sweat washing his shine head and running down his bald face.

Little Loriel frighten till she throw her two hands over her eyes when mi power-raged by her and down the isle to lick the sadamite gal in her face. Munchy take one picture again, nobody love mix-up more than Munchy, not even Raga, not even Biggy and things about to get real nasty in here today. Church or no church.

"No Pinky!"

Aubrea exclaimed, charging behind me, but not before mi tear off a piece of this sketel gal face. Mi kick off one of my heels and the entire church had their eyes on me now, not Qwan on the floor. I kicked off mi other heels, speeding up my strides and dragging out my earrings. People stand-up out of their seats and tipping over each other's shoulders and head-tops to see the clash of the Titanics. People start beg and desperate outbursts of pleas scatter-scatter all 'bout in the crowd.

"No! Don't bother with that!"

"No Pinky! Leave her!"

The loudest voice was Pastor Frog-face

"THIS IS A CHURCHHH!" clutching his Bible tight, stomping one foot and raising one hand to the ceiling. That didn't damp my flaming temper much less cool me down. No. A violent belch of wind busted through the church and cla-clammed the huge window shut. Two fierce clapping sound behind each other 'CLA-CLACK! ... CLA-CLACK!' and the rattling sound of the windows followed after, 'Tiltltlll'.

I couldn't care less about any damn church, for all I care, all the church do, is rob up people money, and from the gal diss mi sister, mi going to kill it. Church can't save her, neither frog-face, him can go on shaking the Bible in the air all him want. She dead.

I bent and grabbed up a green flowers pot in my hand, charging to the gal and she like an idiot, charging full speed at me, like the little imbecile don't see mi with a big tough flowers pot in mi hand for her face. After her head not hotter than mine. Watch the two of us going to clash now, she not easing up and mi definitely not easing up. She shouted out,

"The little dirty whoring gal just fuck with mi man in the bathroom, mi see the pic..."

And before she could finish say anything cantankerous about mi sister, mi give her one solid bloodclawt lick with the flowers pot. Right in her face. The pot shelled out and Munchy catch everything on camera, live and direct, like she working with The Jamaican Star or TVJ.

Nathan was tearing towards us faster than a jam-packed, speeding coaster bus on the Constant Spring bus route. The little short coward tearing through the church door to rescue his little slut. A few other people ran to help her too. The pot split into pieces on contact with her face. Black dirt ran from the pot, spilling and nastying up all of her face and ran down into her heavy bosom. She drop on her back, 'DOOP!' and things start fly. Her jeans skirt button, flew off and rolled on the floor. Her black and burgundy wig took a flight off her head, flipped a couple somersaults through the air and sprawled out beside another green flowers pot in the isle. On top of her head looked bad; it badly wanted some sort out. Leelia would say it was an 'horrendous atrocity', 'cause Lee obsess with doing everything neat. When her wig flipped off, the tacky and tear-up tear-up top of a black wig-cap was over her dry and frizzy cane-row hair. Some of the cane-rows looked like them pull out half way because of how long she had it in. Her face looked lifeless, it was just big and there on the floor, fat and round like spare wheel for the tractors on construction site, her neck was blacker than the rest of her body and had about four fat folds on each side.

I jumped on top of her, sat in her high-rise stomach. A small fart got lose, right in her stomach. What a time for the ice cream to start work mi. It couldn't come at a better time. Poop on her yes. Mi hope the fart blind her. Her breathing not visible. I thought she'd be puffing and breathing hard, but there was no sign of her breathing. She looked unconscious, her eyelids batting but not opening, like she wanted to open them but like she was battling to find the energy to lift her eyelids. She didn't have the strength. I heard a woman's voice,

"Oh God no! No Pinky! Don't kill her!"

It sounded like my mother, Aubrea, but mi never looked back. I grabbed the other flowers pot, raise it with both hands high above my head. I heard fast pacing footsteps charging from behind me. I didn't look back to see who it was, but I knew they were coming mighty fast and I knew they were heading towards me to interrupt me smashing her face again, trying to save her. Mi use all of my might and brute force and bashed the other flowers pot again in her forehead. The pot splintered into pieces and more black dirt buried her face. Her head twitched, her body jerked, then stiffened, got lifeless. I rubbed the dirt in her face. A trailer fart came out. Mi think everybody hear it. Loud and clear. Makes no sense mi try cover it. If mi fart, mi fart, is what? Everybody do it. Don't? Ice cream working mi belly and mi can't control mi bottom. The farts slipping out like as they like, as if they have a mind of their own.

The second blow to her forehead bust open above her eyebrow. It was wide and open and long. The blood gushing from it soaked some of the dirt on her face and some ran down her face to the floor. I reached for a next flowers pot, mi breath, mi blowing short.

"No! She's too wicked! Hold her!" I heard from standing witnesses in the holy church. Confusion. Mayhem. Chaos. DISGRACE.

Vance was the one running behind me. He had ran back into the church and now he wanted to create peace, part the fight and stop the pandemonium. I was a raging torpedo with only one thing on my mind, mash-up this gal face, smash, grab, squeeze. Mi just couldn't cool down.

"Lord have Mercy!" Ms. Merl cried out as I took the third flowers pot that was close by her feet. Her feet as skinny as cat whiskers .The french-coffee coloured stocking fit her fine legs loose with much room around them as if the stocking was worn two hundred times more than it should be worn, stretched out, and at her bony knee caps it fitted her even more swingingly. I raised the green pot high above. Ms. Merl smacked her forehead with her palm, her glasses tilted. She shut her eyes. Mi bite mi lips with monstrous force, gathered all my strength in my arms and swung mi hands down with all my might, right down into the E.T. face.

But there was no pot.

Mi hands empty.

I swung my head back to see which idiot wasn't in their right mind to come snatch out mi weapon. Whoever it was, mi going to sheg them up royally. Proper. Watch.

It was my brother. Vance. Cho man!

I spun my head back around, and all I knew was that, I didn't see the person, or better yet I didn't know who it was. All I saw was the shine bottom of a brand-new, made-in-China boot with the heel powerfully sailing directly into my mouth. It looked like I saw a size eleven and a half or maybe it was a thirteen on the boot bottom, it was coming so fast to my face I was confused. I couldn't even duck the kick. Mi did just have to take it. Mi never know who it was but mi did sure he could kick better than Beckham. I felt the heel rammed into my top lip and some of the heel caught just below my nose too. And even if there were ten JPS in Jamaica they couldn't have enough energy to fuel the light I saw flash right before my eyes; it was the brightest light ever. I swore I felt some of my teeth shifted. Instantly I started to fret about my smile. As white as my teeth were, my smile wouldn't look so lovely with two missing front teeth. Just Picture mi with the smile. I saw only the blackest blackness after the bright light flashed. I dashed my two hands over my blinded eyes. Vision slowly blurring back into them. I removed my hands and squinted my eyes over and over to find out who it was. Who was it? I saw. And him certainly dead.

The Heart of Revenge

I couldn't believe it was the coward. Nathan. What a short man foot big! Mi going to kill the short little tokoo-tokoo fucker. He had no idea what he just did, he must have seen a pretty little lot by Dovecot that he couldn't wait to be buried in. I sprang up off the bitch and Nathan gave mi the other boot heel solid, kicking mi right under mi eye, nearly slipped out mi jawbone like the great King Yellow-man.

It didn't slow me down. Before I could bite out his eye, fool-fool Vance that again, with his soft heart, always helping people and sorrying for people, come and hold me back again. It seemed like Vance working for a beating too or something.

Mi buck Vance in his face. Then chuck it off and almost break off his neck. The flowers pot was still in one of Vance's hand so he could barely manage mi. Mi rail up and wring up miself out of his hand. Vance held his face with his hand that I got out of and shouted,

"Pinky stop nuh!" That didn't mean a thing to me.

"Pictureman! Mi going to wring your neck like farm fowl!" and I meant every D.E.A.D. of what I said.

I flung a full-fledged fist at his right ears corner. I had problems breathing, but I was either going hard or going hard, so I chose going hard. I felt a big Goliath hand snatched me by the wrist, lifted me off the ground, spun with me and threw me away in the other direction, away from the pictureman. Is who this now? Them want dead?

I couldn't believe that such a thing was done by him. Didn't Daddy see the rawtid-hole kick mi get in my mouth? Before him pop one of the pictureman foot, him come holding on on people and throwing mi one side. He was limping over to me. I stared at him huffing and puffing but somehow my breathing got easier. I began to gather my head the closer Daddy came. The coward, Nathan, got the chance he wanted and bolted out of the church looking like a midget vampire running from sunlight. Daddy looked into my eyes for a moment without saying a word. Then he asked,

"What happen to you? The devil in you? Saviour divine!" He shook his head with an expression that could have been one of disgust. "You plan to mash up your sister wedding? Eeh?"

"But you don't see that is them come here to mash it up? Is me saving it." Daddy's eyes analysed me as if I had done something wrong and I was the one to be blamed but I knew different. I was the hero of the day. He should be thankful, well at least Leelia.

"What mi should've do? ... Let them mash up mi little sister wedding? You must be mad no blood---" I stifled the last half of the badword, not for the sake of the church, but more for the sake that I was talking to Daddy, in a church.

"So you happy now?" He pointed towards the girl who was spread on the floor without looking at her, still looking at me, "Look what you do to the poor girl on the floor. Look there."

"That's what she must get! She too bright ... And ups!"

At this point, mi start get bringle again. I wanted to curse, and shout, and grab, and fling and mash-up everything damn thing in sight. I tried hard to get a grip of my temper. Daddy always told me 'Never let the tail wag the dog Pinky. Always remember, the dog should wag the tail whenever your temper is getting out of control', and by preaching that to me so often, he meant that, I should never let the anger control me, I should control my anger, I'm the bigger one, so I should take control of it, and not it of me. It's like I could hear him saying it to me without him saying it to me and a feeling began to bud inside me. It was an awkward feeling. One that was embarrassing almost. How I felt was a little stupid, a lot stupid, for being so angry and going so senselessly ballistic, especially in the church.

But I wasn't always like this, I swear. I got this violent from the very first day my man, Finaral, walked into my life. He was shoving a gun in my back with his finger on the trigger, on the very first day I met him. I haven't been the same since that drama, especially what he is making me do just for Aubrea's sake. Oh my, I really wished things weren't like this. I couldn't even let Aubrea know. I really wished I had more control over how I reacted to my temper though. I breathed with a little more ease, took softer breaths and cut mi eyes at Daddy when he asked,

"Who's the girl?" Then he rattled his hand in the air like a tambourine, making a signal to Vance as he instructed him, "Vance, go call back Lee."

Vance didn't move from around the drama. It seemed he too was just as curious about the girl as everyone else was in the church. He too wanted to hear the story, the full story. Too bad, mi knocked the bitch out cold into next summer after next, and mi for one, not saying anything bad 'bout mi sister and mi damn well never was going to make the bitch or anyone else come and talk bad 'bout mi sister, more over destroy her wedding and disgrace her. Never.

A heavy gust of wind blew through the willow tree outside. The windows flung back open and the loudest and longest "Woooeeee," from day, bellowed into the church. The loudest omen of things to come, so it seemed.

Out of nowhere, there was another loud uproar in the church that frightened the shit out of me. The horror filled shrieks the congregation made rose the fine hair on my skin and made them stood stiff with terror. Everyone was screaming. Munchy covered her mouth disbelievingly with one hand and snapped pictures with the other. The shouts were bursting from every corner of the church.

"No! Murder! Murder!... Murdahhh!"

My heart began to quail. I turned around, instantaneously I needed my asthma pump and mi felt a series of farts building up in mi bottom.

CHAPTER 19

Do This For Me
by: Vybz

Her serenading scent fills the air around my face, I salivate, run the hardness of my thumbnail down the cushiony center of her panty, pressing against the meaty plump of her sacred flesh. I put my thumb in my mouth, wet it, drag it down the soft edges of her pink pliable pussy tongue through her panty, her eyelids sleepily, sexually, in a trance-like state, flutter down, she keeps them closed. The flesh inside is pink and her juices begin to flow down slightly, lightly, white, flowing beautifully, dabbing the white lace in her pink panty, moisting her inside, my mouth wetting itself. Her panty so wet she must have had a bad bladder. I run my thumbnail back up her edges, not going inside, outside, trailing along the entrance of her slit, her lips swollen, getting bigger, protruding a slight peep out her engorging pussy cheeks. She moans. My sensually smooth touches quietly stroking along her. I wet my thumb again, press my wet thumb harder as I stroke along her. My thumb bends her panty material slightly into her slit and my thumb gets wet through her panty, her face sweetly winces into a sour expression as the words softly whispers from her opened mouth,

"Mmmm .... mmm."

The ceiling above us in the warehouse is a great distance high, a mile high. The walls are a cruise-ship's length apart. People are still here at work. I suck her juices off my thumb. I go down lower, kneel before her. Kiss the curving front of her peach see-through underwear. My big lips presses against her, and on my lips I can feel the temperature of her pussy, it's high, boiling. Her vagina milk seeps through as she awaits my long horny tongue. I make playful sexbites at the front of her panty with the hard edges of my teeth, her pussy turns into liquid. Her juices soak a mark at the front of her panty, I have to taste her. I suck on her pussy through her draws, suck her juices through the panty material, tongue kiss it. The white lace of her panty tickles the corner of my mouth, brushes against my mouthstache. I press my French kiss into her draws, my mouth milking her pussy, sucking her pussy through her panty. Tingles ripple through her spine, she involuntarily her kicks, her spine twists, her whole body twisting, her legs wide apart and trembling. Face flinches when she begs,

"Suck it, suck it please, suck mi pussy, move the draws and suck it now."

I can see her pink clit already protruding from between her chocolaty pussy cheeks. I wonder what her puffy cheeks taste like. Honey? Sweet? The mouth of her pussy is juicy, but stifling by her tight squeezing undie. She wants to take it off and just feeds her pussy in my face, her raw naked pussy. Grind my face. Just grind in my face.

"Just suck it baby, suck mi pussy, suck it real good..." Body sexually overcharged, she gasps from the electrified pleasure running through her, clamps her teeth together, through her clamped teeth she sucks in a long breath with a, 'HEHSSSH' sound then command impatiently..."SUCK IT... HEHSSSH ... SUCK IT."

Her hand roughly shoves me in closer to her drippings, her hips rising closer, nearer to my mouth, forcing it in my face. She wants to sit in my face; she gets aggressive, pushes me down, pushes me hard. I fall. Land on the carton box. I sit there. A box tumbles over, makes an unwanted echo. I look both sides quickly, again over my shoulders.

"Ssssssh."

She doesn't look around. She walks over to me, stands over my head, both legs opened above my head leading all the way up to her drenching underneath. A single sticky drip of her transparent and glistening juice stretches from between her legs, lands on my forehead. Fuck she's wet. She's about to take a comfortable sit in my face. I look both sides again. No one.

She stoops down into my face, her juice runs on to my chin before her pussy reaches my face, she rubs her pussy unto my happy tongue, her taste, ... her taste, she has her own taste, its more delicious than rice and peas. Her pussy covers my mouth. She slathers my lips, my nose, my chin, works her loin in my face, sits her whole body weight onto my face, squashing my mouth broadly. I feel her weight flattening my lips and her vagina together. She grabs the crown of my head, grinds my face, swings her hips rigorously on my face, with a smooth looping motion of her loin, grinding into my mouth, rough oral grinding. She stands back up. Turns around. Turns the other direction over me, her ass to my face, bends over 6:30 without bending her knee, swallows my cock, her pussy above my head like a pink yummy halo. Still sitting on the box, I lean in towards her naked pussy, suck on her pink softness, her legs opened above my head, knees still straight. I'm sucking on her, she's sucking on me. I call this the 6:30-69 position.

She takes me in deep into mouth, chugs it down. I voyage beyond her tonsils, she murmurs a nasal humming noise

'Mhhhm' as she slurps. Floats her tongue on me, affectionately working, mouthing the full length of my cock, flicks her tongue at the cusp, circles it, swallows me deep. A bright lightning of pleasure strikes my body. I jerk and I rock and I kick and twist, and bite, and flinch, and I cringe, the feeling rocketing through my whole body. She pulls me out her mouth, spits on my chocolate cock, wipes it off with her fat plumpy lips, drags her tongue on my balls. Licks along the straightness of my cock, at the side, at the main vein. She flips my cock upward, does a long slow lick on the underside of my cock, curving her soft broad tongue in the V of the penis cusp, swallows it in her summer-like mouth, a shiver runs from my balls to my ten toes, my toes curl. I see Moses in full white speaking to me in seven different languages. Heaven. I'm in heaven. My eyes roll and flutter and roll. God this feels good.

I return the favour, barely skim my tongue over the entrance of her pussy, and without warning, flick my tongue at an unhumanly fast speed, flicking over her pussy lips, tongue, cheeks, labia, clit, just to get her body excited. A helicopter-propeller-tongue swirling. I spread her pussy open, spread one cheek before pulling away the other, both lips apart, sluggishly lick upward with the point of my tongue, lick from the base of her clit right up the center real slow, up to the head of her clit, flicking over her clitoral hood, lick it again, slow. I flatten my tongue, my pliable tongue bending. I make broader wetter licks, licking all the sweet frosting off, swallow up her clit, inside my mouth warm, a sensation warps through her, twists her knees, I spit out her clit, slide inside her with my tongue, soft, warm, slippery, swooping in her. I slow down, linger my tongue on her petrified clit, the center of my tongue sinks deeper as the two sides curb upward, the point of my tongue stiff and hard, flicking it viciously smooth against her swollenness and shove my finger in her warm hole unexpectedly. She jumped, clasped her legs, tingles erupting through her belly. I flicker my tongue up and down and only my lower jawbone is moving. She wobbles, can't stand, spins around, sits on the box, I take out my wet finger, she swallows it, spreads her legs east and west and I bury my stiff pink lively tongue six foot six in her pussy. Her breathing is ragged. Her breathing slows.

Her whole body is getting stiff. Her lips apart, breathing stops, my soft tongue renders her speechless, her eyes hazy in confusion. Her body folds, hands gripping my head between her legs, her shoulders hunched forward in intense pleasure. Her belly goes flat, bracing her pussy forward into my mouth, forcing it forward and forward and forward, her body making waves like a belly dancer, feeds her pussy into my mouth. I eat her. She whimpers,

"Eat it, eat it, fucking eat it!"

Her hand pushes my head hard between her thighs, she twists her closed legs with my head fastened in between them, twists her closed legs the other way, I keep sucking, she pulls me away, slaps me across the face, buries back my lips into her pussy, winds in my face, humps my face off, fucks my face in a horny-can't-get-your-tongue-deep-enough tantrum, twisting wildly, pushes me away, smacks me across the face again; it hurts, forces back my face deep into her tush, takes her hand and pulls on my tongue, her thumb squeezing ontop, pulling my tongue. I flash my head; she grabs the top of my head, fierce, shoves my head back into her, winds in my face, winds in my face hard, wines wildly, never stopping, forcing her cunt into my mouth, humming in pleasure, moaning, feeding me pussy, stuffing my mouth, pussy gags me, corking my mouth. I can barely get air to breathe between her edible thighs, but I keep sucking on her pussy, I never stop. Don't you dare stop forcing it into my mouth. I keep sucking on it, sucking, tongueing her velvety-smooth hole, swiping my horny tongue inside, flicking it up with a bending curve as it touches inside her, a continuous waving swoop. I see a small speck of her juice on the outside of her brown cheeks, I kiss the speck off, a freaky kiss, wet kiss, keep kissing. I get ravish, get carried away, kissing her cheeks with no table manners whatsoever, sloppy, no etiquette about how greedily I'm devouring her pussy, my fat lips clip around her pussy lips, suck, form soapy spit in my mouth, smooth, gentle, I won't stop, determine to find out if I can suck all the skin off her pussy lips. I slide my lips up and down her labia, wanting to take all the taste off her lips and paste it onto my tongue, I keep sliding up and down, her clit fidgets between her pussy lips, it sinks, a contraction, it jumps back up sharply, she can feel a string of tension stemming from the center of her navel to her clit, a connecting jumping muscle, excited from pleasure. Her whole body tremors, like she's freezing, like an epileptic fit, her body twitching and shaking like mad, her legs look as if they are about to fall from under her, she can't stand straight. Her face is the only thing not moving, face twisted but not moving, frozen in a moment of pleasure and shock. A staggering volt of pleasure rises from the center of her navel and spreads up, explodes down in her pussy with a trillion unbearable stings, scorching every nerves they course by in her pussy, torturing her clit, she can't hold back her gushes anymore. It's cumming, it's cumming, the juices charging down in her body, the tingly sensation rips through her nipples, belly, toes and even her asshole tightens, puckers, twitches, her clit twitching so hard her shoulder is shrugging, her mouth hangs open, her breathing is short and harsh,

"Uh! Uh! Uh! I'm cumming, Uh! I'm fucking exploding! Don't stop, Uh! Don't fucking stop! Suck it! Suck it!"

Her fingers gripping at the top of the cardboard box. It slips off the box. She grabs back onto the pointed edge of the box, clings on to it, she's shooting juices, her legs crossing and pleasure paralysing her body, a devastating orgasm. The sensation of cumming ripping from the depths of her pussy, climaxing, magnifying into a maddening pleasure at the pinnacle of her so tender clitoris. Her clit contracts tightly, jumps, a jolt of electric pleasure shoots into her belly. She falls to her knees, shudders, her body nudging in sporadic outbursts, climaxes faintly grazing inside her, prickles under her skin, the popping sensation drifting down her spine. Moments after the tail of her monstrous cumming has passed she's still shaking. Shakes. Shaking. Her body sensitive. She shakes. Her shaky voice utters,

"Fuck, that felt like twelve cums in one."

A high-pitched voice yelled,

The Heart of Revenge

"Who that?" I wasn't sure if the voice was a man or a woman. Sound more feminine to me than a man though. Must be one of her girlfriends that works around the front of the wholesale. I dashed behind the carton. She yelled back.

"Is me."

"Me who?"

The figure swayed closer. It was a straight shaping girl in skin tight jeans with her hair canerow to the back.

"Is Portia, Marlon, you a informer or something? Mi soon come 'round. Mi head a hurt mi man and mi a take a little rest. Mi soon come 'round. You hear?"

"Mr. Yee looking for you from 'bout three thirty till now."

Kiss mi rawtid! I had to look closer. You know is really a man though/ Jah know star, the high-pitch and slur in his voice could've pass for a girl still.

"Tell him mi did in the bathroom. Go on. Mi coming now."

"Alright ... Is you alone round here Portia? Mi never hear a whole heap a noise like you a fuck again round here?"

"You can't stop watch under mi now? Stop watch mi man."

"Is what do pop-down you? Eeh? No bother come try take mi on yaah, mi not able for you mi dear. Mi ask if you a fuck round here again? Talk, talk. Talk up the things them."

"How you chat so much?" She looked at my expression, my expression was stoic. She got more angry at what he just disclosed, she curses "Mi wonder is what you have underneath you? ... Hsst ... You must a pussy-watchman to rawtid."

"Mi watching your sour rae-rae front? Hsst." He braced his chest forward and rocked his head while tracing her. His facial expression over-gesticulated and his mouth formed into many different shapes as he articulately pronounced his words like Shebada would when acting in a play on stage. "Everybody know your clitoris already Portia, don't make mi talk up the things them and do you up bad in here, ooh. 'Cause we all know your first name is Portia and your lastname is Too-Fucky-Fucky. Go on and leave mi yaah."

Is what this man? It look like Portia running her thing red a daytime round here, round the back. Jah know star! Never again, I swear. Marlon dismissed Portia by simply fanning her off with his right hand and as he disappeared from the dark warehouse in the direction he came from he pulled on the end of one of his canerow that hung at the side of his neck. Portia said,

"Come. Give mi a quickie before mi go 'round." Mercy man, Portia could get the lead role in the movie, 'Lord of the Fuck'. How she one love it so?

"You want see that mi don't too feel the vibes again enuh Portia." I began buckling my belt. Portia stared at my hand buckling, she looked somewhat lost.

"Why?"

"Nothing."

"Is Marlon don't? Him can act like a gal you see."

"Not really enuh. This thing has a perplexity to it and it don't look nice. I don't want get in any predicament, better we just call it quits."

"You going to talk to Finaral 'bout the thing for me? ... You must can do that like how mi giving you mi pussy."

"Relax P, meditate. Is not like we fucked, just oral reciprocation. I kissed your pussy and you kissed my cock, that's it, feel mi?"

"Is still fuck that."

"That's foreplay, not sexual intercourse, mi never penetrated you. If mi did penetrate you, you would be on the floor, spread out and in pain."

"Well mi still give you mi pussy."

"Mi give your pussy a favour."

"So you what you saying?"

"Mi can't do it P. Pinky is mi friend too, mi can't do her that."

"You put Pinky over me then?" Everything Portia lead to a diatribe on Pinky. She has such a vendetta against the girl and she can't walk in Pinky's shoe.

"Definitely ... Is a real girl that. Mi chargie that. You feel mi?"

"She giving you her renking front?" This gal bright and feisty, I thought. A couple seconds passed and mi don't answer her, she feel as if she can style mi friend under guise, she better dig out her two eyes and use them watch her mouth. Impatient, she kept hammering for an answer,

"Answer mi nuh, she giving you nothing?"

"No. And don't pass you place with Pinky if you know what good for you. 'Bout the gal front smell renk, fucking bright you bright." I let go my belt, hands formed fists. "And don't even try come with no choose side thing, 'bout choose between you and she, like you think mi is one of you big crotches friend that sit down at street side and chat and lambast and malice people."

"So you really not doing it then?" She insisted on asking again. I released my fist, cooled off my irritation, finished buckling my belt.

"Hear what, better you cease with your persistent inquiry because mi not doing it. You feel mi?"

"Alright. Bet mi catch you and your stinking crotches gal?"

My anger flamed. I shot her a loud as church bell box. 'BOW!' A proper loud up earzass.

The skin of her face twist and her head almost spun right around.

"Don't diss Pinky! You a idiot?"

Her hand flew to her jaw, eyes red with shock, no tears in her eyes, she shouted,

"Bloodclawt Vybz, you really box mi for big hole Pinky?"

Anger blazed higher. I shot her a even louder box that echoed loudly in the warehouse. Still no water in her eyes, she screamed at mi,

" How you so hurt? Eeh?"

"Mi tell you don't pass your place enuh gal."

" Little liar! You fucking Pinky! Don't?"

CHAPTER 20

The Heart of War
by: Pinky

Everybody in the church hung their mouth wide almost touching the floor. They screamed, faces dismantled, nobody moved. Everybody froze; their eyes big and open, two pools of alertness. They were petrified to see what will happen next. Some covered their eyes.

When mi look at it, it look like it's just the people that Qwan bring that covering up their eyes, or were looking away in disgust, like they were all virgins to these things, first time they witnessing these hooligan-ish behaviour up close and personal, but my friends different. All of them shuffled up to the front and at the edge of the isle, closer to the action, don't want miss a thing. If a pin drop they wanted to see. Munchy was the closest, almost in the middle, despite the deathly danger approaching she wanted to be the referee, right in the middle.

Mi did hear the footsteps bolting behind me, but mi never expect this, mi never prepare for this calamity. He wasn't slowing down, he came closer and closer and the crowd got even more frightened crying out,

"Jesus Christ! No! She dead!"

"Murder! Murder!"

Mi want run but mi can't move. My belly moved, griped, a fart slipped out, loud. His tie was blowing over his shoulder and in less than a second, the coward Nathan reached mi with a broad sharp machete in his hand above his head. A next fart went off. Bad gas. From mi look into Nathan's eyes mi know something wrong with the man, Leelia would describe Nathan's eyes as inoculated with manic dement. I say they looked like a mad man on the loose.

Mi foot couldn't even budge, right or left, none of them could move the way I was frightened stiff. My eyes went wider as he swung the machete down to chop me. I wanted to run like a thieving rat for my life, but somehow, I just couldn't move. My feet ceased up and were glued down to the tile. So too was the rest of my body perfectly unmoving. I saw Mr. Death grinning at the tip of the machete and my heart galloped straight through my nose, but my feet still wouldn't gallop, it would not move an inch. Doomed.

The machete swinging to my face. Helpless. My hands empty, no flowers pot, the blade looked sharp enough to slice hair. I do the only thing I could do. Fart. Mi Shut my eyes and wait on the chop as the blade is about to chop my face. Then I heard a,

'DOOP! DOOP!'

Ms. Merl collapsed and hit the benches at both sides of her before hitting the floor. My heart start shit up itself when I opened my eyes and saw the machete was almost into my flesh. Memories of my sons flashed infront my eyes as the blade was getting bigger and bigger in my eyes. Who would take care of my sons? I wanted to piss in the church when I felt the chop, before it even reach mi, landing right into the center of my forehead. A fart broke loose. The ice cream working mi belly mercilessly. I heard a deafening outburst,

"Call the police! Murder Oooo! MURDAHH!"

This was it. I shut my eyes tight and I heard some noise but I didn't feel the chop. It sounded like a collision of some sort. A crash. Pieces of something falling to the tile. Then came another loud,

'DOOP!' and from that solid sound, it hit into the floor real hard.

Mi hear the machete dropped from Nathan's hand. Its metal blade clinking and skittering on the tile 'Cling. Cling. Cling' as it tumbled. What happened? Then another sound, loud, bashing,

"SPLA-SHY!" It sounded brutal. I opened my eyes. Some old women were fanning Ms. Merl with the wedding program, desperately trying to revive her. The holy spirit touched a granny that was over Ms. Merl and she jumped and twirled and bounced up into the other elders standing close by her, causing one hell of a commotion. She was shouting some ancient language or one she just made up, and kept getting louder and louder

"Alla-ma-shalla. Alla –mama-sha. ALLA-MA-SHA!"

I felt a sharp stinging pain in my leg. My skin was open, my flesh too. Where was the chop I was suppose to get? Why didn't I get the chop? The falling machete blade had caught my leg and cut it open. The slice looked deep, wide and exposed my flesh as it bled.

Vance had totally shelled out the flowers pot in Nathan's face. Nathan fell to the floor and Munchy had given him another flowers pot right after. Nathan was flat on the floor in front of me. I felt my blood flowing faster down my leg, it was a warm trickling feeling. The cut was right in my tattoo on my leg, where I already had a horrible scar and fucked up my tattoo on my leg. Water wouldn't come to my eyes, only a raging fire that only Capleton, the fireman, could understand. Nathan almost chopped off my head clean. The cut was stinging with a burning sensation, but my anger was burning much more. Mi head get hot. Hothead. Head ablaze.

Mi grab up the machete off the floor, looked at Nathan's neck, head, neck, aimed and swung the machete above my head. Swung it back down at his head, with every might in mi body, shutting my eyes tight for the blood spill.

You can hear the angry winds outside, a turmoil, her the tense vibration in the air. The windows slammed with the sound of a judgement day drum, echoing through the church. The wooden cross on the wall swung, slanting out of place. It was almost upside down on the wall. Mi feel one hundred hands holding back my arm. The machete would not swing down. Looked who they were. In my rage of a temper I thought what's wrong with these idiots? I saw who it was. It was Daddy and Vance both holding on to my arm. Munchy snapped a picture of the three of us.

Mi wrestle in their hands, fighting to free up myself, so I could chop Nathan in him short rass. I was wild, wheeling the machete aimlessly between Vance and Dad knowing very well the sharp machete could swing and accidentally chop anyone of them, anywhere but more than likely in their face, since the machete was being wrestled at face level. The wild tussle between the three of us fiascoed all over the church, the blade dangerously swinging all over as I wildly buffaloed to get the machete for myself. I knew one of us would get a decent chop from the machete and I was certain it wasn't me, the best thing for them to do, was let go the machete and leave me with it. They wouldn't let me go instead they wrestled harder and wilder, I wrestled back wilder and harder and determined. The wheeling machete brushed the pastor glasses off his face. He sprang backward and chanted with fright but with greater anger,

"The dev---vil is in this child. The dev-vil!" Everybody heard him already and he still went on to holding up his Bible high in the air maybe to get everyone's attention and hear him chanting again, like the people were deaf,

"The DEV-VILLL!! ... I say the DEV. VILLL, is in this CHILDDD!"

Mi step on his glasses. Crush it out. Good. Like crushing out weed and grabba.

Vance's grip loosened. Both his hands freed up from around mi. I wrestled with Dad as Nathan tried to get back to his feet. I kicked him back down. Stomped in his face. Wrung my heel in his jaw pretending I was still crushing the pastor's glasses, crushing his face.

He whacked my foot off his face. I lost my balance, farted, fumbled to stand straight and Daddy held me firm. The fart smell bad this time. I heard something fall to the ground. Or maybe it was someone as the 'DOOP!' sound was loud. I walloped another loud kick in Nathan's soft throat, 'WHOOP!'. He grabbed around his neck with both hands. I snatched another flowers pot with my free hand that Vance had let go, bashed his head good with it. It made a loud thwack sound. He wasn't moving anymore. I looked around to see what or who had made the loud dooping sound before.

I saw who it was. I tried to control my fart-ish feelings. I got stiff with shock. No. No. No. It was my brother on the floor, both hands squeezing his chest trying to grab hold of his heart. His knees curled up to his chest as if he were trying his hardest to curl small enough to fit into an oyster's shell, or trying to fit back into his mother's womb, a fetal position. He kicked with small surges of epileptic-like shocks, eyes looking beyond the ceiling. I remembered Dr. Reid saying that the next heart attack he got he would die. Vance lips trembled out his last dying words,

"Uh... Uh." kicked, blinked a thousand times, "Uh." he couldn't breathe, squeezing his chest. Mi bawl out,

"Nooo ... Vaaance, Vance. No! Noooo!"

His hands fell from his heart. Screams of pain flooded inside the church. There were unconscious bodies laying all over the church's floor. Five bodies on the floor if you count. I heard another loud fall.

'DOOP! DOOP!'

I dropped the machete from my hand at the sound. I hoped it wasn't anyone hitting the floor again. Snapped my head around, my head thrown out of thinking straight, fright crawling in my belly and up to my heart. I looked in the direction of the pulpit where I heard the sound, in my heart I was clasping my hands and closing my eyes, praying it was the pastor who called me the devil. It wasn't the pastor. My eyes opened as wide as my mouth when I saw it was Aubrea. She fainted, slamming the side of her head into the tough edge of the pulpit floor. Her head was not bleeding, but it had a long swelling at the side of her eye, even though mi can't stand Aubrea, mi hope that it was just a cocoa and not internal bleeding. Six bodies were on the floor.

Mr. Douglas held his phone in place at his ears with his shoulder as he lifted Qwan off the floor and carried him out of the church.

Vance baffled to speak,

"Mi... heart" gasped weakly and even his gasped seemed interrupted by not having enough strength, "Mi hea—" Then he couldn't speak another syllable. His lips moved, trembled, no words came out his mouth, only spit and frothing at the corner of his mouth closest to the floor, and there on the floor his spit leaked. It formed a a small watery spit puddle by his unconscious head.

No one made a move around him. I dropped to the floor, felt his chest, his heart, it wasn't beating, no heartbeat. I didn't wipe his spit and froth before I performed mouth to mouth resuscitation on him. I tried. I tried. I tried. Oh God I tried. Pumped his chest, pinched his nose, blew air into his lungs. Pumped his chest, blew. Blew, blew, blew. With all my might I blew. It wasn't helping. His heart already stopped. My tears came. Washed down my cheeks. His eyes were still looking beyond the ceiling, still opened, looking at God. Looking at death. Dying. My tears falling on his dead chest. I looked to the ceiling, cried out,

"Why Lord? Why? Oh Lord why? Please."

I was too weak to stand. Crying, crying, crying till I couldn't see anyone, just water in my eyes. Please God. Please. Pleeease.

Nothing we could do to save him. His eyes opened. Dying. Gone.

CHAPTER 21

The Broken-Hearted
by: Leelia Lexings

My wedding day was like a bad episode out of Gossip Girls. I was crying, shaking, hunched up, sucking on my thumb in Gloe's room. Her room was a little bigger than a closet, barely had elbow space. I was tearing up inside. The door closed and the windows shut. The room dark and I am all alone sobbing.

(((Rrring. Rrring)))

(((Rrring. Rrring)))

I was too shaken to pick up my cell. I only wanted to speak to God, not a soul else. My chest, my head and my eyelashes hurt from crying. Instead of helping Vance, I blew his only chance he would ever have at saving his life. I didn't know what I would say to Vance tomorrow, didn't know how I would ever face him again, or Qwan. I had no idea where Nathan's girlfriend came from. But I was sure she must have preached disgraceful inequities about me, to the entire congregation, all my family, friends, to Qwan, to Qwan's friends and she didn't know my circumstances, but she was going to judge me right? And talk all manner of crap about me. They all at the church now just sitting and chatting shit about me, I can bet. I tried not to let it get to me. I was so sorry Vance, I'm so sorry Qwan. Maybe I should call Vance now. Later I would. I just wanted to cool off for the rest of the day. My head was splitting. My heart felt heavy. I looked at my phone ringing, it was Pinky. I didn't answer.

Not now.

CHAPTER 22

Full Heart Attack
by: Pinky

Mi hate hospital bad. If death had a scent it would smell like hospital. If that smell had a taste it would taste like the yellow fester-poss being squeezed into your mouth from some old sore of a rottening foot. The scent of disinfectant, medicine, raw open cuts and stale sores make me want to fill my mouth with my own vomit.

Vance was unconscious on a hospital mattress that was as thick as a BNS credit card. The shiny aluminium base has four wheels. The white pillow cases seem white straight through but it's the white sheet spread that's getting to me. It has a pale brown spot that just freaks me out looking at it. It just says death. Makes mi wonder who died in this bed? Did they make that spot? How many died in this bed? Mi can't get rid of thoughts like these whenever mi inside one hospital. The last time mi get one asthma attack, mi ask Daddy to carry my own sheet. Mi think 'bout death and mi heart start behave bad, get weak to know my brother battling for his life in the said bed.

Whether or not mi did lick Nathan's galfriend in her face and mash down Nathan, Vance heart would still attack him. It was just its time to attack him. It's God's works. It was all written in black ink in God's book of life. Anything the big man write in that big hardcover book is destiny, must come to pass, and we little earthlings can't do jack to change what the Lord ordains. We can't rub out what God had written and we can't change the date. If it's written, it's written, mi never give Vance a bad heart. Mi can't manufacture heart and if mi could make hearts, mi wouldn't give Vance or anybody in my family a heart that's working bad. I would give it to Portia, she love take people man too much. Is she must get that.

I can't stand that little dash away belly gal. Because of she, right now mi fretting and worrying about this big hell of a dilemma that she made so much worse on mi now Mi don't know what to do. Mi wish mi could just done her and nobody don't know is me get rid of her. She just come spoil mi fucking life.

Mi never know a little gal that love go dance like Portia. And every dance she go, she have to go on her head top and wine-wine up her skin and just dash-out dash-out like she a go-go. Even after she did breed for Finaral, and dash away the baby, she tell the man that is lose she lose the baby. How Finaral find out now that is lie the gal was telling, was two days after she dash away the belly, she gone party at dance and dash dashing out and wine-wine up her little fine self. She end up start bleed, bleed, bleed and they have to rush with her go down to KPH (Kingston Public Hospital).

The taxi that bring her go had to take out his car seats and go wash it out how bad she bleed-bleed up on the seats. When she go to see the doctor she had to talk up the things 'bout her recent abortion, she couldn't tell no lie. When Finaral go find out he left her at the hospital and didn't pay her hospital bill. Her two partners in crime, Syreta and Nash make up them money together, and pay the hospital bill for her.

When she reached home, Finaral pulled his gun, he shot at her twice. He shot at her nose-bridge and chest. It caught her ears, taking off a piece and the other ripped though her shoulder. She was on the floor bleeding. He came over her and gave her another shot. Shoot her in the chest. The old tough turbit never dead. She survived and to think that would make her stay a hundred miles away from Finaral, it's like she take a set on him. Mi almost sure she and Finaral start fuck back again. And mi know she up to something, nobody can't tell mi nothing.

With all that went down at Lee's wedding, mi never did have a choice. Mi couldn't make the slime bucket diss mi sister and spoil her wedding, not under my dead body. Mi mind flash back on Vance. Both his arms had needles in the main veins. The syringes were hooked up to clear tubes that swirled to the drip. The drip was hooked up to a slender stand that reminded me of a mic-stand on four wheels, but this one was in all chrome. When Vance's heart sent him folding on the floor, his heart stopped beating for about six minutes. After not quitting the mouth to mouth resuscitation, I did get some breathe into him and his heart beating again. But he had not blinked since.

Everybody's face in the hospital looked like zombies, like they already dead, and the walls too. They looked plain gray and dead. The faces of all the nurses were naked of smiles. Dad was not the type to cry, his eyes had in tears. His stance was uneven, easing most of the weight onto his good leg, holding his black jacket in his hand, his face looking as if he were at his son's funeral and the hospital bed he was standing over was actually the grave that his son was in. Mi feel bad for Daddy. Mi feel worse for Vance. I stepped closer to Daddy. I felt the worst about what I did. I held my head down.

Mi try to chase away the worst outcome of this situation from out my mind.

"Daddy everything will be good, don't worry 'bout nothing." I reached for his hand and held it, he looked away from the grave and looked at me.

"How mi mustn't fret? This is the second time this year."

"Mi know... but still ..." I tried my hardest to up my spirit and keep positive so I could say positive things to Daddy, "Don't God bring him through the last time? Don't Dr. Reid said him would be dead? Don't he's still living?" All these words just poured out off me without me even thinking about what to say, it just came naturally, "Leave it to God ... he controls all things."

"Yeah ... But .. I don't know," he shook his head, "This worse than ever. If he lost two weeks memory the last time and suffered minor brain damage, what will happen with this big one?"

"How can you know that this one is worse and he only here less than an hour now. The last time he was in a coma for six days, you can't know the outcome of this so don't try predict the worst. Things gonna be crisp man."

"Dr. Reid said that if he doesn't get an ablation treatment done on his heart in less than an hour, he's gone for good."

"Mi don't understand you, what you mean gone for good?" My anger jerked inside me.

"Gone, gone. Dead."

Mi couldn't even talk. Even though mi know his condition was life and death, I just had it in my head that everything was going to be good. God won't let a good person die young, more over die a virgin. My man is an old murderer and he is almost twice Vance's age. I know Vance won't die

The Heart of Revenge

but .. but... what Daddy told me, gave me a bitch lick and frightened the hell out of me, it's kind of like walking casually in the street, chatting and laughing with your close friend and a man screechy up behind you and fling one, rawtid, river stone and bust your head. That was the sudden fright and pain I felt. Dad was looking up to the hospital ceiling as he mouthed,

"All the talk mi talking to Dr. Reid, showing him that he will get the money, just go ahead and do the surgery, 'cause as soon as we get through to Leelia, he get the money. But all him keep saying is that him can't start that surgery without it being paid for beforehand."

"Wait there. Stop right there so. Him know it's Vance?"

"Then nuh must. Of course him know, his exact words were 'I'm sorry Mr. Lexings, I can't administer any of that drug or start the surgery before payment, that's the company's policy, can't break procedures.' No matter how I pleaded to him he just kept on repeating like a robot. ' I can't break procedures, I can't procedures. I can't break procedures Mr. Lexings.'."

"Bet if mi man roll up in here he would run go do it fast. Or bet if it was his uptown friend son dying he forget about procedure, procedure," vexation was wrathing through my body, I got louder,

"Or if a money people him start operate long time before him get the first dollar. BUT WE NOT IMPORTANT. DON'T ?"

"Pinky just relax."

"How much for the operation?"

"Sixty-four thousand."

"Sixty-four thousand! No ... but look how much money we spend with dry-up Dr. Reid already ... We ever owe him a dollar yet ... NO!" My breath got heavy and my voice climbed higher,

"And my brother must bloodclawt dead, over sixty-four fucking thousand dollar? After we spend over a million dollar in here so. And with him same one! And you gone tell me that my brother going to dead over SIXTY-FOUR THOUSAND DOLLAR!" Mi wanted to mash up every rass thing in the hospital, "Must Belleview this 'cause they must fuck mad in here." Mi hands start squeeze itself angrily. "Where Dr. Reid?"

Mi start map out the place to see if mi spot Dr. Reid.

"Where him gone? As a matter of fact ..."

I walked off. Daddy grabbed my hand, the only one person in the world that can cool me down, the one person who thought me never let the tail wag the dog. The dog should wag the tail. He spoke to me firmly,

"Pinky control your temper." I replied,

"Control mi bomboclawt!" He stared at me with huge bulb eyes," Yeah I cursed badword to Daddy, so what? It's not the first. Mi is mi own big woman. Mi have mi own kids, mi live on mi own. Mi is an adult. Daddy curse them too. No disrespect because I love Daddy till the day my bones turn to dust, but right here now, mi vex till mi couldn't even control what was coming out my mouth. Mi try to rivet the situation in his head. "You a idiot? We spend almost a million dollar here on Vance, Dr. Reid know the youth and that's how him gone deal with us?" I yanked my hand out of Dad's grip.

"What mi should do? Stand up here so over mi brother and watch him dead?"

"What you doing won't solve anything either Pinky. Don't?" Mi never answer. He rask again, "Don't?" Mi still never answer. "What you gone do then? Fight? That's what you gone do? That'll make anything better or worse? Think nuh."

"You want bet? Bet Dr. Reid have to come in here come do the operation right now. Just watch." I stormed off.

"PINKY!"

"Mi not standing over any bedside and watch my brother dying, and the doctor and medicine is here, you must be sick in your head. After Dr. Reid don't want dead in here today."

Dad caught up with me, grabbed both my hands. I wrestled hard to get loose. All that was on my mind was to wring Dr. Reid's neck till mi hear 'POP!'. If mi have to haul Dr. Reid by his tongue to get the operation done on my brother before him dead, well, by all means, the pleasure is mine. Vance getting that operation today.

Mi talk on top of my voice so that even the dead at the hospital think mi too loud.

"Let mi tell all of you this." I raised my voice and my face gesticulated the wrath I was in. "Anyhow ... My brother ... Dead in here today." mi pat my chest three times hard as when mi cursing, "Me personally killing everybody who work in here." Mi sweep my hand infront me from one side to the next to gesture the everybody, "Everybody in here! After mi done murder the one Dr. Reid."

Dad shook me and my weave became a mess. Mi tussle, twist and turn in his hand.

"Let mi go Daddy. None of them don't have no respect for life. All of you in here sell your souls and you don't even know it. Before you work to save a life, you rather watch people dead if them don't have the money. Money! ... PAPER! ALL OF YOU SELL OUT YOUR DIRTY SOUL. To be poor really is a fucking crime in Jamaica."

"Pinky! Settle! Control your temper."

All were staring at me as if I got out the insanity ward and I was the dangerous type. The nurses' white hats that were moving about and the ones that were at the patients' bed all faced me, and the patients who couldn't sit up, merely turned their heads slowly in pain to face me.

"Lost something? Is what all of you looking for? Which part Dr. Reid? Him mi want find."

The nurses who were with the patients behind the green curtains, drew their curtains a tad and peeped their heads out. Whenever I looked their direction they would try to hide their faces so I wouldn't see them.

A security was marching towards me in seriousness, taking militant strides. Mi yell out,

"Ooooiie, Rambo, where you going?" He kept coming to me as if I were issuing out free U.S. visa and greencard. "Please just touch mi. Please, mi beg you."

Dad used one hand to put up a stop sign to the security, him stop and observe from which part him did stop. But God know mi did want one of them just touch mi. Daddy shook me for about a minute straight.

"Just control you temper little girl and make we try to save Vance life, not try go jail ... Time's running."

Mi draw out mi asthma pump out my handbag, take two puffs, two more puffs, one more. Settled down against my will, still mapping the premises to see if Dr. Reid was insight.

"Your mother alright?"

"Don't ask mi anything 'bout Aubrea."

Daddy stared at me and was just looking like him lost something in my face. Everybody was returning to what they were doing, the look of excitement left the nurses' face, and a look of tiredness took back their seats in their faces. The sick patients returned to being sick.

"You bought the coconut water for her right?" I didn't answer.

"She get it?" Daddy snapped tightening his big jawbone

"No."

"What you do with it then?"

"Mi leave it in the fridge at the receptionist on her ward, the nurse said I should just leave it there since Aubrea still sleeping. She will let Aubrea get it when she wake up."

"Then from the time you gone, what take you so long to come back?"

"Mi go pee-pee ---"

"Pee-pee so long? Is what you pissing out so?"

"Listen nuh, you never make mi finish. And then mi was trying to get a light."

"You won't stop smoke weed?"

"You won't stop go rum bar?"

"Everywhere you go, you have weed hitch up between your breasts."

Mi push down the weed deeper in mi bosom, hissed my teeth, 'cause mi not seeing him, 'bout stop walk with weed.

"You know how much time my weed save mi out of trouble on the road?"

"Stop chat foolishness. What kind of trouble? Hsst!"

"All type."

Daddy hissed his teeth again. "Anybody answering my phone?"

"No. Look like them take out the chip."

"Call it again."

"Them take out the chip already, it just going straight to voice mail when mi call. Look like them take up you little piece of Nokia and gone with it."

"Call it again nuh Pinky."

"For what? It gone Daddy, just call that George." Dad shook his head in regret as he came to grips with reality that his little old piece of Nokia 3310 that him love so much really gone. He stilled his head and sped out the question,

"Get through to Leelia yet?"

"No. Mi not getting she either." I didn't even look over at Vance on the bed, I dialled Lee, praying to God she just answer her damn phone this time. It's not like Lee to leave her phone anywhere. Time was ticking away. I stared at Vance as I put the phone to my ear.

(((Rrring. Rrring.)))

CHAPTER 23

Emergency, Just Pick up
by: Leelia Lexings

    Honestly, I don't think I'll even get my stuff from Qwan's house. I'll stay here by Gloe till I get somewhere to rent, definitely not going back to the ghetto by Mom. The only problem is how will I pay my school fee? Where will I get that money to finish up UWI? Where? My clear blue sky was turning gray to black to shit. The more I thought, the more my inside tightened. I felt like my whole inside was getting smaller. The tears stormed down my face. I pulled my thumb out my mouth, wiped more tears with the tissue.

    (((Rrring. Rrring)))

    I picked up my phone. Pinky again. I didn't have the courage or stamina to deal with Pinky and her bombastic drama right now. All she was calling for was to curse and exaggerate everything. Or maybe to blame me. Whatever was her drama I didn't want to hear. Pinky didn't understand what I was going through and she's only going to blast things even worse. I wanted to hug Mom, I want to lock myself into Gloe's room forever. I never wanted to see anyone again. Jump off a cliff. Kill myself. My crying got loud, and breathing was like an asthma attack.

    "Vance ... Oh Vance." I sniffed, wiped, patted my nose. The flints off the tissue aggravated my sinus.

    I was gonna make it up to Qwan. That's the only way out. What would I have to do for him to ever forgive me, and forgive me soon. He would never forgive me. He never would. What in the world could be worse for a bride to do to her groom on his wedding day? Fuck seven cameramen? I must have given him the worst day of his life. The only way he would forgive me, the only way I could think of, was his father, Micheal Douglas. Yeah, that was it. Mr. Douglas owes me that much to be quiet. He must. Or else, I would tell everyone about what he did. A man who was so proud of the reputation he had spent years building would do anything to keep me hushed and having me publicized what's hidden in his closet. I knew he didn't want that. No way. That's the plan.

(((Rrring. Rrring)))

I looked at the phone's caller ID, it's sis. I can't manage you now Pinky, my head was in too much of a shamble. Ajrien. With everything tumbling down around me with this marriage, I thought about what's real love. I was stupid to have been keeping my feelings for Ajrien closeted up. Should I let him know I still think of him a lot? Or do I even have the courage to let him know? What the hell, I've been keeping it buried forever. What's wrong with a little harmless text to a childhood friend? I texted him a message with only two words in the text. ***'Miss you'***. I didn't want to say too much. I hoped it was enough to let him know that though I hadn't spoken to him in years, I had his number, would never lose it and I still thought of him.

(((Rrring. Rrring)))

(((Rrring. Rrring)))

I shut my phone off.

No more calls. I just wanted to breathe, clear the noisy confusion out my head. I fell myself backward, flat on my back on the bed, spread my arms wide, staring up into the zinc roof and thought why didn't Danielle at least made it concrete. It was the least she could do to upgrade the place and make it a little more neat and presentable. It looked so messy, and it's not like she wasn't making good money. My feet hung from the bed and was almost touching the brown wood of the old dresser infront the bed. I kicked off my heels. Shut the world out. Alone. I just want to be alone. No calls.

No world.

Just alone.

No calls.

CHAPTER 24

What Now?
by: Pinky & Leelia Lexings

"Get her yet?" Daddy asked mi.
"No. She lock off her phone on mi." Dad shook his head.
"Can't believe she turn off her phone at a time like this, when her mother and brother in hospital one time."
"Remember she don't know Daddy."
"How you know she don't know? Somebody must call and tell her."
"Well mi don't know 'cause mi never get to talk to her, so mi can't judge and say nothing."
"Stop you noise Pinky, big rawtid mix-up like this and she don't hear. Have sense nuh. If Thomas can call you from England 'bout it, how on God's green earth Leelia don't hear yet and it's her wedding it happen?"
"That don't mean she hear. Thomas hitch up on Munchy twitter, so him must hear and see everything the way how Munchy was taking picture and posting them on twitter. But you don't see Leelia phone lock off? How she going to hear nothing?"
"Mi don't understand this twitta or twippa thing whatever it name."
Well Munchy was broadcasting every piece of mix-up that took place at the wedding and posted over thirty pictures. Now it's spreading faster than when Lisa Hype sex pics when them did just bust out. A concern came to my head. I put one hand in the air at Dad, trying to break the conversation.
"No, wait ... wait." Mi scroll through my phone for a number.
"Mi Gone call Gloe. Is must over her Leelia gone. Let mi call and check."
Mi get Gloe on the second ring. Gloe said, Leelia was locked up in her room. Mi tell Gloe it's a life and death matters we dealing with. She must tell Leelia that. Let her know that she must call back immediately.
Mi did have to hang up in Gloe ears when she was blowing me kisses through the phone. Mi eagerly wait on Lee to call back.

The Heart of Revenge

Adele. That's what I would love to soothe my mind, and a bottle of Apple Vodka to drown my problems. Escape this mess. On the battered nightstand to the side of the bed was a small silver radio and stacked infront the radio was a messy pile of CD's, some in cases, some not, none of them in original album cases. On the face of the CD's were the ugliest and most untidy crab-toe handwriting, some written with black marker and some with red. Gosh, this could never be my stuff so unorganised and untidy. I breathe out a puffy breath as my mind thought about what I would love to listen.

Let me see. I got up. Tried my luck, knowing pretty well my chances are slim to find any good music in this pile, Gloe and her girlfriend, Danielle, we call her Danni, that she lived in with, listened to the same type of crappy music like Pinky. Gloe and Pinky were such close friends. I couldn't understand why Pinky had avoided Gloe so much. Ever since Gloe became open with the fact that she was a lesbian and moved in with Danielle. It's not like Gloe still wasn't the good person she was. Nothing about her had changed. But you couldn't tell Pinky that. Pinky discriminated and stayed away from her ex-bestfriend, like she had the bird-flu. I grew to become close to Gloe. She was more than my bestfriend, she was my rock of Gibraltar.

Qwan hated Gloe and insisted that she shouldn't come to our wedding. He despised gays so much that he idiotically and most annoyingly called his e-mails, she-females.

I skipped through the pile one by one, nothing with sense, pure boogie-yagga, boogo-yagga. Not one Adele, no Katy Perry, no Pink, just Busy Signal, Kartel, Mavado and DJ Kenny mixes. God, I wished I had my ipod right now. I neatly organised all the CD's, the way they ought to be. The ones with no case at the top, the ones in thin cases next, then the ones in the thicker cases final. I placed the pile in a more orderly position beside the radio instead of infront it.

I lay back down thinking, Danielle must be allergic to anything original. She made good money from whipping up fake passports, visas,

CXC certificates, driver's licence, death certificates, you name it, she could cook it up, trust me, she's the best at it. Gosh. Only heavens know why I didn't just say 'I do.' It wasn't like I didn't love Qwan. He and Mom were the only persons on earth who understood me the closest enough to Ajrien, but with Vance's situation in the picture and knowing that that was why I had proposed to him so soon, it just felt like the marriage was not about the love. It felt wrong. I didn't want to do him any wrong. I was sure if Vance wasn't dying I wouldn't be marrying at nineteen. Maybe Ajrien would be a bigger part of my life since I wouldn't necessarily be needing to be with a rich guy. Not saying having a rich is a bad thing though, cause I really don't mind, and Mommy always warned me against talking to anyone without money. Was just saying that I could be with the one person I loved for who he was, Ajrien. I didn't want to use Qwan, but Christ, I wanted to save my brother. Tears formed in my eyes.

I lay down, turned on my side, staring blankly at the white door, my two hands clasped under my cheek. I closed my eyes and tried to sleep.

It was impossible. I couldn't sleep. My mind won't stop talking with itself. Disturbance. There was someone at the door,

'Knock-knock' ... "Lee."

The call wasn't loud. It was as if she really didn't want to disturb me grieving. I rolled and turned on my side, away from the door, facing the blue wall, lap my gown between my knees.

'Knock-knock.'

"Leee."

I looked back at the door, then turned my head back and around to the wall, reached for the flimsy pillow, covered my ears with it. It smelt of a stale body odour, kind of dingy or something. I closed my eyes.

'Knock! Knock!" It was louder,

"Leee!"

I didn't budge. I wish I could close my ears too.

"Leee!"

I grabbed the useless discoloured pillow from over my ear and answered,

"What?"

'Knock!-knock!'

"LEEE!"

"WHAT GLOE?"

Gloe eased the door open, pushing it with caution, peeped her head of natural hair that was braided to the back, between the door and the jamb. She reluctantly crawled into the room. She had on a black merina and the waist of her plaid underpants could be seen above her football shorts.

"Yow, sorry Lee, mi never want disturb you, you see mi, but ... but ... she said it's very important."

"Who?"

"Your sister."

"Pinky?"

"Yeah, she said you must shout her immediately, it's a life or death thing."

"Hsstt ... I'll call her tomorrow"

"But ..but ... she sound ---"

"Gloe, that's how Pinky stay, after no one's dying, she just always full of excitement, it's just about what happened at the wedding today. Tomorrow when I clear my head I tell you all about it."

"But what if it's something really ---"

"Gloe just let me clear my head nuh, please. You have no idea what I've been through today, trust me. Talk to ya in the morning."

"Sure you don't want to at least call her back? Just to find out?"

"Believe me, things can't be worse than what I'm going through. So anything happen I'm sure it can wait till tomorrow."

Gloe paused for a thought, turned the door knob in her grip, turned it the other way, then back the other way, stared wordlessly at me, turned the knob again and it made a click sound, she made a single step back and spoke,

"Zeen, a true that still."

I didn't look back as I heard the door close, wondering what if it were Vance that got an attack on my wedding day? What if Vance was actually dying? I should call. I turned on my phone to call back Pinky. As the phone screen came on, I thought, but Vance had left the wedding, he wasn't at the church, it couldn't be him. I turned off back my phone. Why on God's green earth was Pinky pestering me then?

CHAPTER 25

It's in a Nissan Sunny
by: Pinky & Leelia

'Bout ten minutes passed and all now my phone didn't ring.

"She don't call back yet?" I don't know if Daddy really expected me to answer that question and he was right beside me all the time and witnessed that my phone hadn't even vibrate much less ring. So I sarcastically replied,

"Yes Daddy. She call back and we speak in a silent language to each other that's why you didn't hear the whole time mi stand up right beside you." I kissed my teeth. Daddy shook his head and managed a small smile. It quickly disappeared.

Mi know anything we doing it must happen fast, real fast.

One nurse pushed an iron trolley by me with a yellow medicine in a clear glass jar. The jar had measurements running up its side in red print. Beside it were balls of cotton, syringes, a pack of drip, and other hospital stuff that mi never like see, were on the top of the trolley. But it was the bag of drip, identical to the one sending fluid into Vance that sunk my heart.

Almost nobody spoke, everybody whispered and you could hear the low murmurs all about. You couldn't hear a conversation only murmurs and it were interrupted by splices of complete silence. It makes me think hospitals are one of the eeriest place on earth. I was staring at the TV above the receptionist who was sitting close to the main entrance. My mind was thinking hard on how mi can get through to Leelia since mi wasn't getting back any call. Blank. Not a single idea hit my brain. I was getting pissed again. The medicines were here. What kind of blood ran through these doctors' veins? They were really heartless creatures. Vance lay coma-stiff and these doc.... Dad interrupted my thought,

"Here's what, call the friend and tell her to tell Leelia that her mother is trying to reach her urgently." Daddy spoke with urgency as he knew the time was going and Vance was going with it. Why didn't I think of that,.

Leelia will definitely call back Aubrea. I dipped into my handbag, redialled Gloe,

"Gloe look here, don't bother with the sadamite thing. Serious things going on here so. Just listen. You tell Leelia to call her mother right right now. It urgent bad, do it now and don't tell her that is me call you. You hear? Tell her is her mother call you. You understand Gloe?" Gloe's voice came through the phone confused,

"But... Bu... Mi just did ---"

"Stop you 'but-but', mi have less than one minute left on mi phone."

"But Pinky. Listen nuh, I just tell her and she not ---"

"Gloe just do that right now and stop chat off mi little credit." I hung up the phone same time. Daddy chuckled under his breath.

"Is what Daddy?" He shook his head. He couldn't hide the small smile that was growing on his face as he spoke,

"Nothing man."

"Must something why you smiling like that."

"No... Is like you always have less than one minute on your phone. And you always sending 'Please credit me' or begging credit. Is what so with you and credit?" And his smile got wider.

"What happen to you? Have to try save back at least four dollars on mi phone so mi can at least send a text. Don't? Nuh so?"

"Misses, you cold. All when it's something this serious you still thinking 'bout saving credit."

"Then must. Suppose any emergency reach, at least mi can call somebody phone and tell them to call mi back. Don't?

Something dawned on me. Something I hadn't think of before. The thought hit me so hard I blurted out a big long,

"RASSS!"

Everybody started looking my way again. I guessed they were not used to hearing mi talking loud or maybe they thought that a little badword or even a big one gone kill them, or send them to hell on Judgement day. Them lucky, mi not looking on them. Mi sure every single one of them curse a badword before somewhere or another. Daddy asked,

"Is what?" A horrible Dettol scent rose up in the hospital ward and breast-stroked its way up into my nose. Mi want spit. I replied to Daddy,

"Mi don't have Aubrea phone and is it Leelia calling back on."

"Then run go get the phone before she call it nuh, or you waiting on the phone to run come to you?"

A white bed on wheels exactly like the one Vance was unconscious on which was identical to every other bed in the ward, barged through the main entrance. Two nurses, uniformed in white and wearing white stockings under them, were charging alongside the chrome rails of the bed with their hands busy on the patient. A third nurse was pushing urgently and shouting from the foot of the bed,

"Clear the way! Clear the way! Emergency!" The old man who they were wheeling in on the bed was frothing. Dad and I looked at each other and the frail smile disappeared from our lips.

Mi make a dash out of the ward for the phone, immediately mi felt the burn on my skin from the parching 3'o'clock sun. I slowed down, took some deep breaths. Mi not too fit at all. The car was parked all the way at the front, and there was no cool shade on the premise, just the wickedly hot tar. Mi get frazzle out in less than two minutes, breathing shorter than usual. Mi run little bit, stop, take breaths, walk briskly, run again, stop. Run again. Boy, mi really need a little exercise.

My blood was seeping through the gauge bandaged around my foot when I was stepping swiftly through the iron gate into the parking lot. The security sat up straight and observed me as I jogged to Daddy's car or rather Aubrea's car, a 1991 Nissan Sunny, with two different shades of gray and the driver's door was a half-white one. The only white on the gray car. Micheal Douglas had given Aubrea the car to help her run his errands on the road while she was working for him. He didn't take it back when he fired her. The back window wasn't rolled right up.

Mi reach the car just in the nick of time. As I reached by the white door, I heard Aubrea's phone ringing in the car.

(((Rrring. Rrring.)))

I looked through the glass, her blackberry was vibrating and ringing on the backseat. My hand went to opening the door. Locked. Tried again, almost popping off the lock in my hand. Locked. It was ringing like a house phone.

(((Rrring. Rrring.))) The same ringtone as Leelia's phone.

(((Rrring. Rrring.)))

Knock! Knock!

"Lee!"

"Knock! Knock!"

Holy Christ man! Them must set Gloe on me today. Why she can't just leave me alone to clear my head. Gosh.

She entered the room with unconscionable intentions to disrupt me. "No, Lee, it's really serious. It's your mother, she said you should call her right now, right right now."

"Oh Jesus! Could be what now? I searched the sheets for my phone, the damn BB take forever to turn on and load, it's up, I dialled Mom.

(((Rrring. Rrring.)))

(((Rrring. Rrring.)))

(((Rrring. Rrring.)))

(((Rrring. Rrring.)))

Aubrea's phone ringing in the car on the back seat. Leelia's calling.

Mi squeeze mi heavy hand through the back window that wasn't wound up properly, desperate to reach the phone. Mi wrist went inside the car, a little pass my wrist and no more, my arm was too big; now I wished mi hands were fine like Leelia own. Mi forced my big hand forward, it barely went any further. Mi force and force and force it till it inched forward. Not even an inch good, 'bout half inch. Mi forced it forward again with a large portion of my strength, well desperate.

'Creeeak!'

I heard the glass strained under pressure. Mi will just push through and break it up this old piece of crosses window and done enuh. I pushed again. Hard. It was impossible. Mi fight to haul out back my hand. It's stuck. Can't get it out.

(((Rrring. Rrring.)))
Stopped.
One missed call.
Shit!
A security was walking over to me. Frisk and brisk.
He drew out his baton.

    How Mommy asked me to call her and she's not answering her phone. If anything she will call me back. Gonna keep my phone on for a couple minutes, before I turn it back off. But ... How Mommy just asked me to call and now she's not hearing her phone ringing. Something's fishy.
    Gonna call one more time. If I don't get through to Mom, I'm shutting off my phone and spinning the lock on the door. I ain't stupid. It must be Pinky trying something or another. One last call.
    Redialled.
    (((Rrring. Rrring.)))
    I hope I get her.

    The light was fading from Aubrea's phone. Mi stare at the phone's screen, looking at the missed call from Leelia. The time on the phone was 3:13. Less than thirty minutes left before Vance's time to be up. Even if mi do get through to Leelia now it still too late already. The security got closer. My hand felt even tighter in the window, and mi blood circulation in my hand was cutting off. Mi hand start turn red like Santa Clause' pants.
    Mi make one big drag and dragged out my hand. The whole of my hand start burn mi like mi lotion it with the real country scotch bonnet pepper or chilli pepper. Mi wipe mi other hand over it to try cooling it off. Is then it start burn mi. Jesus man!

The Heart of Revenge

Can't believe mi missed the damn call. I cursed and kicked the white door , forgetting my leg was sliced, it sent a sensation through the cut. Mi start get into a piece of temper. I lifted my elbow to ram the glass and saw the phone lit up again. The security started walking over faster.

(((Rrring. Rrring.)))
(((Rrring. Rrring.)))

The screen had incoming call from 'Honey'. That was the name Aubrea saved Leelia's number as. Ever since Mom tried to coax me to sell my soul to the Douglas to save Vance, which never made no sense to me, losing one child for the other and selling out myself for money. So mi did refuse, and from that day mi swear up and down Aubrea start treat mi like mi not her child. And because Leelia eat the bait, hook and line, selling herself to help Mom save Vance, Leelia turned her air that she breathed, her Honey. How can you sacrifice your own child's life entirely to save another? Six is one and one dozen the other, because Aubrea running the chance of losing two of her children. What if the Douglas decided to do anything terrible to Leelia? God forbid. To me it just didn't make sense. I wasn't going to sell my soul, deceive people to get their money. It was just wrong. However, God wrote my life that's how mi taking it. Pray and leave things to God. Just have faith and believe, 'cause to be using people is wrong. And wrong is wrong. Mi wrong?

When I smelled Mr. Douglas' cologne the early morning, coming for my little sister, I cried, cried till my chest turned red, literally. Aubrea took mi to the hospital minutes later for the asthma attack I came down with from the proper piece of cow bawling mi put down over my sister leaving. It wasn't fair. From that day until now I don't call Aubrea Mommy again. Because it's not a mother that. Mi start call her just Aubrea. I didn't even want her to touch me that morning. Mi did rather she left me at the house let the asthma kill mi than to touch mi.

(((Rrring. Rrring.)))

The security reached closer. Him face look serious. Mi turn round and run off, not from the security, 'cause you know mi not afraid of no security with baton, but to get the keys from Daddy. I saw Daddy running towards me, his limping was barely obvious in his strides, he held out his hand with the keys dangling in front him. Shouting

"You forget the key."

(((Rrring. Rrring.)))

"Hurry up! Hurry up!"

'Doop!' Daddy's body bounced against the white door on the driver's side, he looked out of breath. He was fumbling with the key at the keyhole to open the door.

"Oh Shit!" Daddy said, limping in haste to go around to the passenger side.

"What's wrong?"

"The key can't open that door, is a different door that." The security was coming faster towards us.

"Hurry up! Move your hands fast old boy."

(((Rrring. Rrring.)))

Inside my mouth felt dry and upsetting, like I had some dry fish scale in my mouth or pregnant feeling. I spat to the side of the car and it landed on the car tyre, bright white. Daddy hassled with the key to get it in the hole. The bunch of keys fell. The security was at the car. Daddy bent for the keys while the security coarsely asked,

"Excuse mi big man, what you doing? Is your car?" he stepped over to Daddy to remove him from the car. I didn't say a word to him, I doubled my fist and get ready. Daddy didn't give the security an answer either. He was focusing on the keyhole like he needed his glasses, he turned the key in the lock.

(((Rrring. Rrring.)))

The door opened finally and the phone was still ringing. The security stopped in mid movement and turned back around. Daddy didn't waste a second. He snatched up the phone just in time to miss the call by less than a second. It was the second missed call. We waited on Leelia's third call.

(((Rrring. Rrring.)))

See there. Mommy not answering her phone. Nothing more than the genial Pinky up to her antics and ism-skisms again. Hsst.

I locked the door. Not calling back a third time. Shifted the pile of CD's neatly in a straight line by the side of the radio. Shut off my phone.

CHAPTER 26

Use your Head
by: Pinky

We waited and waited and waited on the third call 3:18, Less than twenty-five minutes to go. No call.

Daddy had the unringing phone in his hand. We were slogging in bottomless despair to Vance's bedside, not looking at each other, not speaking to each other. Dad stopped.

"Why you don't use Aubrea's phone and call her back?" I didn't know why I hadn't thought of that. She'd see the call coming from Aubrea, and we all knew that once it was Aubrea calling and Lee saw, Lee would answer the call no doubt. Because Aubrea was Leelia's beginning and ending like quotation marks.

"But what if she lock off back her phone?"

"Just try it Pinky, how else you gone know?"

"But through she did ---"

"You head tough? ... Just call the blasted thing. Hsst. You wasting time. Call."

"But suppose ---" Daddy's patience was sitting on the edge of a cliff and my questions were pushing him over the edge.

"JUST CALL ... CALL ... HOLY NAZARETH MAN! "

Not another beat went by. I dialled Lee's number hoping Leelia had her phone on. Daddy eyes were glaring impatiently. The call was unsuccessful. Aubrea's phone had no credit.

"No credit not on her phone."

"Then transfer your credit to your mother phone quick nuh."

"But when mi send my little credit to Aubrea phone, how mi get it back?"

"Christ man! Mi will buy back a credit, just do it."

Mi *128* off my credit to Aubrea's phone. A notification came on my phone, advising me that my balance was $26.23. I needed at least $27.00 to transfer credit. You see if mi did just hang up in Gloe's ears a little earlier, mi could've make the transfer. Mi wonder if Digicel realised this was an emergency.

"Mi can't transfer it Daddy, mi don't have enough. You don't have no credit on your phone?"

"You deaf or something? Mi said mi run out leave mi phone at the church. Is not you same one say that them must thief the little piece of old Nokia?"

"You gone bite off my head? Why you acting like so for?"

"Stop chat frigging foolishness man. All of this is your fault."

"My fault? My fault? Is me tell Vance to born with heart problem?"

"If you never ---"

"Don't bother try come pin no blame on mi, 'cause mi don't do nothing. The all of you stand up in the damn church like poppy-show and not doing a thing after the gal come to mash up Lee wedding."

Daddy squinted his eyes to narrow slits, grabbed my arm. Mi flash him off.

"You think mi is a little child? Is who you think you can just come grab up so?"

Daddy didn't use his mouth, annoyance and chagrin in his knitted brows. He snatched my arm again, unspeaking. Mi flash out his big burly hand, shoved him in his pigeon chest with a force that could flatten the Hylton's Hotel. His strapping body staggered backward in an awkward motion on his bad leg. The inquisitive security was scampering over to us, shouting with one hand waving at us and the other hand holding down the peak of his security cap.

"Yow! Yow! What happening over there so? ... None of that! None of that!"

Daddy shattered my face with the hottest box I had ever got in my entire life. I felt a burning heat almost pulsing like a heartbeat out the red fingerprint marks that wailed my face. It was burning so much that the slight breeze against it stung me. I could not touch it. Water came to my eyes. Daddy stood stiff and spoke stern.

"Have manners little girl, you still mi daughter."

Mi spit to the side. It was a mixture of white and red. I looked at a big rock stone on the ground, but ... I didn't bend for it. I hugged Daddy and cried. He hugged me, rubbed my back. Mi rested mi head on his shoulder, he rested one hand at the back of my head, hushing me. The security walked back to his station glimpsing over his shoulder at us several times.

"Sorry man Pinky, but sometimes you need to think before you do things." I leaned off his shoulder, fixed the weed in my bosom and replied,

"Yeah, but mi never want mi sister wedding spoil." Mi wiped my lips, and as my hand went down to my side. He held on to both my hands and held them steady at my side.

"Well if you did talk to the girl or even just hold her back, none of us wouldn't be here so now."

Daddy didn't argue further, instead he asked,

"Is what time now?"

"Three twenty nine." Less than fifteen minutes. Vance was a goner. No way on earth Leelia could reach in less than fifteen minutes, it was not physically possible. I spoke with strong hope and determination in my voice,

"Alright. Let's run go buy a credit to put on Aubrea phone, hopefully Leelia phone still on. Because if she got the credit card number we can still make it."

"It can work so? Mi never know that."

A twinkle was in his eyes. The same proud twinkle that was in his eyes when mi get the highest average in the entire eighth grade, ninth grade and eleventh grade. I guessed he was proud of my wits. We rushed outside the hospital, looked right and left and spotted a Digicel poster sticking out the side of a blue board shop under a huge guango tree down the road.

We hurried over. I stood by the red igloo that was on four blocks. You could pick up that the cover of the igloo was originally white, but now it looked closer to black dirt color. Dad stretched a five hundred dollar bill to the heavy-breasted old-lady. The sleeve of her oversized t-shirt, with Digicel printed in the chest, caught in the lollipops sticking up out the jar by the counter as she served the card. Dad handed me the card, staring blankly into Mars. I scratched the silver off the back of the voucher with my false nails and punched in the voucher number to Aubrea's phone. The time on her phone was 3:36. I hastened to call Aubrea. Daddy spoke with the old lady.

"You don't have anything strong to drink in there?"

The sound her thin lips made when she smacked her toothless mash mouth was louder than her shaky voice. "Like what mi son?"

"Like some rum or so."

"No, but you can go check the bar down the road."

"Where?" She stuck her saggy neck through the opening of the blue counter door. Her voice got even more wobbly as she spoke,

"You see where that man stand up in the blue shirt?"

"Beside the orange container?" Dad asked. She shook her head impatiently.

"No, no. Watch mi where mi pointing nuh." She pointed with one finger, the deep wrinkles wrapping around her knuckles looked like seasoned creases in genuine leather handbags. "Right at the red awning, you don't see the police car and the man in the blue stripe shirt beside it?"

Daddy was nodding yes while she continued to direct him. Mi couldn't move as I saw what was in Aubrea's phone. Daddy answered her letting her now that his head not that thick.

"Yeah man, yeah man, mi see is where. Thank you Grandma."

"Yeah man sonny."

Mi just staring on the phone and can't believe this all now.

"Pinky call Leelia. You don't realise that time going?"

Mi dial Lee, before mi go checked out what is going on in Aubrea phone. Lee's phone did turn off. Mi dial again. Off. And again. Still off. One more time. Off.

"Same thing Daddy, her phone turn off."

Daddy didn't answer, only stared. Mi know he couldn't bear to go back to Vance's grave. His face was falling apart. The time passed and we never got to Leelia. Vance was and should be dead.

"What now Daddy?" Daddy's mind went fishing. No response. Body froze. "Daddy!" He jerked and jumped back into reality. "What now?"

"Come we go get a little sip and come back."

"Daddy? ... Now? What's wrong with you?"

"Yeah man. Now. Mi stress out Pinks." I akimboed.

"Is joke you making. Don't? Mi not going inside no bar with you enuh. Try know that."

"Alright. You can wait here so then."

"What's wrong with you and rum? You don't learn from what did happen? It spoil your life and up to now you still paying for it and you still won't stop drinking. You need to stop!"

Daddy's mind went to a small town in China, deep in thoughts as he stared through my forehead. His head slowly went down and then he waltzed off, almost in a trance-like state or doing some deep reflection. He headed in the direction of the bar.

I looked shockingly at Aubrea's phone.

This couldn't be what I believed it was. Aubrea wouldn't even dream of doing this. Would she? She must be frigging mad! No way.

CHAPTER 27

Vodka in My Heart String
by: David Lexings

Pinky can't even begin to understand the heap of stress mi going through. How mi mustn't have a drink? Mi head feel like it's busting up to bloodseed. Mi can't even gather myself to go back to the hospital. Vance out to die and it feels like is mi dying. Even though I don't think Vance is ... well, at least mi still not sure that Vance is my child, and the rumours make it even worse. You know, the more mi think 'bout this, is the more mi want... the more mi need a drink. Vodka. No ice. Maybe Pinky's right. I should try and slow down my drinking. Mi stop in my tracks, turned 'round, looked at Pinky, and my body swelled then deflated as I breathed out with a big round puff, dropped my shoulders. Bloodseed yaah man, Hsst ... Mi need a strong drink. I turned back around and walked down the scanty street, heading straight to the bar. Vodka.

I stopped at the bar door. Right by the door was a chalkboard, it was about waist high, it stood on two thick wooden legs. The writing on the black of the chalkboard was in two colors, white and pink. Written in pink, big and bold and in all capital letters was, 'WELCOME TO YOUR FAVORITE RUMSHOP'. I nodded my head, yes. Underneath it, written in white was, 'Rum on Special Today and Everyday.' I smiled, nodded, ahhh, my kind of place.

You know what, I still wasn't so sure if I should go into a bar now. You know. My mind was cloudy about the decision, I thought twice before I set foot through the rumshop door. Looked across the street at the police car parked up. Looked up the road at Pinky again; she was pressing the buttons on Aubrea's phone as if she were searching it. Just one drink won't kill mi. That would help, Just a quick drink, one or maybe a little more than one. Mi head mash up bad yaah man. Mi just going drink till mi satisfied, blurt-naught man, drink till mi red. I felt someone pounced into my back as they walked by me, it was a young man, he was apologising,

"Sorry sir, sorry."

The Heart of Revenge

What's wrong with this brother man? Hsst, I wondered, why young men wouldn't wear their pants on their bom-bawt waist? The youth was wearing a long sleeve beige shirt and his beige jeans shorts was one shade darker than his shirt. His pants was buckled almost exactly where his shirt tail ended, mid-way his thigh. Lord these young men need Jesus. I shouted at him,

"Draw up your backside pants man! Look how the sidewalk big and empty and you still come and bounce up behind people, with your pants draw down to your knee. You is what? Faggot?" He didn't look back.

That couldn't be me just awhile ago. It wasn't like me to lose my temper. See, I really needed to wash this stress away in some white rum or something strong. I sucked in a deep breath, shaking my head, walking into the bar and stepping out the bright sun.

After one step into the dimly lit bar, I stopped, looked around. Inside the bar looked like midnight to my eyes freshly leaving out the blinding sun. I squinted my eyes to see as inside slowly got brighter and brighter to my vision. Maybe because it's early Sunday evening why inside this bar so empty. I looked to the left, towards the L-shape bar counter. Mi come here already. Or so it seemed. Mi sense something kind of familiar, the feeling, a vibe, the place, something.

But then again, when you drank in as many bar as mi, they all seemed familiar, a strange umbilical-cord or navel-string feeling to it, to me, it felt like ... like ... my second home. Only without the quarrels and nag-naggings from my ungrateful wretched wife. Ahh ... Bars ... What an escape. My escape.

I strutted over eyeing the few rumheads that sat close to the window directly ahead of me. Took a seat on a high stool at the counter. The short bartender wearing green blouse with splices in the back, tight green batty-rider shorts, green bangles and green earrings turned around from the sink when she felt my shadow on her. She was chopping a green bubble gum like cow chewing their cods. I ordered a drink and smiled at how she was severely green like a fifty dollar bundle of callaloo. Mi laugh out loud. Big laugh.

Rawtid. It looked mi did something wrong, or as if mi mustn't smile. The short feisty green leprechaun looked me up and down, up and down again, knitted her thinly shaved brows that was very obviously over-brightened with eye-brow pencil, and said,

"Is what sweet you? Which part the joke?"

I made my order.

"Yeah, aahm," but the look mi go look on her again, her mouth chopping away, tongue as big as a cow's, and swirling the little piece of green bubble gum round and round in her mouth, made me chuckled. Mi skin my teeth all the way through my order "A drink ... tehehe ... of Vodka ..tehe ...No ice."

I lifted my other foot up an rested it on the cross bar of the stool as I begun to relax, gave it a slight swindle, facing the bar head on. The only place that seemed to relieve my stress. Bars. We go way back don't we? Ahh, yes, we have a history. The bartender tugged at the big knot of her blouse that she tied to her side. A quick tug just to keep the knot tight and in place, right above her belly, making sure she expose her soft porridgy belly along with a few stretch marks mostly to the side.

She poured me a drink quite professionally. I, in return, gwapped it down professionally, one drink, shook the glass, drained it, slammed the glass down on the counter. I Clamped my teeth together, the skin of my face pushing down from my forehead and pushing up from my chin to form all the folding in the middle of my face, widening my nose. The harsh vodka flamed in my throat. I cringed. Shut my eyes, hung my head down, shaking my head side to side as the fire of the vodka spreads in my stomach and burns inside my belly, warm, hot,

"Awsh!" I grunted through tightly gritted teeth, "A next one baby-love."

A familiar feeling. I sat here before, said those words a thousand times before. Was it this very same place? Same face? Did I dream this before? Lived it before? The familiarity of it was so close I could touch it, grab it, squeeze it. Deja-vu? I searched my memory but all that was flashing in my head were pictures, scenes, still shots of my most haunting memory twenty-one years ago. It was me and Pinky. Pinky was only three year old and underfed.

I drew the glass closer to me along the wooden counter. Dazed down at the clear vodka in my glass, so pure, so smooth, so calming. The light dancing ripples spreading in small circles and running from the centre to edge of the glass. A peace formed within me. I took a relaxed breath. Took another deep one and my body swelled as I inhaled deep. I drifted far in thoughts, reflecting on memories. Cold harsh memories. That night in the kitchen. It was dark, and Aubrea's voice was in the background. I felt like choking the bitch to death.

CHAPTER 28

Dig Up in Mi Mother's Business
by: Pinky

Booming loud and bass kicking. The blaring music got louder and closer, Kartel's song 'Back to Reality' blasting out the speakers. I turned around on the sidewalk, faced the road in curiosity, eyes searching to see which vehicle was playing his new song that he did from in prison, the tune shot. I saw a white extra-large Avalanche van. Mi jiggle mi bottom to the rhythm, not even realising it.

Mi vision concentrated deeper in the vehicle to see who was the driver. His little round head was the size of a sea-shore pebble, bopping terribly offbeat to the music, a big spliff hanging from the side of his mouth that could be mistaken for a white ice-cream cone with a big orange fire at the head. Mi laugh to myself, thinking, watch the little mawga stickman in that rhinosaurus van. I laughed harder when I saw how he was trying to look cool but looked so damn funny, bopping his head completely offbeat. Watch the idiot. Watch him. Mi bust out laughing when the spliff dropped out his mouth and he was hurriedly brushing out the fire from his crotch. Damn fool. Hsst.

The old lady's voice was trying to get someone's attention,

"Hey! Hey!" Flagging her hand through the counter trying to get Daddy's attention. Daddy kept walking down to the bar. She turned her head to me and spoke.

"Sweetie, shout the brown man for mi."

"Is what?"

"Him gone leave him change. Him soon come back?"

"That's cool man Mama. Just give mi a pack of cigarette, Matterhorn, and a pack of Rizzla with the change. And you can give me some icy mints if any jinglings leave."

Mi really want know why Aubrea doing this. Why this morning she'd be calling my man? But hold on there, if this last dial time saying 8:38 a.m. that mean to say, is just before Leelia wedding start. Something just don't look good about this call here. I didn't even know Aubrea had mi man number much less to call him in early tea time hours. Mi don't trust a bone in Aubrea; that's why mi searching through her whole damn phone. Mi need to get down to the bottom of this today. Mi going into her messages to see if mi see anything suspicious, mi have to find out what's up between them.

    I pressed, 'OK' to open her inbox messages. So said, so done. The third message on top, that was staring me in the face, was from my man. The second message on top was from my man. The last message on top, him too. Kiss mi clitoris! What they could be texting one another so in the early morning. I wasn't laughing 'bout the situation. I was fuming, not over Finaral but over my mother's betraying me. Mi dying to find out what the messages say, because mi sure is must some snake-into-grass, schmoozing thing them up to. Mi select 'Open' on the last message.

CHAPTER 29

*** Pack Your Belongings***
by: David Lexings

That night, my eyes were fixed on the black scandal-bag on the floor at the side of our pop-down cupboard. The scandal bag was being used as our garbage bag. Mi see a small frisky rumbling of the bag, heard the crisp dry sound of scavenging rats as they scuttled and rummaged through spoilts and scrags of garbage. A roach scurried to the edge of the cupboard, then another crawled to the edge behind the first roach. Then there was a third roach. A small teenage one. My blood crawled internally. I frigging hate roaches. My kitchen.

The biggest cockroach of the three was at the front with its long feelers probing for crumbs of food, it widened its wings in flight mode, and the hair on my skin turned yellow, thinking about him flying about and pitching on me. Or even just his wings batting against my face. I even hated the dry buzzing sound that their wings made flying through the air. These small insects horrify me. I wanted to do what all humans want to do when they are scared of anything, any insect, any unknown. I wanted to destroy it. Kill this roach before it took flight.

To my eyes, I could almost see through their mahogany brown wings. It looked like more than one pair intertwining with each other. My skin crawled. It didn't fly but just anticipating it pitching on my hand, or neck, or face with its sharp nasty legs is the most blood curdling feeling. I hated roaches. What had my life gone to? Eighteen and things were getting worse and worse and hell-bottom. Ever since Micheal Douglas started his landscaping company and his workers using lawn-mowers, which I couldn't afford to buy, me and my little cutlass got less and lesser lawns to service. The brute drove me straight out of business. Back then he was the big cheese and he still was ontop. I used to get at least twenty jobs per week, now it was more like three per week maximum or so. Aubrea's ranting voice nagged me in the background,

"Mi not use to this!"

The Heart of Revenge

The leptospirosis rat dashed out the scandal bag at the speed of a snake's bite. Another one followed, a bit slower, fatter, longer, bigger, more disgusting. The stench from the sour garbage was trapped inside by the closed windows and doors of the kitchen, rottening the inside tunnel of my nose. I knew Aubrea had a nose-hole too and that she smelt it, and she knew the stinking garbage should have been taken outside. But as usual, there it remained until I came off the road in the evenings and took it out. Her voice sounded even more annoying as I thought about what she did all day – nothing. Absolutely nothing. Not even the dishes. Her voice was driving me up the frigging wall in the background. Please shut up. I was in no haste to take a breath in my smelly kitchen. My life.

I bought myself nothing. Every dollar I earned I spent into the house. Made sure Aubrea and Pinky were taken care of. Aubrea's savings was similar to what she did in the house – nothing. She wanted to keep on living the life she was grown up in, which we couldn't afford. And now that I wasn't getting any jobs, she had transformed into someone new. A lazy spoilt bitch who cursed everyday about what she didn't have. About what she wanted to have. What she should have. She had transformed into someone I never fell in love with. To be quite honest, if years ago someone had said to me,

"You know when life gets tough Aubrea gonna be your biggest adversary, she won't stand by you but against you."

I would look at them without smiling and say something sarcastic, like,

"And you know that before I die a black man will be the president of America." Or maybe something more off like "A woman will be the Prime Minister of Jamaica before I die."

Just say the impossible because I couldn't believe how much without money Aubrea changed. She hadn't lost feeling for me, it was just that her love had changed to something else, something cold. Maybe ice. Or maybe hate.

The roach's sharp prickly legs began to crawl back into the crease of the old piece of cupboard. Mi eyes search the floor like mad for a slippers or shoes, anything to clobber the roach before it escaped. None in sight. I slithered closer, eyes fixed on this roach. I wanted to smash this roach, kill it, kill it. I doubled my fist, scan the floor again, squeezed my fist. I stood still, watching the two smaller roaches escaping, crawling into the board wall above the cupboard. Aubrea's voice continued to bicker from in her room.

"When you gone get money to buy gas and put in the house? Look how long the stove don't turn on!"

Aubrea damn well and know I wanted a better life too, yet she emptied all her blame on me, cutting me deep with her tongue, over and over again,

"You too worthless. You damn cruff! Mi know is this here kind of life you want live longtime."

Aubrea knew my buttons and she was pushing them well. I gave Aubrea the solution to solve our position, but no, she refused to do it, I yelled it,

"Aubrea sell the car!" It wasn't the first time mi telling her to sell her car. "Sell your car and make we buy little gas put in the kitchen!"

It made sense to me. It was better that we sold the car and bought food for the fridge. Food for the baby. And buy mi one of those lawn-mowers so mi could get more work. It would make mi work faster and I could pay her back for the machine. But Aubrea's head was manufactured out of the same steel that made lawn-mowers. With all my talking to her, trying to show her the light, she wouldn't take heed. She wouldn't sell the car, not because it was her father who had given it to her, as what she continued to use for her excuse to not sell it, but because Aubrea looked richer in the car than she looked in walk-foot. Better yet, she looked better off than people, that was the bottom-line. She wanted to impress everybody in the community to believe that she was better off than them. We had the only car in the community and she wasn't giving up that hype. Although she never said this outright but to me, Aubrea rather to look and make people think she was in a better position than them, rather than to have a bottle of syrup in the cupboard, some yam and potato in the old fridge, on our plate, on our scrape-up table and in our hungry bellies. Her reasoning was never too logical to me. Her damn voice sounded like fingernails making that squeeing annoying sound on clean glass, it got louder, sickening, I couldn't fucking stand it no more and like a lighted match thrown in a full gas cylinder, she exploded in utmost rage,

The Heart of Revenge

"Mi sick and tired of you! Why you don't leave? Eeh? LEAVE! Just fucking leave the house an go on! LEEAAVE!"

One swift grab. I snatched the fat brown cockroach, squeezed. Squeezed it in my fist till the feeling of its stabbing sharp pricks on its legs scrawling against my palm to escape was gone. Its wings crushed. Its feelers stopped twitching and scrambling against my thumb, just stopped moving. It's feelers touching my thumb felt light, yet so sharp and stiff as if they were two thin brown bones growing out of its head. I needed to leave this house, now. Now. Before I explode. I needed a drink. Vodka. Aubrea's door slammed and her footstep clummed louder and louder as she blazed to the kitchen. The little devil woman lighting her tongue on fire, her antagonising voice pelting out at me,

"Answer mi nuh worthless boy!"

I gritted my teeth. Squeezed my fist tighter. The dry crushy sound was louder than the wet squishy sound as I squeezed and burst the disgusting roach's bottom with a splashing 'pop-pluck' sound. The semi-solid cream from the roach's soft ass spewing into my hand felt not wet, put icky-sticky, a nasty type of clammy feeling as it stuck unto my hand. It wasn't warm, the white mush felt almost cold. Some of it dropped to the floor. The devil-ridden woman marched into the kitchen, shoved me on the shoulder. I turned around. She spat at my left eye. Her spit landed on my cheek. This was more than nag. Her words sliced me like a sword. Her spit got me violent. She cursed,

"Mi don't want you in mi house! Come out! Loser! Fucking worthless!"

I rather to be chewing on tin foil paper than to hear her words. I was silent. But I squeezed. Muscled my hand. Squeezed. Squeezed. Squeezed the last of the white marshy shit, squirting it out in my hand. Squeezed. I couldn't stand it. I wiped some of her spit off my cheek with my clean hand. I needed a change. I released my fist, filled my lungs with air, let it out. Crumbs and white fell to the red floor. A piece of its wing, feet and head still stuck in my palm. The perfect condition to shot Aubrea a box that people in Hong Kong could hear. Aubrea cursed,

"Come out!" Shoved me again, in my chest, "Come out!" My anger built. Shoved me again. I open my hand. "COME OUT NOW!"

I chanted inside my head,' Don't let the tail wag the dog. Don't let the tail wag the dog. Don't let the tail wag the dog.'

I looked at the scandal bag of garbage on the floor, then looked at her, not seeing her eyes in the dark kitchen but penetrating them as I asked,

"You want mi to leave?"

"Mi regret the day mi never listen to Daddy!" As she screamed those ruthless cruel big stones into my feelings, I folded back my hand into a hard fist. Her mouth would be the perfect target. Don't let the tail wag the dog. Don't let the tail wag the dog. "Don't know why mi ever did go married a poor man! Is the worst thing ever happen to mi in my life!"

"Mi trying every bloodseed thing! What else you want mi to do? Eeh? Turn water into Hennessy? Eeh? WHAT ELSE?"

I stomped out the kitchen into the livingroom. Walked away. Best thing to do. She followed. Raging.

My brain wasn't the size of a football, maybe a hollow ping-pong ball, but even I could figure out why Aubrea was truly sick to her stomach of me. All her life she was used to having more than she needed, excess. Luxury. Without having to lift a straw. Now she had less than she needed to survive. Poverty.

Her parents had warned her over and over again.

"Lee, if you choose to be with that poor ghetto guy you choosing not to be a part of the family. And we're serious about this. We can't afford to ruin the family's reputation by choosing to stoop so low and mingle with that kind. The Lexings are beneath us. Moreover, for you to have a baby with that trash. We will pay for your abortion. Leave him."

Aubrea didn't choose to not be with her parents. At sixteen, she was choosing love. She was choosing to carry her child. Drop out of school and fight the storm with me, her teenage love. But now the storm was a mercilessly freezing blizzard. Her reality was cold. It was poor. It was frightening. She wanted to undo everything. Wished she didn't have Pinky. Wanted to go back home to Daddy, to luxury. And she could. If this were a game, but it wasn't. It was reality. It was her life. She had never seen hungry days before. Never had a belly full up of gas. Never seen toilet paperless days. It was a cruel awakening that proved smiles were scarce with poverty, frowns were plenty and anger was high and peaking. Poverty was hell. And for the poor, money became your only saviour to living like humans. Money became God for many. Steal, kill, prostitution for salvation, for money.

Aubrea didn't believe in love any more. She believed in money. How far would she go for money? I didn't know. It depended on what heavens her new God offered her in return. Cheat maybe. Lie maybe. Give up her child maybe. Save a child maybe. Kill?

The fury was getting redder and redder in Aubrea. Her voice rang out in a condescending tone, loud enough so the neighbours could hear clearly without cocking their ears at the fence.

"You call yourself a man? ... And you can't take care of your child. Mi should've had an abortion! I would have been much better off." She shoved me from behind. I felt it through my back all the way through to my chest. " You can't take care of mi!"

"Why you stay with mi then? Mi tie you down?"

"Young mi young and fool! Mommy was right, never talk to a poor man!"

I snapped around in one spin, facing her, eye to eye,

"Leave then nuh!" The scent from the kitchen was high and as strong as the scent of gasoline at the gas station but if this scent was gasoline it was the stinking-est one. The scent travelled into the living room. The moon was in the sky but in the living room felt like the parching sun was in the kitchen. My neck began to sweat. I felt hot and clustered and stink.

"You leave! This is MY house. You don't own dry shit in here. Leave. Leave. JUST LEAVE AND GO ON!" I believe the entire neighbourhood heard her loud and clear, but it still didn't register in my ping-pong brain. It was easier for me to swallow her whole than for me to swallow the news. I had nowhere to go.

"You want mi to leave? Want mi to leave?" Fire blazed out my eyes into hers. But my flame was a baby pup to her roaring lion. She was always better at getting angrier than me, even if she was in the wrong.

"Yes! ...Now!... Leave now. Come out of mi house! Get out of my life!"

Pinky burst through the blue curtain that was hung at the door entrance to the livingroom, running towards me and collided her underfed body with my leg. She feebly hugged around one of my legs.

"Mi not leaving mi daughter." I placed a hand on Pinky's head, covering one of her big plaits in her head. She stretched up her two anorexic arms. They looked like two flimsy shoes string attached to her shoulders for arms, wanting me to lift her up. Mi wipe the crushed roach out my hand on the batty of my shorts, all over the back-pocket. Mi use the back of my hand to wipe the rest of Aubrea's spit out of my face.

"Daddy ... Daddy" Pinky's voice was whimpering. I stepped away from her.

"Pinky, go sit down." I said to her, I was busy cursing and still angry.

"Mi hate every single bone that make you up old cruff! My life was perfect before mi meet you. You destroy mi life! Mi have nothing now. Nothing, but that damn red child that looks so much like you that it hurts." I looked down at my baby Pinky "Mi sick and tired of you talking 'bout you trying, you trying. When you getting nothing done? We starving."

"You starving little liar gal?"

"Yes mi starving. When last you buy piece of mutton? Look on Micheal Douglas them. Look at Daddy. When you gonna be a real man and stand up to your responsibility like them?"

"The same year you stand up to yours. You don't have no responsibility too, eeh? It's me one?"

Mi don't know what was wrong with my lulu wife, but I was always standing up to my responsibility, she made it seem as if mi didn't do nothing since we were together. With the little mi made, mi take care of her the best way mi could afford to, she and my little girl, Pinky. Mi just never have nothing and couldn't afford nothing right now. Mi think she was confusing responsible with rich, with money, excess, luxury. She always had a lustful eye for Douglas' things.

"Go sleep with Micheal Douglas then since you love call up him name ... and you love him things Ms. Pretty-car-and-big-house-eye. Is rich man you want? Go lay down with him then nuh." And I forcefully added, "Make his coolie woman chop you up into eight separate pieces like Dominoes pizza. Since is that you want." Pinky tottered over to Aubrea.

"Yes. Is that mi want. Mi wouldn't be suffering like dog now."

Pinky began to cry with a sour face.

"Little gal, shut up your mouth!" Aubrea screamed at my baby and pushed her away. "You and your Poopa is the same damn thing." Pinky ran back to me. "Mi could just stab you right in your face right now for what you putting mi through. GET OUT!"

Aubrea was offered a heaven. It was to let me leave with her only child, our child, so she could get her freedom, pursue money. Her decision was already made. Her happiness. She was already taking out a lot of her bottled up bitterness on Pinky. She had grown to hate me so much that the very sight of Pinky irritated her because Pinky was the splitting image of me. When Aubrea looked at Pinky, she didn't see her child, all she saw was me. What mattered more was that if she didn't have Pinky with me she could have been up and gone her ways already. Wouldn't have to be in this situation now, living a life of sufferation. She wished she didn't have Pinky. Wished she had listen to her parents and did the abortion. Pinky was the crosses that helped tie her down in this. Pinky was the best thing to ever had happened to me.

"Let mi ask you this Aubrea. What you doing to help? You don't even want to wash out the baby clothes. No matter how the garbage stink, all if it's stinking up the whole house, and you here whole day, you rather dead first before you just take it out!" Pinky clung on to my leg and her malnourished hand tugged at my shorts, "One hand can't clap. Help out nuh. Everyday you get up with the same bloodfire thing. Look how much work you turn down. You ---"

"You breed mi and drop mi out of school, how mi to get a decent job and mi never finish school idiot? As the man, you suppose to take care of mi. That's what a real man does."

"Nothing not wrong with the jobs. At least you could buy gas now. Don't? Any work is work, you have too much pride?"

"That's all mi have left after you turn mi into a pauper." She started crying as she talked. "Mi wish God would just take mi life sometime than to live here so with you, God know. Mi fed up, mi fed up, mi fed up."

Pinky was crying louder, her face turning red and her whole face wet.

"Daaddy ... Daaddy." She buried her head in the back of my shorts. I remembered I wiped my roach splattered hand there, I grabbed her, pulled her around, her forehead plastered with crushed roach. I stooped, wiped and picked it off. Stand. Her puny shoe-string arms stretching up, I lifted her and she was so light; filled with more air than food, like a bag of O'lay's potato chips is filled with more air than anything else.

Aubrea got fired up looking at me and Pinky together. She stormed off in a tantrum into the bedroom, rooting out all the clothes out the chestnut draw and throwing them behind her across to the bed. Most of the clothes landed on the floor. None of them I had bought for myself. I had bigger responsibilities to take care of with my small earnings. All the clothes were bought by Aubrea, with some of the money her father had given her before totally cutting her off and forgetting he ever had a daughter named Aubrea.

"Leave. Come out. Mi don't want you in here!"

I didn't want any of the clothes she had bought for me. I didn't need her handout. All I wanted was my daughter.

"Keep the fucking clothes, make them full your belly." I walked out into the black night with Pinky hugged in my arms. I had enough money in my pocket to buy chicken-feed.

Nowhere to go.

I went back inside, stole Aubrea's car key. Drove away with Pinky, stopped at a bar, got drunk, drove drunk, lick down a little boy without knowing, stopped, wondering what I had hit and reversed the car over him. An angry mob came to chop me up. I slammed my foot on gas, sped off to escape, ran head-on in a lightpole, crushed Aubrea's car and it caught ablaze immediately. Pinky was unconscious, she got a big hell of chop on her foot. A nasty scar for life. The blood was spewing, my foot was broken in two places. I never walked the same again.

CHAPTER 30

What Kind of Secret Between Them
by: Pinky

Mi push down the pack of Matterhorn in my bosom, my eyes glued to the message in Aubrea's phone from mi man. Mi not sure what the messages mean but mi blood start bubble like Konshens tune, just to see that they texting each other behind my back, worse, mi never like how the message sound. Mi read it again, just trying to figure out what it mean and what them could be up to. The text from my man read,

'Tonight zeen. Make sure.'

What the rass was happening tonight? What's happening between the two of them that I don't know 'bout? What kind of secret thing is this? I take two slow steps away from the blue board shop because the old lady was making me uncomfortable from staring at me. I walked around to the side of the shop by the lightpole, out of her sight, Mi going to buy thirty-six in Cashpot tomorrow, old woman. Mi open up the message Aubrea sent him. This mi have to see. Her text was plain and straightforward; it didn't need any second thought. She was the culprit, it read,

'Finaral Please don't do that. No games, real thing tonight sure. Linking you at the same place, same time. Pinky in the room, so mi will shout you later.'

What that could've meant? Why the fuck she sending mi name in her text to mi man for? And why she can't talk to him when mi around? Mi squeeze the phone tight and a single word jump out mi mouth,

"Whore!"

Mi snap mi head around to see if the old lady heard me. Her head was peeping through a side window of the shop, the window had a Mandingo calendar pin up on it. My eyes and hers eyes made four, she was just staring in mi morning. I thought to myself, what an old woman inquisitive, at the same time contemplating going back to the hospital, over the ward Aubrea was on. War was on my mind. Mi read the text one more time. Whore.

CHAPTER 31

Pay Me or Get Shot
by: David Lexings

"You not drinking?" The fully-green bartender's voice woke me up out of my memories. I still held the glass of vodka in my hand, waiting to drink it down. She blew out and swelled a bubble between her crusty lips. It popped and she dragged in the thin splashes of green bubble gum off her lips and bit under her lip to get a stubborn piece that would not return into her mouth.

The vodka in my glass was calling. Something deeper inside me didn't want it. I had enough. That accident had affected my life entirely, my role as a father, my money, my walk, my marriage, my son, Vance.

"How much mi owe you now baby-love?"

"One fifty."

I stood, dipped my hand down to the bottom of my pocket to pay her. She eyed me from head to toe.

"So watch here, nothing not wrong with the vodka enuh, you not drinking it?"

"No, it's alright. Mi have enough."

"You still have to pay me for it enuh. Once you order it and mi throw it out, you have to pay for it."

"So that's not what mi doing now? You blind?"

I didn't feel any money. Strange. I dipped my hand in the other pocket, anxiety building up. No embarrassment on me today, please.

"And make sure you tip mi too."

"Hold on nuh Green-Ranger," I stopped digging down in my pocket and stared at her in disbelief. "You don't see mi searching for the money, just let mi find it first." What a bartender cold. She didn't even tell me good evening but now she was demanding a tip. She must see a big round red nose in the middle of mi face. Mi not tipping her a cent. I shook my head.

"What you shaking your head for? You not tipping mi broke-pocket?"

I dug in my pocket faster. Let mi just pay this young miss and leave 'cause she mad in her rass head. No money. Pocket empty.

"Is what? You don't have no money? You a real broke-pocket enuh"

"Hold on nuh ... Just easy." I searched again. Thoroughly. No wallet. No money. I sank through the earth.

The bartender called the owner of the bar, who happened to be the police man in the car across the street. Police. Damn. He roughed me up for the money. I tried to explain to him that I was picked by a young youth in full beige but he didn't believe me. I was dealt with like an animal. Embarrassed in the one place I loved. My place of escape was not escape any more. I knew it was my sign. A sign that I should give up bars, and drinking. Pinky came to bail me out the crisis with no money. The little girl spend it off. Jesus Christ man, it was calamity on top of calamity. Even though Pinky had spent my change. What she did was give Mr. Mathias, couple bills fifty bags of weed out her bosom. And of course you know she rubbed it in, that the weed I was cursing her about came to my rescue. I replied to her,

"If you never spend off mi change mi would be ok, you know you don't bother send mi no 'please credit me' for the rest of the month though, cause you spend off mi change."

"Oh to rass, Daddy look here on 'em text messages here that Aubrea send mi man." Her head was down looking at Aubrea's phone in her hand and pressing the buttons to bring up the messages. She didn't looked up. "Tell mi what you think, cause is kill mi want kill the one Aubrea she." She passed me the phone.

I read the text, something definitely was up, I answered Pinky

"Well it could mean anything still."

"You blind? What else it could mean? It say them linking up tonight, what else that could mean? You act like you don't know is long time Aubrea fucking on you, you need to stop deny it, the whole community know. Mi love Vance but mi sure Vance is not ---"

"Shut up your mouth nuh! Mi ask you anything? Mi ask you nothing? You just don't know when to bloodseed chat, that's your problem. You think anything come to your mouth you must chat, shut up man."

"Daddy you know! Why you don't do a DNA?"

"I don't need to do any DNA. He's mine."

"Well sure as the sun rise, tonight mi will find out what Aubrea up to, and trust mi it won't be pretty."

CHAPTER 32

Be Warned
by: David Lexings

When Pinky and I reached by Vance's bed at the hospital, Vance wasn't there.

Empty bed.

I found out in the evening, according to what Lee said, that she had locked herself away and turned off her phone. Gloe then logged on to twitta or twippa, whatever it name, and people were having a blast with the pics Munchy uploaded. The pictures were funny and some unbelievable. They were retweeting most of the wedding pictures Munchy uploaded, they were just too funny. Browsing through the pictures the first one to make Gloe laugh was the one with the frog-face Pastor Ellis which had gotten the most retweets so far. Some persons were asking if it was photoshopped or real. She saw some more hilarious shots of Pinky fighting and thought it was pretty damn funny how Nathan was running away like a coward. It was one hell of a wedding and Pinky had some flowers pot to buy back. She saw the picture of Vance getting an heart attack and her heart stopped. She knew Leelia had left the wedding before this took place.

Leelia didn't want any disturbance. Gloe disturbed her persistently, insisting that she open up. Leelia looked at the tweets. With only minutes remaining. Leelia called Dr. Reid and paid for the Vance's treatment by maxing out Qwan's credit card. Dr. Reid had already began surgery on Vance when he heard of Pinky's earnest devotion to ending his life. News had already reached his ears of how much damage she did with several flowers pot, he didn't want to cross her path. Vance was held under observation for three days before he was sent home with the warning that he need to do the surgery by Thursday, latest Friday, or else he's dead.

Aubrea left the hospital the same day. She didn't drink the orange juice. She was to meet with Finaral in the night.

Night came.

The Heart of Revenge

She didn't leave the house.

Pinky was angry, because she was time-pedalling the two to see what they were up to.

Aubrea didn't leave because I warned her that Pinky had read her texts.

Pinky said that she will never stop until she got down to the bottom of everything. She vowed if she didn't catch them today then she will catch them tomorrow. I agreed with her.

But I still warned Aubrea about Pinky's intention.

CHAPTER 33

Keep Trying Till Never
by: Leelia Lexings

Eleven days out of this week I've been trying to get through to Qwan's phone. This was my twenty-ninth time calling his phone today without getting any answer. He wouldn't take my calls and he still wasn't sleeping at his house. I just can't get through to him, no matter what I tried. He was too devastated from the wedding. He had nothing to do with me anymore, nor ever again. He didn't want to see my face or hear my voice.

I tried calling for the thirtieth time. His phone rang.

(((Rrring. Rrring.)))

Still no answer. I tried calling with Gloe's phone, I put my number on private, I called at nights, mornings, evenings, days, blue moon, full moon. No answer. I gave up.

I resorted to my only other option, Micheal Douglas.

I didn't want to blackmail Mr. Micheal Douglas to persuade Qwan to get back with me but my brother was depending on it. Time was ticking away, every minute counted. I was desperate, and desperate situations demanded desperate things. I dialled Mr. Douglas.

(((Rrring. Rrring.)))

No answer Yet.

(((Rrring. Rrring.)))

Got him.

"Good morning Mr. Douglas, it's Leelia. Can you talk?" He went silent then answered.

"Yes. Yes." His voice then went up, "What is it?" I felt his voice searching with curious eyes but with more fear in his heart than anything else knowing I held the handle to things and he held the blade. Just where I wanted him, pinned. My next sentence proceeded to tactfully corner him.

"You remember that thing from the other night ---", he interrupted me
"I can't talk to you about that now."
"You better listen to what I ..." Something's wrong,

"Mr. Douglas? Mr. Douglas?" No answer. A couple seconds passed before I heard the empty tone humming through the phone. Shocked, I still held the phone at my ears listening for his further response, waiting on my opportunity to talk. Did he really hung up? I spoke in the cell.

"Mr. Douglas?" Continued nothing. Unbelieve-fucking-able. That!.. That! ... I pulled the cell from my ear and held it directly to my mouth, screamed,

"Mr. Douglas!" Only the annoying tone. Son of a motherfucker. I yelled again, more angry

"Mr. Douglas!" Flatline sound. He definitely had disrespectfully hung up. I heard the connection got cut. My face slackened, astounded by his brute rudeness. Some nerves! He can French smooch my ass!

I pressed the redial button with hard force. His phone rang. The tip of my nose grew some tiny marbles of sweat.

(((Rrring. Rrring.)))

I'm going to be blistering cold with him for dealing with me like crap.

(((Rrring. Rrring.)))

It rang right out. He didn't answer.

I called seven more times. One right behind the other without break. The scum didn't answer. How can he be so disrespectful? The small fire in me blazed into a big flame of rage. My brother situation in the middle of my thought and with time running out, it was overbearing on me. And now Mr. Douglas disrespect? Just when I desperately needed his help? I was being pushed pass anger. Some nerve! Some fucking nerves! I've dirt on you and you know this and you gonna disrespect me? Disrespect me? Fuck, I wanted to hurt him. Hurt him real bad. Real bad. I'll show him.

I try icing my temper. Went to the fridge, poured myself some Dole pineapple juice, sliced a piece of cosmopolitan cheese cake. I couldn't finish the juice. My mind was stomping too much. I was so pissed I must have had a weak bladder. I didn't know what to do to diffuse my anger, my thin legs was making a heavy thud noise every time my heel hit the floor as I walked over to the dresser. Picked up the brown furniture-color comb, combed my hair, combed my hair straight through, harder, rough, more like raking it than combing. Dragging the teeth of the comb through, the comb tugged my scalp when it encountered any tangling of my hair. I didn't stop, I dragged it, ripping, brute force, breaking my hair, tearing out some of my hair from the root, hurting my scalp but I didn't seem to feel anything. I continued raking, raking, raking through my hair. I dropped the brown comb back on the dresser, a tear fell. My eyes murky with tears. Why? Why? Why?

I looked at me in the mirror. My tears flowing freely down my face. Why must this happen to Vance? Why God? Why? I won't give up. I won't give up. Lord give me the strength to fight on. I know there is a way.

An hour passed. I privated my number, called Mr. Douglas. His phone rang twice. On the third ring I successfully got through to his voicemail, not him. I dialled again, and speaking loud to myself, like I was a mad woman, as if he could hear me threatening him 'Answer the phone nuh, you little wretch!' Nothing. No answer. Waited five more minutes. Called back. This time was different. His phone was off. I vexedly hoofed off into the kitchen. Lord, I'm not giving up. I just won't. If Mr. Douglas want to play hardball, well damn-well hardball it will be. Back to my dresser, looked in the mirror, picked up the brush, brushed my hair. Again. Again. Planning.

My mind's all over the place. I really needed to talk, so I dialled Pinky.

Pinky picked up and I went straight into venting,

"Pinky I don't know what to do again, it's like everywhere mi turn mi get dial-tone. I really want help Vance but nothing's working. I feel like giving up. The whole drama thing with the wedding, now this."

"Give up? Just have faith in God sis, mi tired to tell you, you can't control things, just leave it to God. And stop fret 'bout the wedding. God know what him doing, even mi did know that is never Qwan you was to married. From six years aback mi always think Vybz was the right man for you."

"Ajrien? Hsst, him get too bad, he got all his subjects and throw them away to go run up and down with gun like an idiot. Childish love. He's just in the past. I got over him longtime."

"Hmm. So you say."

"What? Him tell you him still like me?"

"Not really but you sure you over him Lee?"

I stopped brushing my hair, froze with the brush midway the length of my hair.

"Of course I'm sure." I got back in action, finished pulling the brush down the length of my hair slowly in thought while I answered. "We living in two different worlds right now, it would never work ... I think you should be with him. Both of you really compatible and look good together, plus, both of you live so close already like husband and wife. I think you should leave Finaral and be with someone who you're compatible with like Ajrien since you always complaining about how much you don't like Finaral."

"You sure you over him Lee?"

"Pinky don't add to mi stress! I said yes ... Sound like is you who like him?"

"Mi kind of like him yes, but mi couldn't sleep with him because mi never sleep with a younger man than me yet, plus mi wouldn't comfortable sleeping with my sister one time man, is dirty life that."

"Look how long that pass and gone Pinky, from I was thirteen, fourteen. Try it. Perry and Dushawn love him. What's stopping you?"

I forced my voice to sound like I really wanted her to be with him. I couldn't admit to Pinky that I was still madly in love with Ajrien. It wasn't right for a girl like me to like a guy like him. Well not anymore. What would people say about me? I know people gossiping and chatting about us wouldn't hurt me literally, but come on, what's the benefit of being with Ajrien? What good will I take all the prosecuting and chatting behind my back for? And how would things work with me and him if he doesn't have any money? He has a daughter. Sigh. It would never work.

But what if in some strange magical way it could work? What if he stopped the night prowling? What if ... aahh, this was just wishful thinking. It would never work. It would work better with Pinky. Sigh. But could I live with that though. Jesus mi would dead inside if Ajrien ever married Pinky. I know Pinky good enough, she'd never go to bed with my ex-boyfriend. Ajrien. You know, Ajrien thuggish ways kind of turns me on. I wonder if, naah, no, no, it wouldn't ... sigh ...

"LEE. You listening to mi?"

"Yeah man, I'm listening. What you say again?"

"Mi say, it look like a big hood man your thing at, Vybz things suppose to long like a church tie when it pull out. Don't?"

Pinky paused for me to answer. What she took me for? I didn't answer. She didn't stop,

"It bigger than Nathan own?"

"How mi must know that?"

"Talk nuh man, whose cocky longer, for Nathan or Vybz. Vybz own. Don't?"

"Stop call him Vybz nuh Pinky, his name is Ajrien. Anytime you call him Vybz I think of bleach-out, good-for-nothing Vybz Kartel, and Ajrien don't look anything like him, they just tall alike."

"Don't diss the Gaza Don. World! ... Boss! Is mi artist and mi don't care 'bout what anybody want to say. Mi artist don't bleach out, him just tone. And it fit him too."

"Stop it. You don't see that Vybz Kartel turn white, till people start mistake him for Justin Bieber?"

Pinky exploded into laughter. She tried to stop laughing but couldn't. I didn't know it was so funny, especially that Kartel is her artist, but she was laughing away and gasping. She repeated

"Justin Bieber ... hahaha ... Raaaements! .... Justin Bieberrr! ... No sir. Big man thing, Kartel don't cute so... Wwooiiee, mi can't stop laugh to rass! ... Tun upp! Mi tight hole a squeeze mi to rawtid clawt!"

Pinky's laughing was contagious, I had a mighty big smile on my face. I rested my hand with the brush on the dresser before me. Ran my other hand over my now neat and relaxed hair, looking in the mirror to see if it was looking all good and neatly in place.

I chuckled harder at the joke. At the same time it crossed my mind if Kartel will get charged. Pinky continued to talk, asking,

"So whose cocky bigger?"

"How would I know Pinky? I was thirteen, I never had sex with Ajrien."

Though I think about it everyday of my life since Mommy sent me away to Stony Hill.

I wondered if I should open up to Ajrien. Wondered if Pinky took what I said serious. Wondered if I should make a move before she tried to make a move. Wondered if Vybz ever advanced at Pinky before.

"Pinky?"
"Yow."
"If Ajrien tried kissing you would you kiss him back?"
"How you say you don't like him?"
"Just answer nuh, or him try make a move at you already?"
Pinky lips were quieted. I knew what that silence meant, I asked her, "So what you did? You kissed him back?"
"Mi say, how you say you don't like him again?"
"Hear what, forget it, just forget it. Bye!"
I hung up. Threw my phone on the dresser. I felt uneasy inside my heart. Damn, it hit me. I know what to do now.
Mr. Douglas can't escape.

CHAPTER 34

This is the Plan B
by: Leelia Lexings

I knew Mr. Douglas managed all of his businesses from his office at Douglas Arms' Security. So, I chartered a taxi there in the evening, at about five thirty. That's the time I knew he usually leaves the office. Let's see what he would say to me now, in person. That prick!

At his office, the receptionist was standing and searching through the slots of a crammed accordion folder. She greeted me with a courteous and over-processed smile, her mouth speaking through the headpiece that she wore, it reminded me of the attendants at the KFC drive-through.

"Hi welcome to Douglas Arms Security," There are sometimes in life when you just see someone and your spirit doesn't take on to them, you just don't like them especially if you're upset, and this was one of the moment. The receptionist teeth was a bright beautiful yellow, like that of a sunflower. The red lipstick was applied unevenly to her thin lips. She strained another stiff smile, just as she was trained to greet. I didn't smile back. I nodded. The air conditioner was blowing cool air on me but I was still hot and tempered.

"How may I help you?"

"Here to see Mr. Douglas." I was looking beyond the receptionist desk and down the cream corridor. I could barely see through the lightly tinted glass door, but I saw that there were persons moving about in the office, walking, maybe getting ready to leave, it was about that time anyway. Two females came out wearing identical navy blue blazer and skirt. And a guy in a Dockers khaki pants trailing behind them wore thick lenses and struggled with both of the ladies handbag as well as his laptop bag. The ladies held their head straight, conversing with each other as they passed by me, the nerd nodded at me and politely greeted 'evening'. I didn't reply not even nod. I was angry with everyone in the building.

I strained my eye in concentration trying to see through the door that they just came through to see if I could spot the son of a swine. The receptionist toyed on the collar of her navy blue jacket, close to where the Douglas Arms Security round white logo with D.A.S. in the center was embroidered. She took up a long black hardcover book, the spine skirted with a thin strip of red. She leafed through the old written pages to the fresher pages until she reached a page with only half of it written up. Her index finger slid down the page as she read. Not finding what she sought, she clammed it close. Almost pleased and definitely feisty, said

"Sorry, you have to have an appointment." As she talked, she rocked pressed her lips together, opened her eyes full and then asked, "You want to make one, lady?"

"Listen. Ms. Spotty-Spotty-Pudding-Face, this important." Her fake smile evaporated, her face became blank, measuring me up with shaky eyes.

"Well, we close off dealing with cheques from four thirty. So you would've to come back in the morning anyway."

"Mi don't come here 'bout any frigging cheque. Tell him Leelia is out here. Do that NOW!"

The receptionist went down slow in her black chair, her eyes never leaving mine. I could see the black hair glue in her weave and the black chord used to sew down the weave at the edges of the part in the center-front. It looked awful. The part in her hair was too wide, and looked like when Moses parted the Red Sea, in the Jesus movie. She dialled an extension, then stand up straight from out her chair, one hand with a black Papermate pen just doodling on the desk like she was writing something but not actually writing because the pen still had on the cover. Her other hand held the office telephone at her ear. Three seconds later, she stopped swirling the pen around and spoke through the phone,

"There's a Leelia .." She stopped and cupped her hand over the phone's receiver, turned her head to me and asked quietly,

"What's your surname Ma'am?" Her tone was more impolite than helpful, before I answered her she added "Give me you full name, just in case ..." I swear to God this bitch testing my faith,

"Lexings. Leelia Lexings."

"I'm sorry pretty Miss, is that Sexings?" I knew she heard me the first time and was just being disrespectful. I gritted my teeth,

"No, academically unattained dunce-bat! Lexings. 'L'. Lexings. Can you frigging hear me now?"

She narrowed her eyes at me, I return the narrowed eyes, she cut her eyes, I remained narrowed and staring. She removed her hand off the receiver and continued to speak.

"Yes there's a Leelia LEX—ings here to see Mr. Douglas." She glanced up at me as if she could feel my stare was burning into her, then added, "She said it's very important."

She waited some more time. Tapping the desk counter with her black pen. Waited longer. Patted the side of her weave with her flat open palm. Her head was more than itching her from how powerfully she was beating her own head. Her un-cared weave was digging her. Or maybe it had a bad case of lice. She slipped the head of her pen through her weave and scratched her head, shaking the pen rigorously. Furiously. Viciously. The entire weave on her head shook as she bored through the weave scratching. It must be scratching her worse than leprosy. The pen wasn't enough. She began pulverizing the side of her head with her hand again, battering, winking only one eye shut with every clap that her strong manish hand clobbered upside her dry head. Gosh, her head must smelt funky. She needs to wash her hair with some strong shampoo and disinfectant.

Finally, she realised where she was, or that she had a client infront of her, processed a stiff smile again, held up her index finger to me, as her lips mimed 'One minute'. She switched over her weight from one leg to the other, switched over again, glanced up at me,

"Coming, ok ... Just one minute." I was impatient and wanted to grab the phone from her and scream at Mr. Douglas to get the fuck out here now. She listened in and stopped chewing her gum as the information from the other end of the phone arrived at her ears. She nodded her head, nodded again, then replied,

"Ok." She hung up and her hand still held on to the phone on the desk. "I'm sorry Ms. Lexi, Lexings right?" I didn't answer her bullshit question. She continued, "Mr. Douglas is not here."

She swept her hand behind her skirt as she lowered herself to her chair. Took up her stuffed accordion folder and rested it into her lap. Began treading two fingers across the slots of the folder in concentration. Finished with me. Stopped midway the folder, dragged the slot open wider and her busy fingers began skipping through the invoices between the slot.

"Not here? NOT HERE? Don't let mi get dark in here. Think mi stupid or something?" Her face went slack and mouth O."Isn't that his van in the parking lot? Tell him I'm here or else it won't be pretty in here today. Get that?"

Her fingers stopped moving. Her voice was slim,

"Yes ... But he drove is other vehicle home."

"Right! Alright then." I didn't waste any more time with the nincompoop. I charged off from infront her desk and stormed down the cream corridor. The receptionist sprang out her chair, the accordion fell. Landed on the switchboard. Papers, invoices and cheques spilled all over the switchboard. Slid to the floor, scattering. The receptionist yelled,

"No. Ms. Lexings. You can't go in!" I sped up down the corridor to the door. "Miss! MISS! MISS!" I didn't look around, I knew the jerk was in there. That cunt! "You CAN'T." That damn conscienceless cunt! "SECURITY! SECURITY!"

Reached the glass door. Pushed the steel bar to enter. Door wouldn't open. Pushed harder. It rattled. Pushed. Rattled with resistance. Locked. I wanted to rip off the blasted door to get inside there. I rocked it harder. Longer. Shaking it. Locked.

I saw a security key pad to the side of the door. I'm familiar with this pad, used it before. It's the same pad by Mr. Douglas's house. I knew the code. I punched in the security pin 4927#. Pushed the door. Still locked. I entered something wrong in the code. Entered it too fast. Slower now. 4. 9. 2. 7. #. Wait for the green light to blink at the top of the keypad. The light blinked. Red. Wrong code. I entered it again. Faster. Wrong code. Banged the door with my fist. Bang! Bang! BANG! Beat it down.

Someone came. It was an overgrown man, decked out in a full navy blue security uniform, with a white name badge, pinned to his left chest that read 'Tobias'. The name sounded old and country. He had a gun at his side. I quieted down.

"Ma'am you can't enter," He was definitely country, and his accent sounded as if he originated from the farthest region of the country. Far, far. "Move from the doorway Ma'am." This is really how Mr. Douglas gonna deal with me? Really? He's making a sad mistake because it won't go down like this.

"I know the little .... I know Mr. Douglas inside there. Sitting around a big desk watching me on a little TV. Tell him to get outside this very minute." I wanted to say, tell him to get outside now, let mi rip him up. But I couldn't let them know the plan, or else I wouldn't get my chance. "Tell him Right now, right- right now." I pointed to the security chest. "You do that." The security deep country accent sounded out of place in the office when he replied

"Ma'am you have to leave, or else you forcing mi to fist you under your belly."

Another security came. He was shorter and had more belly than muscles.

"I'm not leaving this building till your boss come and speak with me. Tell him that a mad woman out here to him." The shorter security informed me that,

"Ma'am Tobias is right. If you don't leave, one of us will have to punch you under your belly and haul you outside."

"Dream on, I dare one of you to thump me today. You wouldn't see the end of! Just touch mi." I begged them to. The security eyed each other and walked over to me. "Don't you dare touch mi enuh!" The receptionist smiled.

The stout security grabbed one of my arm and the overgrown Tobias grabbed my other arm and swung his big fist in the air to thump me. The shorter security grabbed his fist and said,

"No Tobias. You too wicked. Look how she mawga she can manage that ...," Swinging his chin up in the air pointing at Tobias fist in mid air. "that big fist, she can't manage nothing big." Tobias really wanted to fist me. He pressed on to argue,

"But Sup .... mi have to do it. It's procedure ... It's in the manual."

And before the shorter security could reply, 'PLOW!' right under mi belly for true. I saw the moon and the stars, all blinking. They escorted me off the property. Where's Pinky when you need her?

By seven thirty in the night, the light of the day was fading to the dark of the night. I was still by the gate, waiting. I watched all the vehicles drove from the property and at 9 p.m. I was still waiting. Everyone was gone. Only Mr. Douglas Range Rover remained in the parking lot. The receptionist spoke the truth. He really had driven his other vehicle home.

I privated my number, dialled Mr. Douglas. Changed my mind, cancelled the call. It was useless anyway. I made a big sad sigh. With my head down I prodded off slowly from the gate. I live more than four miles away from here, but I felt like walking home. No taxi. No passenger. No talking. Just a quiet lonely walk home. I prodded.

My phone rang. Gloe. I didn't answer. I thought long and hard and short and wide; how else could I get that kind of money before Thursday. There's no other way I could think of. Not giving up, I said to my heart, but it sounded much weaker than when I said it this evening. All hope is slender. I will return to Mr. Douglas's office everyday until he pays me some attention. But Tobias. I doubt he will let me step foot back on the property. My hand went to holding the remains of the cramp under my belly.

Then came a mechanical sound behind me, a continuous tone, sounds electronic. The automatic gate was opening and the army green Range Rover was driving through. I squinted my eyes to see if it was really Mr. Douglas driving. I couldn't really make out who the driver was. But who would be driving his vehicle? The dry hair secretary? Or?

I kept my eyes focused at the windscreen through the night's smoke of darkness. The windscreen was tinted and that didn't help in me trying to make out the driver. The van came closer, and as whoever was driving saw me, they stepped on the gas. It must be that bitch of a secretary. He must be sleeping with her for her to be driving his vehicle. That's the reason she has so much attitude. Why didn't I picked it up from the way she spoke about the vehicle? The vehicle sped closer. I could see the silhouette of the driver more clearly now, it was like a 3-D shadow image behind the steering wheel, Mr. Douglas bald head, but couldn't quite make out the features of his face. How can I get him to stop? I don't know. Think. I do what I had to do. Sprang right infront the speeding vehicle.

I heard the engine revved louder and the van picked up more speed, a trail of furry dust behind its wheel. I'm not moving. I wasn't moving. He'd have to stop or run me over, but I'm not the one moving. I closed my eyes. One second, two, three. His engine roared louder. He was not slowing down, he was gassing it. I popped my eyes wide open like big round bug-eyes. He wasn't easing down. The van raced closer and closer. Closer. Bulleting full-speed with no intention whatsoever to touch his brakes. Oh shit!

Ran. Jumped. Got out the way, running out of my shoe, chucked into the bushes at the side of the road, landed on my side. My hip hurt. One of my shoe left in the middle of the road. The van tore over my shoe, swerved to the side I chucked. So close to me that the breeze from the van blew my well combed hair to a mess. Dust covered my face. My shoes laid dead in the road. Dead. That could have been me. I pranced up to my feet, took off my other shoe and threw it through the plague of dust at the long gone green van. I screamed, rather yelled out

"Battyman Mr. Douglas!" the van shrunk smaller and smaller down the road as he sped on and zoomed around the blind corner, vanishing.

I heard the frightening screeches of brakes. Then a loud mighty clap of metals, a deafening collision. Someone's definitely dead. The first thing that came to my mind was, great, I hoped he's dead. Dead good. He just swerved at me. He killed my shoe. The jerk wanted to run me over. But when I thought about the money for Vance, I prayed to God he saved the bastard. My only chance. Did he survived the crash? I kicked off my other shoe, raced barefooted down the road and around the bend to find out. There was blood all over, and a dead body.

CHAPTER 35

Got To Go
by: Vybz

Murdered. Couldn't Sleep lastnight. Too much to sleep with, just too much. Killed. I didn't know how long before I even returned to Jamaica when I leave. I put my journal in my red suitcase on the bed. Got to let at least two years blow off before I set back foot in Jamaica. That's if Portia pull off the other half of the link that she should. She gave me a link to a bandoloo-ist girl name Danni to buy a fake U.S. Visa. If I get to California on this Visa I'm hoping the other link Portia said she lined up for me over Cali come through, then I could settle down in Cali, sort out my papers and join the California Police Dept. Use that clean money to start a brand new crime-free life. I put the key to my journal in my wallet, back-pocketed my wallet. I reached to close the suitcase but picked up my black journal from among the few clothes I packed, held it in my hand, stared at it.

Leaving someone you love behind, with you being their one and only support is a hard decision to make. Leaving Mama and Tatiana is a huge decision for me. My life. A big deal, but Mama will be proud of me once I get the link from Portia and settle down. Tatiana gonna miss me but eventually she would understand that her Daddy looking for a better life for him and her. And as soon as I earned my citizenship, I'm filing for her and Mama. Just as I got a text from Lia, this happens. I think when she hears of what happened lastnight she'll lose all hope in me. Her text was a strange one, the other day. I wondered if she still thinks about me romantically like I do her. What the hell, I shouldn't even care what she thinks anymore, she's uptown, belong to Qwan, and only see me as her friend, not even a close one. She would never give me a chance. I have a daughter and she was as good as having a husband. So why she texted me that?

Definitely gonna miss my chargie, Pinky. Most people think mi and Pinky doing things, not a relationship, but because we so close people think that we must have sex already. Maybe that's the reason Lia standing off. Naah, couldn't be, Lia knows Pinky is not my type, doesn't she? Let's be honest with myself, me and Pinky would make great partners, she's my kind of girl, that's why we so close. I could spend my whole life with Pinky, but she is with one of my closest friends, Finaral, who is one of the most murderous man I ever heard of. So even if we would, I wouldn't. You feel mi? Lia I wished we had gotten to talk before I leave. Lia, Lia, Lia. Still staring at my journal in my hand, I remembered the poems I wrote her in my journal, but had never given any to her. I made a breathy sigh, a feint scent of tin mackerel was still in the house though we ate more than twenty minutes ago. I put the journal in my suitcase.

Knowing Portia I can't depend on her link but it's better than no link at all, right? How Portia stay, she love to hype up things and talk 'bout she's going to get this and get that artist to pass through, and this and that selector, cheap link to bullets, links with this and that Don, and most of what she says never come through. Not saying none didn't come through before, because couple of them did. Like the one she made at the wharf, with the barrel of Blackberry Curves, that was legit, but most time, she just love chat and hype things, so it's hard to know when her link legit or not. I'm praying the one in Cali legit, because what will happen to me in the future all depend on this. Mama hobbled through my room door.

"Ajrien you don't think you should give Agri-Processors at least a week notice before you resign? Can't just burn your bridges behind you enuh." She began hobbling from the door towards me by the bed, "Don't think you should just up and leave just so. You don't even have any friends or family in Cali, why you taking that job?" She hobbled closer, "Tell them give you a week to sort out things in Jamaica, any company dealing with immigrant labour must can understand that. From when you applied?"

I couldn't look in Mama's eyes. I didn't turn around, I told her too many lies. I had no choice. I had to in order to hide my underworld life. Mama have no idea what a young youth had to do to prove himself in the ghetto, just to not become the next beating stick of the ghetto. I had to be gangster, even if I rather to not run the streets. I had to show Finaral was tough. I had to lie to Mama about it even if I rather not to. Told her so many lies about where I went at nights – parties, friends, girlfriend. All lies. To her I'm Ajrien her intelligent and ambitious son who works an honest nine to five to support her and my daughter. To the streets, I'm Vybz, the gangster with the brain. Except for lastnight. And even though I don't want to, this afternoon I'm telling Mama the biggest lie.

"If I don't go to Cali today, I won't get the job, it pays eight hundred U.S. per week. I got to go Mama."

I wasn't going to Cali to any job. I pulled the zip around the suit case and lift it to standing on its wheels on the floor.

"Mama, meditate. This is the best way to take you out of the ghetto like you've always dreamed. I'm doing this for us. This is the opportunity of a lifetime. For us, and Tati. I got to go."

"It just look strange for you to get a call late in the night and you packing and leaving already, the next day. Something just don't feel right 'bout this thing and you know my feeling usually don't wrong."

I turned around, looked at her withered face. I should just be honest with her, tell her I was going up to escape my guilt and this gangster life, a life that had gotten way too far lastnight. This life wasn't me, just wanted to prove to my friends that I was thugged. I couldn't afford for anyone calling me Sissy like Vance, or let no one ride my back with ridicule. I had to show them that I'm tough. So of course I hid my journal from them, the only friend I showed my journal was Pinky, she knew I wrote, but I never gave her my journal to read. I hide it from all my brethrens, they'll think my stories and poetry is too sentimental, girly and soft. A thug can't have that. I couldn't tell Mama I was a gangster either, it would make her angry. Make tears come to her sick eyes, have her wondering what have she grown her boy to become, but it wasn't her, it was the streets. I was the streets. And I couldn't tell her about what happened lastnight, it would kill her the very minute anywhere she stood. I pulled the handle of the suitcase and it extended out for me to haul.

"Mama, got to go." I was striding by her, wheeling the luggage.

"You sure you not lying to me Ajrien? Look at me." She touched me at my waist as I hauled the suitcase by her, tried to subside my emotions. I couldn't. I stopped. "Who's going to be here with us if nothing happen, God forbid?" Her eyes were weakening. "What if things don't work out up at foreign? How mi and Tatiana going to eat?"

I couldn't look back at her, I gazed ahead at the door. I'm usually an optimist, but in reality things could get really atrocious. Portia link is my dying straw of hope. I really want it to come through so I can really uplift Mama's life. Turn this negative that had happened to me to drive me into a positive. Mama been suffering long enough.

I looked at my hand, my fourth finger, it had a plastic ring. Lia had given me the ring six years ago. We were kids, playing, but serious. Marriage. I was so right for her then. Now I'm so wrong. I guess that's how life is, people change as time goes by. Situation and circumstances change people. We have grown to be two different persons. She went uptown, I went gangster. I ran my hand over Mama's wrinkled hand at my side.

"Everything will be alright." I remembered the card, "Almost forget." I brushed the left side of my blazer open and went into the top pocket of my button up shirt. "Here." I handed her my bank card, "Use this till I get myself together up there."

I ran a quick mental check to see if I was leaving anything that I would need. No. The four things I valued the most I had, my journal, a wallet size pic of Tati and Mama, my credit card and my white plastic ring. Nothing else mattered that much. Time to leave.

Tatiana rompingly skipped through the door, vivaciously hopping in the same spot. Dropped her blue Dora the Explorer Lunch-pan at her feet and clapping with her tiny finger spread wide apart and missing the clap on some occasions. Her blue and white uniform bouncing to the rhythm of her energetic hops, her forehead sweating from the hot sun outside. One of her pink knapsack's straps slinking about to fall off her shoulder, you can actually see the dry dust on her blue socks and black shoe, except for the silver buckle at the side of her shoe. She swung both hands up to me for a hug. I smiled, hugged my little princess.

"Monster Daddy, plway monster ... tehehe" The Monster game she was talking about was Hide and Seek, but I'm the monster looking for her, and when I found her I gobbled her knees. She giggled loudly when she hid so I could find her quickly and eat her knee. That's the part she loved. She absolutely loved it, eyes became sparkly, giggled endlessly as I playfully gobbled her knee.

"Can't play now sweetface. Got to go."

"Tehehe ... Daddy where you going?"
"Remember what I told you this morning sweetface?"
"Yeah ... You going in the sky."
"Not in the sky baby, in a plane." Tati had a slight lisp from the couple of teeth missing from her mouth, her voice was mostly sing-songy when she spoke,
"Really really and truly ruly going on plane Daddy?" She pointed one finger up to the roof. "Up there so? In the sky?"

Maybe leaving wasn't the right thing after all. I frisked my hand in her thick head of hair, nodding, yes. She asked the darnest questions. Her round face as broad as pie, her cheeks puffy, smiling and wiggling her head out of my frisking hand,

"Stop spwoil my hairstyle Daddy. I'mma hot girl." This little big woman was so cute, and seemed smarter than Google for two and a half years old, a blessing to me.

"Who tell you that you are a hot girl?" She fixed her knapsack's strap properly on her shoulder, akimboed and rocking, said

"Aunty Pinky!" She smiled, her eyes proud, "Daddy, want come with you, plwease, plwease." She grabbed onto my suitcase handle, started pulling, helping me with the suitcase.

"Oh, no, no, Hold on, you can't sweetface. Well not yet. You have school tomorrow."

"No. Not sweetface Daddy, hot girl... Is your plane? You must Brwing back ice-cream and cheese-balls for me." I watched her in awe, she was just in my scrotum like yesterday. "You want mi give you money to buy ice-cream Daddy? She generously dipped in her uniform like she had money. Mama smiled, my heart smiled, my face smiled, "You soon come back Daddy?"

We stopped smiling. There was a sudden eruption of silence in the room that was heavy on our hearts and awkward. She looked at me. Mama looked at me. I gazed at them both. The cataract was spreading in Mama's eye, almost covering half of her pupil. I replied,

"I don't know."

"Come back tomorrow Daddy, or else mi ..." She lashed her hand by her bottom suggestive of whipping me. "beat your bottom." She smiled, she was so joyous. "We can play Monster tomorrow when you come back Daddy?"

I didn't want to lie to her, but I couldn't tell her the whole truth. My phone beeped. A text. It was Portia. I read it. It read

'You have to link mi right now. Stop by at work before you leave and how you never answer what mi ask you lastnight? You doing it or not?'

From the tone of the text I knew it spelled some disaster. I hoped this had nothing to do with what happened lastnight, or worse anything bad about the link in Cali, or worserer bad news about both. The taxi tooted its horn outside. I looked at Tati waiting for the ice-cream and Monster tomorrow, looked in Mama's cataract eye, kissed Mama. Kissed Tati.

"Have to go."

Tati was no fool. she sensed it was more than tomorrow, by the look in my face and by the aura around us. She felt it. Her face changed, her smile disappeared. She stepped towards me. Her feet bounced her Dora lunch-pan that was on the floor. It fell over, spilled opened, her lunch container an juice bottle rolled out. She didn't look at it, she looked in my eyes and insisted

"Daddy don't go."

"Got to go sweetface, I got to go."

CHAPTER 36

Who Dead
by: Leelia Lexings

It was a surprise how huge the crowd was already. The accident was a lot nastier than I had imagined. There was a river of blood on the black tar. A totally dismantled red Suzuki Swift and a white coaster bus. The coaster crashed head on with the small Suzuki Swift . The petrified crowd surrounded the dead body. A bald head gentleman.

The driver had smashed through his windscreen and was laying against shattered glass from windscreen, headlights, and orange and red indicators. Blood pouring from his split skull. Instantly my mouth and stomach felt provoked. I tasted earthworms in my mouth and felt them wiggling. I covered my mouth. A young girl probed up-close to the disgusting sight of the dead body, curious to see more clearly in the night what the body looked like. She vomited lumpy chunks of pink, orange and brown slush in a watery mixture at the sight of inside the man's head and the raw smell of his blood and brain. She spewed one more mouthful of vomit slush on top of the already colourful muck on the ground.

The witnesses all seemed more angry than shocked. The bus driver walked in every direction and in circles, his two hands on his head, his fingers squashed down into his huge afro. He was chatting non-stop.

"Is swing mi did have to swing out of the green Rover boy that run through the redlight enuh. Suppose mi never did swing? With the speed him come round the corner the whole bus load of people would've dead off to pussyclawt." He stopped and looked at an office attired lady that must have been on the bus, seeking her approval "Don't? You see that is Jah-Jah guide the bus though mumma?"

My eyes instinctively searched the surrounding for the Rover that caused the accident. Nowhere in sight. Gone.

"Him not even stop after him ram up in the little youth vehicle and kill off the youth."

The driver took one of his hand off his head. Shoved his hand down his big jeans with its waist two times the size of the driver waist, hauled up and draped up around his belly by a slim belt. He shuffled his hand up and down his pocket. Took out a slim silver phone. Dialled, one hand still on his head. A market lady asked aloud,

"Nobody don't catch his licence plate number?"

"Mi catch the number." A student still in his khaki pants and white shirt said.

Mr. Douglas had no conscience. He could run but they still gonna find him anyway. I bet he must have raced home. I hurried my barefoot across the road to the red plate taxi and chartered it straight to Mr. Douglas' house.

I reached. The crushed Rover was there, parked. The property was closed. The steel gate padlocked. The guard, Mr. Willie, was in the white guard room to the side of the wide gate. This is a problem. I wondered if Mr. Willie knew I was no longer entitled to enter the property without consent. My wedding drama was the hottest mix-up in the entire area, because of how popular the Douglas family were and to have such a propaganda at Mr. Douglas' son wedding was headline mix-up. Well apart from the dirt I had on Mr. Douglas. Mr. Willie must have heard about the wedding, of that I'm sure. How should I approach this? Shoot. Only one way. Here goes.

CHAPTER 37

Persuasion
by: Leelia Lexings

"Hey, night Mr Willie. How things man?"

"Goodnight Ms. Leelia, longtime mi don't see you 'round this side."

"Yeah. Been up and down. Busy. Really been awhile for true. Can you believe I left my keys at home? Oh silly me. Let me in please."

Mr. Willie put down his Pepsi on the guard table, turned the volume knob down on the small radio. His black rubber watch was buckled in the last hole on the watchband but it's still swingled around his fine wrist. His navy blue guard uniform was baggy and slinky on him. He definitely didn't have the built to be a security.

"You leave your keys? ... How?"

"The haste."

"Boy Ms. Leelia, mi hear 'bout what happen at the wedding. Sorry to hear that man. Up to this morning mi and my wife was talking 'bout it." He spun the silver key in the huge padlock, unchained the gate and opened it.

"I know right. It's Ok still, we worked it out." Walking through the gate with a feeling of relief, yes I got in. Mr. Willie wrote my name down in the visitors' log book. Stopped writing. Looked up at me suspiciously.

"But wait ..." He paused, "Come out back one second Ms. Leelia."

"Why Mr. Will?"

"You just come out back little."

"Why?"

CHAPTER 38

Mr. Willie Hold the Keys
by: Leelia Lexings

I stood inside the property still. Staring at Mr. Willie in disbelief.

"Mr. Willie? Do better than that, don't treat me like mi a thief."

"You is not no thief Ms. Leelia, but just come back out one second please."

I looked to the apartment complex. It was a lengthy dash from here. I'm not in heels, barefoot. Should be able to sprint leave Mr. Willie. I thought hard. Looked at Mr. Willie back at the complex, back at Mr. Willie. My steps towards the gate and back through were slow. He spun back the lock close. But why should Mr. Willie treat me like a stranger? We cool. I made him lasagne for lunch every Saturday when I lived here. I glared at Mr. Willie in disbelief. I was no thief. I touched between my bosom.

"It's me enuh Mr. Willie. Leelia."

"Yes Ms. Leelia, mi know is you from you walking come up the gate..." His small eyes were like two black beads staring at me through the night's darkness, his face shaved clean and his receding hairline an ill-shaped semicircle, "But mi not sure mi can let you in?"

"Of course Mr. Willie man. Why not?"

"Mi don't want get in no trouble."

"What kind of trouble? It's me. What mi going to do? Rob the complex?"

"Mi doing mi job. Mi following procedures. Mi just get some orders and mi have to check out something first. It alright with you if mi do my job? Or you want tell mi how to do my job?"

"You think mi would really do you that?"

His beady eyes studied my expression then he sputtered,

"Well ... well ... trouble don't set like rain enuh, you don't know when it coming ... Hear what, just hold on right outside there." He walked back into the guard booth. Today is not my day with securities. Hsst. I Shook my head. Sigh.

"What is it Mr. Willie?"

"Stop pressure mi nuh ... Just wait let mi call Mr. Douglas first to make sure. Mi don't want lose mi job, because it's mi little bread and butter."

I texted Pinky. I wrote in the text

'Sis can you believe is two times today mi in pure problems with security? Can I have so much bad luck?' Mr. Willie was still on the phone.

"Mr. Willie come on ---"

"Just one minute nuh Ms. Leelia, how you in so much haste?"

He dialled again. Waited with the phone by his ear. Waited and waited. Hung up.

"Mi not getting him." He breathe out his frustration loudly, while contemplating his next move.

"It's Ok man. Just trust mi." He dialled again. Waited. Waited. Hung up.

"Him not answering him extension enuh ... Sorry. Mi can't let you in."

"Christ! What would I be doing so bad to make you lose your job?"

"Ms. Leelia, your lasagne them sweet but mi don't want lose mi job. Mi just want be careful. Mi get warning just a while ago from the boss. You think mi would be so hard if mi never get warn. Is three years and little months mi at mi yard not doing nothing, before mi catch this little security work, mi don't want lose it."

"Oh Gosh man, shame on you to even think I would let something like that happen to you. You know if you would get in trouble, I wouldn't even ask you in the first place." I stepped closer to the guard house. "I know things hard, especially with you and your kids and I would never set you up to lose your work, look how long we've been friends."

He hesitantly stepped out the white guard's booth, stared at me, walked up to the gate, shoved the key in the padlock and before turning it said,

"Make sure enuh Ms. Leelia, mi trusting you and doing you this favour. Remember mi job and mi family depend on it."

"Mi sure man, mi sure."

He spun the key, opened the gate. I walked peacefully through the gate. He finished writing in my name, looked back at his black rubber watch then jotted down the time.

"Sign here so." His pen pointed to the blue ruled line in the book. I scribbled down my signature flash-handedly. Dropped the pen down centering the gutter of the open book.

'Beep ... Beep.' Pinky text reply came in. I opened it. After expressing how bad luck I was with securities today I wondered why the hell Pinky sending me this and she knows I won't buy. What the text said was,

'That mean you should gamble a money on number thirteen in Cashpot tomorrow for the morning draw. Thirteen mean police. Set 'bout two bills sis.'

I hissed my teeth as I texted her back,

'KMT! Mi not buying no damn Cashpot and waste off my money.'

I heard Mr. Willie voice from behind me,

"What happen to your shoes Ms. Lee?"

"Long story."

"Hey! Qwan not here enuh, just him father alone here from you left him father run him out." I continued walking to the house, it was all dark. Except for one weak light in Mr. Douglas' room, at top, fourth floor. I replied to Mr. Willie,

"That's Ok, I'm here to see Mr. Douglas." And grumbled under my breath to myself, 'I'm surely gonna teach him.'

All the codes to the doors was still 4927#. I climbed up the tall spinely stairs that wrapped around and all the way up a gigantic byzantine column, it was made of white marble stone. The stairs had wrought iron railing painted in black. Why Mr. Douglas put out Qwan? What a coincidence with the time of me leaving, I don't think Mr. Douglas would put out his own son because I'm not here though, that didn't make any sense. So what Qwan did then? It was strenuous on me to breathe when finally reached the peak of stairs on the fourth floor. The elevator would have been easier but you see, Mr. Douglas had a little TV in his room that showed in black and white the insides of the elevator and various section of the property intermittently, so I took the stairs. Another text came in from Pinky. I opened it and it read,

'Send me $50 credit please.' I shook my head, Pinky knew my phone was post-paid, so couldn't have said I have no credit. I sent her seventy dollars credit. Climbing all those metal steps barefoot made my footbottom tender. Mr. Douglas room door was locked. I banged on his door with my two fist, 'Bang! Bang! Bang! Bang! Bang! ... Bang!'

"Who the fuck's trying to break down my door?"

"Open this damn door! ... Now!" ... 'Bang! Bang! Bang!'... "Open up bastard!"

CHAPTER 39

Back to the Warehouse
by: Vybz

Her hole is hot. Fiery from the friction of bouncing rigorously up and down my dick. Beating my cock to a bruise with every sturdy bounce she makes. She grinds hard and fierce, up and down, pumping on my cock, working that pussy. Sliding down the length of my cock, filling her inside, just the way she wants it inside her. She feels a pleasurable stretching from the length of my cock beating down at the bottom of her pussy. Portia dashes down the full distance, her river wetting my cock like a spitty blowjob. Her white honey smothers all over my sweet chocolate dick, she slides her pussy all the way back up to the top, her parted pussy walls feeling so good as she rides up to the broad head, she didn't pass the rim of the head, she forces back down on it, with a slight forward swerve, making way through her flesh, somewhere in her belly that was sensitive to touch, she jerks and the pleasure sinks down so deep in her, it spreads beyond her pussy, driving her to go deeper, harder and faster, rupturing all the joys in the very bottom of her pussy, pleasures bursting, and filling her hot hole. She pulls her own hair hard, bites the brim of her lip, grabs her left breast, squeeze it, the cock is too sweet, even her teeth is rattling. She bounces her fleshy round ass into me carelessly, making a slapping sound as she hits into my pelvis. We make sex heat, steaming sweat. We are getting wet, sweating. She grabs her other breast and squeezes them so erotically, not giving a damn about perspiration, she goes on riding my cock like there's no tomorrow, it was her last, her pussy depended on it. The splashes of her ass getting louder and faster, her rhythm now rocking forward and backward slapping her groin into my abs as she thrusts forward, riding my cock out her, rocking her ass backward and down on the muscles of my thighs, sliding on my tough veiny cock in her juicy wet flourishing pink middle, moaning,

"Oh God, this feel like heaven ... hhsshh ... aarrhh ... fuck yeah!"

Our bodies colliding, her eyes closed, teeth pulling on her sexy lips, my cock feels so wet, so supple with her slick juices, she rides and rides and rides, pleasing herself, letting the cock rub deep inside her where it sends her out of control. Out of fucking control. I grip the base of her breast, her hard nipples pointing to my face, so close. So close, so fucking close. I lean in and take her breast into the warmth of my mouth, clasp my boiling mouth around her erect nipple, nibble on them with the edge of my teeth, circle the dark rim around her nipple with my tongue, making sure my tongue grazes the edge of her nipple with every slow circle, suck her nipple, all the way up, suck more than her nipple up into my mouth, she rubs her fist on her knee, feeds her breast in my mouth, I gobble them up, flick my stiff tongue on the flat head of her hard nipple, swiftly, a thousand times, over and over again on her nipple, feast on her, feast on her breast. Her silent gasp turns into soft moans every time she slides back and forth on my cock, breast stuffed in my mouth, fingers digging the broad of my back, she rides harder, her strides are vicious as if she is trying to rub out her pussy to dust on my cock. She feels her clit rubbing against me as she sits and presses into me as deep as she can, plunging down on my cock forcefully so she can feel it the furthest ever it can reach up inside her pink palpitating pussy, rubbing her clitoris on me with intense friction, her clit stiff, swollen, big, about to explode into a billion tiny pieces, I groan with her breast still in my mouth,

"Mmmm, mmm!" My mouth releases her breast, put my lips on her cheek close to her ear and mutter in pleasure,

"Oh fuck you can ride cock! Ahhh! You feel so fucking good baby, shhsshh, feels so fucking good, ride it, come on, ride it baby! God damn!" My breath beating against her face as I talk, "Just like that baby. Work that pussy! Ride it! Sshhhshh. Ride it!"

The sensation of fuck, the feeling in her body is more powerful than a tingle, her body is fucking erupting with a million ecstasy darting through her entire body, her toes, her lips, her belly, her fingers, her neck, splintering her spine, her pussy, her fucking wet clit is paining with pulsing pleasure. I check my watch. Fuck, I need to leave now. I suck on her sweaty neck, pull on it. Spank her ass cheek, grab it, squeeze into it firmly. Slide my hand across her back, polish my hand with the sweat on her belly, stir my thumb against her sticky clit, rub it in circles, stir violently, she stuffs two fingers in her mouth. Pulls it out, holds it before my face, rubs her wet fingers on my lips, pushes them in my mouth, presses it against my tongue, drags it back out. I go out of control, sucking her whole body. Drag my soft wet tongue all over her, running it everywhere on her and under her, suck on the hollow of her navel and her body curls. Swirl my tongue lightly in the delicacy of her sinking navel, her knees clash together. She stuffs back her fingers in her mouth and squirms.

    I love the taste of her sweat on my tongue. My licks get wild, I grab her face, lick her jaw-line, up to her ear, lick behind her ear, her hair brushes against my tongue, I nibble her earlobe with my soft, wet ,horny mouth, tongue, lip, tongue, wet tongue, horny tongue in her ears, sends mesmerizing shrills through the hollow of her ear-hole, down her neck, spine, skidding through her body, ripping her nerves to shreds, her mind turns to dust, she yanks her fingers out her mouth, they are wet, shoves away my head from her ear, shoves her wet fingers in my mouth, her body jerks, pushes her shoulder upward to her ears, sheltering her from the intensity and unbearable tingles running through her ears, trembling. Fuck, I got to leave, I got to go … just one more minute, one more. She pulls out her fingers, I go for her neck vein. Suck on it. She arches her neck to my nimble sexbites, arches her back, jerks, slams her opened-legs shut around my waist, quaking with excitement as I suck and nibble the nape of her neck, under her ear. I lick my way down to working on her broadened sensitive nipples. She whimpers and desperately wraps both hands around my neck so tight my face is buried between her bosom, I can hardly breathe as she rides my pole mercilessly, her fingers dig deep into my muscular back. I feel a scratch there, I love it. This is fuck. This is what fuck should feel like. I'm muffled between her breasts,

    "Oh yes, Oh yes, oh fucking yes! ride it baby, ride it" I grab on her hair, pull her scalp back, put my mouth on hers, talk in her mouth,

    "Fucking break off my dick! Please!" My breath and voice running into her mouth, "Fucking break it off baby." I curl my loin into her, my hot breath barging into her mouth. "Fucking break it for mi baby."

    I thrust my hip upward as she slides down on my cock and her mouth gapes silently, I stick my tongue in, suck on her tongue, pull on her hair, she flashes her mouth off mine, her fingers stiffen into a sharp rake, rakes her nails through my back, gasps for breath,

"Huh! Huhuh!"

Her belly muscles flinch, her back curls and she drags her hand up to my shoulder, while sliding down on my cock again. I thrust upward harder, so far gone, above cloud eleven, her body an earthquake, her spine cold as if small pieces of ice were clinking up and down through the hollow of her spine, then hot, then cold, hot and cold, travelling through her elbows and knees, her moans grow louder and her fingertips sink deep into my shoulders, her nails hitch in my skin. She sounds as if she was crying, begging,

"No! No! Don't move."

Her body trembling, she bites her lips harder as the immense pleasures electrocutes her skin, spasms running up and down deep in her body, rippling all the way through her flesh, and through the marrow of her bones, tormenting every single atom of her body into wild senseless twitches, she can't think straight, she can't think at all, all her sexual emotions stirs up into a wild storm. But she doesn't stop. She fucks me hardcore, looks down at her swollen pussy, sweating, groin wet, watching herself riding it, stares in my eyes, her eyes intense, her lips sexually pouted. And the time ticks away.

She rides my dick hard, determined to cum, that's all she's seeing, all she is thinking, all she is feeling, just the sensation of cumming, the electricity of cumming, a titillating feeling of exploding, she can feel it building up in her loin, her clit is unnerved, she sucks my cheek, sucks my bottom lip, squirming, buries my face back into her bosom. I'll just wait one more minute till she cums, she is on the verge. I motion my hip with her ride. But fuck, I have less than three minutes to leave or else I'll be missing my flight, I can't have that. No way. I got to go.

She drags my head from between the bouncing flesh of her breasts, grabs my hair tight and pull it with pitiless passion. It pulls the skin of my forehead backward. She pants while speaking

"No! No! Don't move Vybz, Don't move, Just stay there, don't move."

The cock is in her sweet spot, she is riding her fucking senses out to ecstasy, the big stiff fleshy head of my cock is right in there, smooth and slippery in that sweet G-spot, she grinds on it, the round smooth head internally massaging her deep, rubbing it, rubbing herself on it right there, riding, riding, pleasing herself ontop, it's the best sex feeling ever, her pussy clamps so tight around my cock, jumping with my cock in-between it. I look at my luggage, think about the time. I feel her pussy flexing, grabbing and letting go, she tosses her head back, her eyes closed, she swallows her spit and I stay perfectly still, only her loin moving sweetly, smoothly working, she is in perfect concentration, she swallows again, eyes closed yet still dreamy, she rides her black cock like its a machine, consumes the sweetest black cock into her, tries to fucking destroy her own pussy on my cock. Goes harder, frantic, wild. The flesh of her ass spilling backward on my thighs with every hard thrust she makes and spills back in place with a bounce. I grip at her hipbone tighter, her face motioning closer over my face, presses her forehead against my cheek, her body winds upward with every stroke climbing deeper into her. Keeping myself on her sweetspot, keeping it there. Her moans getting louder, er hair a mess, she goes faster and faster and faster, she lose total sanity. Pleasure takes over her mind, the movements of her body.

   I hope she cums already, please, I have less than a minute.

   She sticks her tongue out an let only the flat pad of her moist warm tongue glaze over my mouth, both my lips, bites on my lower lip and pulls on it hard. The round head of my cock is in her pleasure–nest, her sweetspot. Right there, right where it feels so fucking good, right there, feels so good, so good, so fucking good. Her longing fiery desires swells inside her, brims up to her clit, her head sways in slow motion, in pleasure, drunken in the sweet pleasure of fuck. She feels my cock beating inside her like a heartbeat, hot, throbbing, warm, in her tight enlivened pink flesh. I hear my cell vibrates. She talks sexy, talks dirty and unfiltered,

   "Bloodclawt … you hood feel good! It feel so fucking good in mi pussy, so fucking good!"

   She opens her eyes, looks at me with intense lewdness and command "Kiss mi! Kiss mi now"

   I want to check my phone. Her tongue was out before she got the kiss, my lips touch her tongue, she swallows my mouth. Squirming in a high pitch and riding, riding, riding me. Riding my cock. She's about to cum or explode. Who calling? She makes a loud squirm,

"Mmmhhhmm!" as she feels the cum running down into her loin, ravishing her nerves, her whole body feels like a huge nerve that's too sensitive to be touch, her entire skin arouse with sensual passion, deeper than her skin, down in her flesh, in her bones. She rocks her hips hard ontop of me like a mad woman, sending her tongue far down into my warm mouth, both her hands clamping my cheeks, still squirming, long and loud moans into my mouth "Mmmhhhhmm" she presses her breast against my chest, her breath stops as she kisses me madly deep and fucks the sweetest cock she as ever felt inside her. I pinch her nipple, roll them. Pull them, pinch them, suck them, it magnifies her feeling, she wants to explode. She is squeezes her eyes shut tight, her eyelids is cringe, her mouth wide open as she speaks to herself in a moaning tone,

"Oh ... right there, right there, mi a cum, mi a cum, Oh God mi a cum!"

Finally, I thought. She becomes senseless, in a sexual trance, the wild mad frenzy of cumming, she latches on around my neck, sends her groin slapping countless times into my waist as she rubs off her pussy on my cock with shorter wild strokes, rocking on my thick cock madly, wild, the cum shoots through her, rattling every nerve in her, her cum is on the edge of squirting out her pussy, my phone makes the special ringtone I have for my closest friend, Finaral. What the hell does he wants now? I don't want to hear from him. Damn, if he ever had any idea I'm fucking his ex-girlfriend right now, I'm good as dead. Portia gets louder,

"Yes! Cumming, I'm cumming! Mi a cum!"

And nobody was calling Portia's name.

CHAPTER 40

Heart in My Mouth
by: Leelia Lexings

"Lee?" Mr. Douglas took a pause, then asked "You don't plan to give up today, huh? ... How the hell you get up here by the way? Huh?"

I had to protect Mr. Willie. I said nothing.

"Hope is not the idiot Mr. Willie let you up here after mi just tell him don't even let in mi mother enuh. Or else him just lose him work."

"Is not Mr. Willie let me through."

"So him leave the gate wide open? Huh? Is a worthless at the gate then, is not a security that. Mi and him rass."

Mr. Douglas didn't open the door. He was shouting on the phone, I heard him loud and clear,

"Fucking Novice Willie! Mi in so much trouble and mi tell you one simple thing. Just one, Don't let in not even mi mother and you do the nex thing. Pack up every single piece of you mumma bloodclawt things and leave mi property! Now! You're fired! ... Bloodclawt man!" I heard Mr. Willie slammed the phone down just as loud as Mr. Douglas was shouting.

Oh Christ. Mr. Willie. I felt a huge guilt darkened my inside. I ushered myself, thinking Mr. Willie didn't lose his job in vain, it's for a good cause, your saving a life. I would try to set up a job for him, but right now Mr. Douglas is my focus, trying to save something you can't get a new one of. Lose it and its final. A life. I got straight to the point.

"The driver's dead Mr. Douglas, his head was split wide open."

The door busted open immediately. The room was a clutter, three huge suitcase were wide open like square clam shells on the bed, drawers opened and clothes haphazardly slap-dashed all over the room.

I spoke low with a calm levelled head.

"Don't be stupid." He turned looking at me, "Running away won't help. They have your licence plate. A big shot like you they are gonna come at you hard, track your flight, your credit card, seize your assets, accounts .. . everything." His baldhead flustering, dripping sweat right around his face, "Let me help you."

Mr. Douglas placed his laptop slowly in the red suitcase and pulled out a shiny chrome gun. Aimed it at my head.

A text came in from Pinky. 'Beep ... Beep.' Frightened, my body jumped, finger pressed on my phone, opening the text, it read

'Tanx 4 always helpin out sis!!! ☺ ☺ ☺.'

I looked back up into the gun. I felt my flesh falling off my bones.

CHAPTER 41

Black Heart
by: Leelia Lexings

"What you want huh?" What is it!"

Both my hands reached out towards his chest, my ten fingers pointed up to the high ceiling, my hand trembling out of control. I felt my heart sticking, just sticking me, sticking me, pins and needles, like I too had Vance's heart problem. Uh, damn it pained. I kept my mouth shut, muffled my heavy wheezing that came on, grabbed on my left breast, clenched, squeezed. Mr. Douglas eyes zoomed in at my breasts that I squeezed. Almost as if he enjoyed seeing me squeezing on my tits. Would he really shoot me? I lunged for air. Would he kill me? My heart felt so much pain, as if someone was opening my heart with a chain-saw. Mr. Douglas? I caught my breath, heaved, exhaled, breathe, breathe but my head delirious, spinning, tightened, thinking, wondered, would he? He asked me,

"Huh, What you want?" Mr. Douglas lips drew back in a angry snarl, shook his gun impatiently at me. I raised my hand from my heart and begged. My heart tempo resuming to normal.

"Calm down Mr. Douglas, I'm here to help you. Your brains watery upstairs or something?"

"How? Huh?"

"Just put down the gun so we can talk."

"Chat now nuh gal!" He didn't put his gun down. I stuttered.

"I ... I ... I can help ... I can help you to disappear. Without a trace. Before tomorrow afternoon." He got even angrier, his hand shook visibly in a no non-sense manner, twitching to pull the trigger. The aim of the gun waved all over my face, I squinted as it pointed to my eye. His whole body jerked in a tantrum as he exploded,

"Think I'm fucking stupid, huh? HUH?"

He callously rammed the gun into my face, my cheekbone, the hard metal nozzle slammed against my solid cheekbone, it hurt. He shoved it, it bruised, tore my skin, bled. He kept pressing it cold-heartedly against my cheekbone, kept shoving it, crushed it hard into my cheek, pain, my flesh squashed thin between the nozzle and my cheekbone, pain, my head tilt back. The nozzle slid on my skin, went under my eye. My head rocked backward again, he heartlessly shoved it harder, eager to get rid of me. My heartbeat tripled. All my words were trying to get out in one breath.

"No, no, no, I swear..." My words were racing out before he squeezed the trigger. "My bestfriend Gloe has a girlfriend who's a bandooloo-ist, I mean she can get you fake everything. Everything. Everything you need to escape. Passport, cards, visa, id, anything." The gun was still in my face, the pressure not hard anymore, I felt it on my skin, but not slammed on my bone.

"What you want from me?"

"Look, let's be civil ... we both need help. You got the cash that can help me out with my brother and I have the connections you need to vanish before they lock you behind bars ... your case is a straight deal ... man-slaughter, fifteen to twenty years. You prepared for that? Let's not lose our heads and be reasonable about this Mr. Douglas." His eyes twitched as he came out of his own mind of reasoning, he then commanded,

"State your price. Little Smart-Ass."

"Remember that night." I coolly reminded him before stating the price, trying to win more leverage on a deal, but not to provoke him back to anger. "I'll let that thing disappear too, I will totally forget it ... Especially for your son's own future."

"What's your damn price? You conniving, manipulative SLUT!" He balled his fist and clench his teeth saying 'slut'. That was the first time I was ever looking at the bald-headed Mr. Douglas so closely as to recognise that his teeth were the same color as golden piss.

"Slut? Who you calling a Slut?"

"You! You disgusting ghetto whore. You and your mother is always about getting some money. Your mother did it when she was young, I paid her in full, I was to get you when you were seventeen and the bitch touted you to hook up with Qwan, blighting my chances with you after I already gave her my money. You were to be mine not Qwan's, mine. You two will sell your ribs for money. I know your brother's heart problem is a another big lie that you and your mother using to wring money out of us, out of Qwan. Use you to get money from Qwan and from me ... You low life ghetto scums would do anything for money. Anything! You think you know how big of a slut you mother is? You have no idea. Why you think mi fire her? You are just the same ... like mother, like slut!"

A turmoil of emotions ran through me in every different color imaginable. My mom was never a slut. Never will be a slut. I'm certainly no slut ...Vance heart problem is real. Isn't it? My mom would never. Would she? No she wouldn't. This scandalous bald-head man is trying to play with my psyche, ruin me and Mom. If this were ever true, I would definitely ... no it can't be true. I see Vance at the hospital, I've seen his attacks. Why am I making this corrupted perverted man who can't be trusted let me have second thoughts about something that's clearly facts. Let him pay for his words. Let him pay.

"Sixty thousand U.S.!"

"You out of your bleeding mind slut? Huh? Huh?"

I folded my arms and stared at him. I can't believe someone like him, after what I caught him doing have the nerve to be judging my Mom. I always stood my distance from him, whenever he is at the house, he was just that eerie and creepy and icky that my instinct told me to stay away. Seemed my instinct was right. He was a real low life for calling Mommy that. I bet every other rumour about him is true. So maybe that's the reason he ran Qwan out his house when I left, he wanted me, he didn't want Qwan to have me. I can't believe Mr. Douglas. Gosh! He sickens me. That day would never come in a million years. That sick bastard. What if? ... But I was just fourteen. I should expose this son of a bitch for who he really is to every media in Jamaica. Mr. Douglas tightened his jawbone with dreadful anger, chew on his lip,

"Who you looking on like that huh gal? He raised his gun to the center of my forehead. "Better if mi kill you right now." I didn't flinch.

"Yeah. Go shoot your face! You know you ain't shooting a soul. You wouldn't be so stupid to shoot your only help right now." I slapped the gun out my face. "Take this stupid thing out my face before you hurt somebody. Get this through your thick skull. I. AM. YOUR. ONLY. HELP ... This SLUT! Ok?"

He lowered his gun, his head in a thick smoke of confusion, lost in a florae of thoughts.

"This is outrageous. Blackmail! Can get all this for thirty-five."

"You and this STUPID SLUT both know, by the time you get all the connections to all the persons you need, your name and picture will be on every wall like the great L.A. Lewis ... You should be thanking this ... SLUT."

He became sensible, surrendered. Tossed his gun in his suitcase, rubbed his hand behind his neck, then squeezed on his forehead like it was a stress-ball.

"Get me twenty now and I start the process tonight. Time's ticking away. The sooner the better."

"Ok. K." He looked both sides of the house, grabbed up a small bunch of keys off the top shelf of his black minimalistic-designed entertainment center, glanced at his small black and white surveillance TV above it and muttered,

"Let's go."

We hasted out and into his Mitsubishi Pajero. I hopped into the puffy leather seats and said

"You know, thinking, then you got to give Mr. Willie his job back."

"Why so?"

"Who else you gonna trust with your property when you disappear? We know Mr. Willie very honest and wont filch a thing."

"Mi not hiring back the idiot. Gonna put Tobias from the office here."

"The big country one? Him don't have not a sense. He's the one let mi know you still at the office. Why you think mi didn't leave? Him pinch and tell me, sell you out for fifty dollars."

"What? He's good as fired. Mi firing him country rass as day break tomorrow." I remembered the fist I got under my belly. Revenge was sweet. I smiled and agreed.

"Oh yes you should. Fire him yes."

"But that don't mean that mi hiring back Mr. Willie enuh. Mi still not hiring him back. Willie too soft."

He buckled down his seat belt. I didn't. I felt horrible for poor Mr. Willie. I didn't even wanted to look in his eyes as we drove through the gate. At least I did give it a shot to get back his job. Mr. Douglas drove to the gate. It was padlocked . Mr. Willie had a cardboard box packing his personal stuff into. He had a yellow comb with big teeth in his hand. Half of Mr. Willie head was empty and the other half was stubborn, it would not grow to any comb-able height. Either somebody tricked poor Mr. Willie into buying that comb or he obviously was dreaming big about how bouncy his bad-hair would get someday soon. Mr. Douglas stuck his hand out through the driver's window and shouted in haste,

"Fly the gate Willie."

"Mi don't work here again enuh sir."

"Willie what happen to you? Open the gate."

"You want the key for the padlock boss?"

"Backside man! Willie, fly the frigging gate! Or else ---"

"Or else what boss? You gonna fire mi again?" Willie picked up something off his table, put his yellow comb in his small carton box, picked up the box and clutched it up under his arm, like a ladies would a purse. He drooped over to the van and handed what he took off the desk to Mr. Douglas. It was his name badge and the key for the big padlock.

"Here sir. Come out and let out yourself." His gaze slowly crept over to me on the other side, face sulked, eyes hazy with hurt, lips barely moving, "Ms. Leelia look what you caused on mi." His eyes saddened. He loosened his clutched arm from around the small pathetic box, carefully fetched something out his box, came up with his yellow comb. "You see this comb ... it's from mi daughter, Roxie, the small one." He took a long blink, closing his eyes for a few second as he tried swallowing how deeply hurt he felt, "Roxie did give mi it as a good-luck charm ... say it would make me never lose my job again. Mi did want believe it was really a good luck charm for true. Mi never want let mi kids go through what them go through before. Mi take it with mi every day to work." He slowly raised the comb to his mouth, kissed it, shed tears. The grown man crying, right there at the van. "Roxie baby, mi get fired, mi coming home early tonight." He used the comb to mop at his tears. My heart felt his pain, and inside, I cried for his grief. It was so sad to look at Mr. Willie's face.

"Mr. Douglas, give him back his job. He's working with you over three years now." Mr. Douglas set his eyes upon me. "He's a goodman and his family depending on his job."

The Heart of Revenge

I knew Mr. Douglas heart had no conscience. But I still tried to petition to it, tried reaching to his heart. He looked down from his van at Mr. Willie.

"Willie, Willie, Ooiiie, stop the donkey bawling. You a big man. Go open the gate and go back in the guard booth. And change back in your uniform." Mr. Willie did his job. He was fired and rehired the same day, same night.

Throughout the entire ride Mr. Douglas and I didn't string a single sentence to each other. The ride was silent and mostly awkward. I thought about the number thirteen Pinky said I should buy. Wonder if it could really play tomorrow? A long forty minutes after, we arrived at a ghostly looking quad, in a bushy country-like area that look abandoned, no pavement, dirt tracks, bush height - waist high, creepy noises. 'Ribbit ... Ribbit'. No light. The place spooked me out. Where is this? Why we alone in the middle of the wilderness?

"Wait here." He unbuckled his seatbelt, "Mi soon come back." Pulled the key out the ignition and jumped down from the van. His boot made a heavy thud sound when it landed into the dirt. All the creepy noise in the background got quiet. The silence was scary, felt like someone's out there watching, prowling. He glanced both sides suspiciously, looked again with a more precarious inspection, as if anyone would be here, except us. Walked off into the bushy yard heading to the unlighted quad. I was alone in the van.

I dialled Gloe. There was a feint murmur of mosquitoes and the sharp cry of 'ribbit' from night insects every couple of seconds. The 'ribbits' sounded like a frog's croak but with more rattling and higher shrill in its projection, a longer eerie 'Riiibbit'. Flying insects, maybe they were fire flies or peenie wallie, blinking lights from their bottoms, all over in the dark, in a scattered Christmas light fashion. I reached over to the driver's side and wound up the window more. Gloe came on the phone, I jumped at the sound of her voice, sat up straight,

"You sleeping?" I asked her. 'Riiibbit!'. The insect that emitted that cry was close, it was loud. But I see none in the van. I hugged myself. Looked around, side glance at the ghostly wilderness outside.

"Yeah, just dozing off. What's up?"

"Got a big job for Danni. Ask her to line up everything tonight." Another loud 'Ribbit!' I glanced up through the rear-view, took my eyes off quickly, tried not to look outside. "I'm coming there with the cash in less than an hour."

"What's wrong Lee? You sound nervous bad, you need these for yourself?"

"No man. Not for me. I'm just a bit bombed about where I'm at now. When I reach over I'll give you all the details, just tell Danni she can start ready things right now." 'Ribbit'. "I need everything by mid-day tomorrow."

I snoopingly opened the glove compartment, searching inside while Gloe spoke.

"Goodness Lia you know that's impossible. It takes at least three days tops, it's not like Danni working with herself." I spotted the chrome gun in the glove compartment.

"G, I'm coming over with twenty grand tonight."

"I can't do it. It's almost midnight and that can't even start anything." 'Ribbit!' insects light blinking in the dark. "You know how much people Danni have to pay off?" I swatted my hand that held the phone, I totally missed the mosquito. The darkness around was getting heavier.

"U.S. money Gloe ...U.S." The phone went silent. 'Ribbit!'

"U.S.?"

"Yeah."

"Ok, come quickly then, let we see what we can do. Mi going to wake her up now. Hurry and come."

"Gloe stay on the phone with me a little longer till someone comeback nuh, please."

"Why?"

"I'm a little scared."

"Hsst. Stop being a girl." Gloe hung up. Should I take this gun? 'Ribbit'. What the hell is he doing so long in the house? Will he get back in the van already. I hate it out here. I still tried keeping my eyes from looking outside. What If he left me in the van and not coming back? What if he is gone? He had the key. I opened the glove compartment one more time, looked at the gun, reached for it, left it there, close the compartment. Insect lights blinking on and off, on and off in the thick foggy dark. I rubbed one barefoot on top of the other, hugged one arm around my waist, put my thumb in my mouth.

Unexpected. A rattling. 'Doop, doop, doop!' Out of nowhere. Shit. Van door. Shuffling. Moving. I jumped, almost through the roof. Door eased open . I gasped. "Huuh!" thumb falling from my mouth. My heart stung me. An electrical overcharge. The door pried wide open. It was Mr. Douglas, I tried to hide my spitty thumb. . The door let in a dose of the night's air, it smelt light and clean, not as hot as inside the van felt. He held the door in one hand and held a black pouch in the other. He threw the pouch in at me, it landed between my legs. Twenty grand large. He leaped into the van. If Vance only knew half the shit I'm going through for him. My foot's itching. Why he brought the gun though? I tried to scratch, rubbed my foot on the furry mat, the fur was somewhat stiff and brittle under my footbottom, almost ticklish as my foot rub up and down on it. My instinct told me I should have taken that gun.

"So ... there you are Ms. Lexings. Hope you can do what you say you can. Mid-day tomorrow, huh?"

"Don't worry that's not a problem." 'Ribbit ... Ribbit!'

"Ok then. Time to go." He replied.

Mr. Douglas, leaned towards the dashboard, one hand on the steering wheel, the other turning the key in the ignition. In one brisk motion he released the steering and fanned at mosquitoes from before his face. Spun the key and the heavy throttle of the engine cut through the broad expanse of silence. The engine quickly quieted down to a murmur that drowned the ongoing buzz of the mosquitoes. Switched on his headlights. The two long white beams of light were the only light in the dark wilderness. He switched the ignition back off. Kept the headlights on. No sound came from the engine, no buzz from mosquitoes in the van, only one sound remained in the night - night insects. 'Ribbit ... Ribbit'.

He stared through the windscreen, his face stilled, steady but his brain running, colluding, the unthinkable I thought. I stared over into his sinister eyes, quizzical, my heart stabbing with concern. What is he up to? I asked,

"What's wrong?"

Mr. Douglas shifted around facing me, leaned towards me and rested his forearm on the headrest of my seat. I was certain he was up to no good. I am alone in the middle of nowhere. 'Ribbit...Ribbit.'

CHAPTER 42

Balancing my Heart
by: Vybz

My jeans falls to the floor, the buckle makes a jangling sound, it echoes in the airy warehouse. She shifts slightly on the freezer size carton box. I glance over my right shoulder then look over the other, scanning quickly, turn my back to her and look about. No motion inside the dark room, but my gut feelings tells me something's not right, something's wrong, something just feels wrong. Why? Scan again, piles of motionless cardboard boxes. You know what, I'll follow my gut instinct, you feel mi? It's always right. I bend, grab the zipper region of my jeans and pull my pants up.

"I got to go, mi already late to catch my flight, this makes no sense, you feel mi? Plus mi and Finaral too close. Mi can't do this." I was buckling back my jeans.

"You right." Her eyes gets soft, "This risky, don't?" She places her hand on my buckling hands, holds it there, says nothing.

I take up my passport from beside her, she rocks her hip up and down as she pulls her tight black skirt up. I don't know what she is up to, but I'm not having it today. I push my passport in my back pocket and look behind me. Still no one, just us in the big quiet dark. I wonder if this gal cognisant that if Finaral finds out he's killing us both. Well she, I'm on my way to Cali. Her hand squeezes my crotch. My crotch reacts. Begins to get stiff. She speaks,

"Let me just give you the last blowjob before you go."

"No Portia, what's wrong with you, you harder-hearing?" She massages my crotch. I stiffen.

"Vybz, just let me suck your cock before you go. Mi won't take long."

"What you want to do?"

Oh fuck, my dick wants her, it's paining with stiffness but it's a battle, and my cock has the bigger brain when it comes to the matters of pussy. Fuck it. Finaral treats Pinky like shit. At this very moment of thinking about Pinky with a hard dick, a sexual thought crosses my mind. Only if I ever got the chance with her, she's so sexy, but how would she react if I approach her like that, we been so close so long. God I would really give it to Pinky. Finaral doesn't deserve her. I do. Oh what the hell, if Finaral had the chance to bang my girl he would, without a second thought. What am I half-stepping about? That's the weak excuse my cock bribes my brain with to set it free. Did it work? You have no idea how senseless men become with a stiff dick.

"I want your cock ..." she grabs my buckle, "In my mouth. Please Vybz."

She gets off the box. I help her slide my jeans down. My cock stands solid, spearing through the air long, thick and with a smooth dark purple head that glistens. She's in shock, staring in marvel on how much of a turn on my cock is. I wait anticipating the flesh of her lips cuddling my chocolate stick. She licks from the root to the tip, slow and steady, grabs the head, her hands presses flat against my abs, my hand light against her face. Like a magician, she disappears my cock down her throat, makes it reappear full length in her mouth, her lips kissing the tip, then disappears again, appears, disappears, slowly drags her mouth down the full length to let it appear, slick with spit, rigid with veins. She stops, pushes me down, fly her panty like aeroplane, spreads her legs wide open and says,

"I want to taste my pussy juice on your cock. Sink it into my hole."

I scan around, shuffle closer, my pants bunches up around my ankles. I hold my tough pointing penis, aim it at her pussy, teasingly rub the head up and down against her labia, press the fleshy warm head against her clitoris.

"Push it in Baby, push it in please, just fuck mi."

She's too loud. I forget about the time. I look behind me, all's clear. I slowly pierce through, my cock feels like a sunny day inside her, she feels the heat my cock is emitting on both sides of her pussy, she swerves her hip forward to the head of my cock far down in her zone, the sweet feel of the head sends her to say 'Good Morning' to Jesus, the fleshy soft pad, warm, smooth, the warmth rubs up and down into her, powerfully, power strokes, deep and hard in her and even when the cock slides out to the mouth of her pussy she still feels the heat down inside her. She anticipates so hungrily to have my dick splash back down in the deepest part of her hole, it drives her crazy, a heat of pleasure, she wants more, she wants it harder, fuck her, stroke, stroke it deep, hard. It forces her inside apart, her paradisingly smooth flesh squints around my cock without her intending, jumps, inside her pussy jumping, the feel, her pussy gets wetter, inside slick, slippery, soaking. The boxes rocking are loud, she can't control her volume,

"Fuck it, fuck it. That's it, Fuck it baby."

"You're too loud, sshhh."

"Fuck me harder! Cripple mi."

I look over my shoulders, cup my palm over her mouth, stroke her deep, not pulling out my dick, just deep stroking, just keep shoving it farther and farther down into her, small movements but deep intense penetration, it brings pleasure to her whole body, maddening. Every thrust hitting on that same sweet-spot, hitting it every single time. She swings her arm aimlessly, out of control, it hits a box, she is getting loud, captivated by the deep humping, thrusting down into her, filling her.

"Mi a cum, don't stop! Don't stop! mi a cum!"

I get all the power from my long muscular legs and begin slamming myself into her the hardest way I know how, she grabs my ass and tries to pull me deeper, face twisting, eyes shut, mouth open. She's getting slippery, I slide in easier, her juices cumming, I pump harder, farther. The rattling is loud, she's high-pitched

"Huh-huh-uh! Huh-uh-huhhh!

I muffle her whimper, she fights to get her head free, wanting to just cry out loud with every hard thrust I deliver. I think both my hip bones made it down her passage. Her left hand held on to the edge of the rattling box, her right hand latched the back of my shirt, ripping it off senselessly. I couldn't care less, I'll go on the plane shirtless, my cock pulsing inside her, pulsing with horniness, buckle jangling on the floor. She twists her head side to side, desperate to release her mouth, I savagely kiss her lips off her face. Her hand moves from the box to latching in my back, I slide my hand up her thighs, hold her ass, grip one cheek, squeeze my fingers into her firm flesh, hold it steady for the striking. I pelt my cock down to her oesophagus. She didn't win the lotto but she was shouting out,

"Yes! Yes, yes!" Her mouth gapes, face winces bitterly, "Shit! Shit! Fuck!, Oh Fuck!"

She made her ugly but sexy cumming face, just beautiful,
"Fuck! I'm cumming! Arrhh!"
She grips me tighter and her waist is rolling around in wild frantic circles, small but orgasmic circles that makes me want to die a thousand times how good it feels. She is winding fast on top, my cockhead right in her G-spot, she loves what she feels and the cum swells to the tip of her pussy lips. Her pussy drools sweet milk on my cock. I can't wait any longer. I whisper,
"Stop. I got to go."
"Shut up and fuck me!"
Her panting loud. I grab her other ass cheek, it sinks in a dimple as her pussy squints then relaxes, her ass gets back round, she arches her back, I go deeper, thrust into untouched zones where it hurts sweetly. She bites hard, my neck, making a humming cry, my penis stroking her inside without breaking, a steady hard pattern, a deep thorough straight through and through vaginal tour. She whimpers into my neck,
"Mmmm."
I grab her hair, her weave, fuck her, she squeezes my ass, pulling me, slamming me into her harder, spreads her legs wide, raise them in the air, points her toes to the ceiling, use both hands and pull her pussy cheeks apart, open wide, I lose it. I fuck her, I fuck her, fuck her, fuck her. Long strokes. Powerful strokes. The sweetest strokes. Her skirt rides up her hips, looking like a belt. She sucks my neck harder, her head jerks, talks into my neck, sucking it, I didn't know what she said but I feel the humming vibration, it sends shivers through me, drives me in-fucking-sane. I hold one of her ankles high in the air, throw it on my shoulder, swing the other leg between mine as I scissor fuck her, it feels good, I want more, I lose it, hoist her hip off the box, her feet not touching the ground, slam myself into her, slam, slam, slam, she gets weighty to lift. I put her back on the box, grab her shoulders with both hands, stroking deep and sensually, I wind slow in her cunt, slow and steady, bracing forward and deep into her. I get leverage, wrap my fingers around her neck, I go in farther, deeper, reaching my favorite spot inside, her favorite spot, it is shallow, ribbed and smooth. She feels it there and moves sensually against the head of my cock keeping it in that erogenous zone, her sweet spot, she is pushing up every time I sink it down onto her sweet spot, her tongue

between her teeth as she inhales raspy and ragged. Our swerves become one, in rhythm, and pleasing, the best fucking feeling in life, ten houses of sexual coke, a sexual high. She runs her hand up her blouse, plucks her bouncing breast out her bra, it is still under her blouse, I crane my neck forward, suck on her nipple through her thin white blouse, my wet mouth wetting her blouse, remove my lips, her dark nipple is perking through the round wet spot on her blouse, she toys with her breast, squeezes it, looks into my eyes, pinches her nipple. She flusters to unbutton her blouse, my chest sweaty, she is staring in my eyes, face sweating.

One breast in, one breast out, flesh bouncing, erotic, so beautiful, the beautiful sight of sex in heated bouncing motion. My wet mouth suckles on her breast, swallowing her nipple, devouring her breast deep down into my oveny mouth, gobbling in a famish manner, I had no control, my horniness peaks miles high in me. I crave her. I unmouth her breast, squeeze the soft plump base, getting her hard nipples pointing to the ceiling fan, circle her erect swollen nipple with my moist horngry tongue, slow wet circles. Continuous circles, rubbed her clit, passionately sucking her breast into my brain, fucking far and deep, stroking, sucking, rubbing, circling her wet clit, circling, circling, still fucking, fucking, fucking, deep, in and out, in, out, fucking, all at the same time, fuck, my tongue circles, suck with violent passion. She flings her head back and whimpers

"Oh fuck! Oh fuck! Don't ... Don't ... Mmmm. Cumming, I'm .. cummmm!"

She springs up off my lengthy cock, screams

"Mi want cum in your mouth!"

Braces her thick slice of pussy pudding into my face, so hard I think she is trying to sit in the back of my throat. I grab both of her ass cheeks and force her farther down into my mouth. She says breathily and in some haste before her cum gushes out her pussy,

"Mi want wet up your tongue!"

I pull my head out. I smell her heated pussy in my face, I'm moving towards her yummy pie, slowly, too slow, she grabs the back of my head, buries my face between her legs, right into her pussy, commanding me,

"Open your mouth!" her eyes rolling back, "Wide!" I did, "Eat it, suck my pussy!" she tosses her head all the way back, her facing blooming with unsurmountable pleasure,

"Drink mi pussy soup!" I did, she kept talking dirty,

"Yeah Baby, drink it up. Drink everything ... every... hheesshh... drop. Good medicine. Vitamin P!" I tried my best not to waste my vitamins,

Her pussy melting her sweet hot cream down, running down. She becomes my full course meal, a serving of pussy lips, with hot clits, glazed in her white honey and to quench my oral appetite some pussy milk shake. Mmmm. Bon a petit to the cannibal. Her juices flourish over her labia, so soaked you could bail it out and full a bath pan. I suck her creamed pussy lips, just one lip, a single one, good and proper and smooth suck. It's not enough for her, she forces my head up into her snatch, stuffing my face wildly into her coochie, my nose squashes against her clit, her loin hoola-hooping wildly, wanting my warm mouth over her clit. I can't get oxygen, mouth fill with pussy, I muffle,

"I have to go, my flight."

"Just let me cum in your mouth again. Please." She grips my head in place.

Her pink clit stiff, shooting forward with horniness, blood rushing into her clit, on the verge of jacking off in my mouth. My tongue pesters her panicking clit, suck on it, her pussy gets dreadfully tender, reacts to the slightest touch, my tongue continues to harass in the center of her sweetness, her pussy smells as fresh as rose water in my nose. My lips gently hauls the petal of her pink rose, sucking off the warm slick pussy sippings her pussy dewed on them. I freeze at a noise I swore I heard in the distanced dark, a muffled cough, a person, someone watching.

"You heard that?"

"Ssshh, Shut up. Make me cum!" Probably just a figment of my imagination.

My tongue proceeds to lapping down in her center, mopping her pussy with my tongue, she was nine skies above cloud nine. I shove my professional tongue in every crevice and curves of her shaking wet pussy. She drains the last of her cum in my mouth, down my throat, her juices feels warm as if her pussy were a thermos. I swallow every drop. Lick my lips. Her eyes flutter weakly.

I ease up, plant light soft kisses, all over her arouse pussy, her poor vagina falls apart. My cell beeps twice, a special beep, Leelia's beep.

I heard 'Click!'

The Heart of Revenge

A bright industrial light snapped on. She clutched her bosom. I hustled to drag up my jeans, hurtled behind the boxes. Portia followed. I felt for my passport in my back pocket, look at the time, bomboclawt star, flight suppose to gone seventeen minutes ago, what kind of power pussy has?

"Who's there?" The guy walked forward, stepping towards the boxes. It's the same youth from the last time, Marlon. Deja vu this? Mi can't believe mi in this avoidable predicament again. Boy, Marlon really can watch the B star. A bet mi shot him a box today. Better yet, keep calm, keep cool Ajrien.

None of us answered. We didn't got caught this time. Marlon turned back, walked over to the switch. Portia spread a devilish smirk on her face. Or maybe delight, she didn't seem any at all shocked, like he catches her a lot in here and it gave her the thrills. I got a text. 'Bee-Beep.' Leelia. The world stopped spinning. The beeping sounded loud in the quiet. Marlon stopped, looked around.

"Who's there? Mi know somebody in here. Move from round the box."

I sneaked a quick look at the texts from Leelia, it read,

'Ajrien, don't leave. Please.'

She must be the only one who still calls me Ajrien, aside from Mama. Can't wrap my head around this. What's this? She still wants me or? Misses me as a friend? I mean, all of a sudden, I'm getting all these emotional texts from her. After years? I thought she had totally forgotten about me since she's been uptown. I knew she didn't want me. Plus she's way out my league. I have a better shot at being with Pinky. Well if ... though I rather to be with ... I don't even know who I rather. But, I do think about Lia so much. So ... I rubbed the ring she gave me slowly in deep thoughts. Who am I kidding? Lia doesn't want a guy like me, she wants an uptown guy. Maybe she wanted to use me, for some dirty jobs, or something.

I stared, thought harder. But I just don't know what's up? Since she sent me the 'Miss you' text on her wedding day that was one hell of a disaster ... you know what? I should go and see her, but .. but .. my flight ... hsst ... I knew she was marrying too young. I didn't text back the last time. Now this. Should I text back now? Maybe, no... Wonder if she knows about my incident that I'm running from? I knew she knew I'm leaving obviously, but what if it's a set up from the other crew? No, but she texted mi the 'Miss you' before my incident even happened. I knew if she heard about my incident, I wouldn't have a chance. She's gonna hear about it anyway, I don't have a chance. Better mi leave. I'm leaving. Or stay? I don't even know what to make of this. Should I leave? I missed my flight, maybe it's a sign, and now this text, maybe it's a bigger sign. I stared at the blank box. Portia pulled down her skirt in place, grinned and asked Marlon,

"You catch everything right? Then turned to me, her face instantly changing from a smile to a wry scowl and said,

"'Bout you come fly big box in mi face for dirty stinking Pinky. Mi and you little bloodclawt now." Marlon voice sounded happy when he answered her,

"Yes! Everything mi catch." He held up his recording camera in the air. Immediately I knew what Portia was up to. I began choking the blackmailing bitch. The other bitch, Marlon, ran away without looking back.

CHAPTER 43

The Heart of Revenge
by: Leelia Lexings

I was stupid. I should've took the gun. I should've never trusted Mr. Douglas. His face was close to mine when he suggested,

"I think we should make this deal fair huh.' 'Ribbit.' I shifted closer to my door and away from him. I studied his eyes. I saw evil.

"It's fair Mr. Douglas. A done deal ... What you want to pay then?"

Silence. 'Ribbit'. Silence.

He stared.

Insects light blinking. Mr. Douglas' eyes didn't blink. The silence stood so long between us, I grew a beard.

"No ... Since we are both here alone ... Why not we ..." He rolled both his shoulders upward close to his ears, afterwards leaned forward and twirled his fingers in the ends of my hair, combed his finger through,

"You know .. huh? .. we could .. You know ..."

My hands flashed, strapping across my chest as if to cover my nakedness.

"No. I don't know. Good God! I was to marry your SON. Are you such a pervert everyone say you are?"

I prayed my emphasis on son would touch his conscienceless conscience. Maybe it did. He straightened his spine in his seat.

"You know what Lee, I should be getting you for free!" As he talked, his voice got higher and anger invaded his tone, he got harsh, "Fuck this shit, I already paid your mother five years ago, from you were fourteen. Fourteen! She took my fucking money... I shouldn't pay shit. You're mine! Not Qwan's, not anyone else, that was the deal! Your mother is a fucking bitch to go behind my back and force you on my son, just to save you from me. What? I wasn't too old for you when she was talking my money? Whatever you and your mother planned, it won't work, no fucking way I won't get you, I fucking gave her my money!"

I wish I could, but I didn't have the superpower to disappear. Shamed. Shocked. Mom. The thought of what I went through at fourteen ran over me like a train. I couldn't answer, I could not speak, I couldn't see his face, all I was saw pictures of Mom sending me off at fourteen. The morning, I remembered everything clearly, even the sound of Lassy barking outside when Mr. Douglas had came, my yellow blouse Mommy was buttoning, Mommy crying, me crying. I had a stolid expression on my face. Blank. The silence lasted. Something building up in my chest, building up in my eyes. How could ... I thought ... that means --- . Mr. Douglas got angrier,

"Ok then, have it your way. I'll only pay what I know it's worth. Forty-five thousand ... and your little friend Mr. Willie is losing his job!" He picked up his cell and screamed in it,

"Willie leave mi place! You're fucking fired! FIRED! You heard that huh? FIRED!"

I could hear Mr. Willie's puny voice asking on the other end,
"What mi do Mr. Douglas?"
"Nothing! You're FIRED!"

He hung up in a blazing temper. Wrath bubbling in Mr. Douglas' snake eyes, he looked like the devil. I said nothing. Tried to be brave. Still taken aback by what he had just told me, was it really true? Mom wouldn't. But even if Mommy did gave me up for money, she took me out of the ghetto and she was using the money to help my brother save his life. I didn't think what Mommy did was a bad thing. If it was my only option to save my son, maybe I would do the same thing, it's not like she still wasn't there for me, it's not like I was suffering where she sent me. It's a mixed feeling in my heart. I can't be mad at Mom. Mommy did what she had to, the better of two evils, watch her son die or give up her daughter.

Silence. 'Ribbit' ... Silence ... 'Ribbit'.

He shifted in the driver's seat, placed two hands on the steering wheel. The cushiony leather seats my back I leaned against suddenly felt like solid iron. The bottom of my feet felt as if there were one thousand worms in it, boring their way through to get out. I pushed my courage infront my fears.

"You don't have a choice. Its sixty thousand or nothing!"

My voice came out really bold, I could fool myself that I wasn't totally distorted mentally. I needed that money before Thursday. He could walk away with all his money. Then what would I do? Maybe I should just settle for the forty-five, at least when I pay Danni her twenty I still would have twenty-five to give Dr. Reid.

"Well then have it your way ... It's NOTHING." 'Ribbit ... Ribbit'. "Give mi back my money." He turned one of his palm over to me, waiting and the other hand shifting towards the glove compartment. My fingers clenched tighter into the pouch. I knew he couldn't kill me, his only help. Would he?

"I swear if you try anything I'll let everyone know about the other night." He looked at me with astonished eyes, recoiled, said,

"Sweetie listen huh, after I get the papers, Micheal Douglas won't exist. Do you think I give one red fuck what others say when I'm gone, huh? Do you? Think again." My face slackened like some screws fell out of place.

"What about your son?"

"His problem. He's on his own."

"He's your own flesh and blood. Your only son."

He wrapped back is four fingers around the steering wheel, massaging it up and down and with a miniscule snicker on his face, uttered

"Ahh Lee, you've tempted me so many times in your little .. tiny .. white panties." His eyes rolled over into some sort of ecstasy. "Ohh how I love to sniff your panties like canines sniffing for narcotics. The crotch. The worn ones. Or may I say, the freshly dirtied ones. Stare at your young buoyantly soft teenage boobs, nipples so puffy, so perked, breast so bouncy .. soooo ... sooo .. SUCK ...ABLE."

"You PERVERT! You saw me naked?"

"Oh Lee, Oh Lee, I have cameras everywhere, especially in your bathroom. Watching you bathe is my favorite TV program on my little black and white TV. Your skin ... so supple, so wet ... so tender ... like baby lamb meat ... rotisserie."

The sounds of the night got eerier and his eyes lit brighter than the peenie wallie and fireflies blinking light. His eyes still dreamy in ecstasy. He shook his head slowly, side to side, as he savoured in softly saying,

"Ohh how I want to eat that sweet little pudding pie of yours," His smile spread wide from ear to the back of his head, as he brought back and savoured in the scent he sniffed. "Ohh how I want to taste it, eat it like a warm slice of pizza."

"Oh my God! Mr. Douglas! What kind of perv are you?" thrown aback and almost dumbstruck by his language and mannerism. I've never heard anyone spoke with such intense perversion before over the scent of a panty. My panty. I felt completely naked. I clawed my toe into the bristly fur of the van's mat.

"Lee. Lee, gifts of opportunities are wrapped in disguises of misfortune. This is really an opportunity for you, can't you see? Do you really want to save your brother's life?" he still spoke soft and in control. "I can make you visit Italy, I can have you visit anywhere in the world. Where do you want to have breakfast? Huh? Paris? Tokyo? London? Maybe in Australia? Would you love to clink glasses with some friendly Aussies? Africans? Antarcticans perhaps? Huh? Just say it Lee, Just say it, Anywhere, for that vagina of yours. Your lovely lovely vagina. Mmm."

"No!" I felt disgusted. "Nowhere. I just want to save Vance. That's all."

"Do you? Huh? Really? How far would you go Lee? How far?"

My brother's life. I already gave his son myself to save it, at least I liked Qwan but the father? He made my skin crawled. Gross. This ain't worth it? Is it? My brother's life.

"I'll pay sixty. I'll save him Lee. Only if you will give it up."

A feeling of a nest of spiders swarming my entire body and crawling over my skin took me over. Crawling all over my face and into my nose, into my mouth, I felt yicky.

Ribbit ... Ribbit. The insect cries were lower seemed further away. Silence.

Shudders rattled my thin frame. The rumours must have been true. Mr. Douglas offered young girls money and trips to perform oral sex on them. It sounded preposterous, like just rumours. It was hard to digest as truth, such a respectable and successful gentleman yet so deviantly unpleasant, hid so many dark sides. But here I am. Its real. It's happening to me, now.

The Heart of Revenge

And if the entire rumours were true, he could not have sex for five minutes. Five minutes to save Vance. My soul went dead. It was as if the sky kept falling on my head. I could not hold my tears anymore. I broke down. Should I shake hands with the devil?

"This wrong. I can't, I just can't. Please, please, just have a heart. Please. Have a conscience." I stiffened my upper lip, soldiered my emotions, toughened my voice, "We don't need to do this, help me out. Don't try to take advantage of me Mr. Douglas. Help me help my brother, Please Mr. Douglas, Please, please, please."

"Lee. Lee. Just help me be happy huh. It will only take a few minutes. A few minutes of your life to save the rest of your brother's life. Now, ain't that worth it? Ain't that fair? Huh? Here I am. Your opportunity."

Silence. 'Ribbit'. 'Ribbit'. 'Ribbit'. Midnight blackness was approaching and the night air got cold.

I played tough. Betrayed my cry inside. I was faced with saving my brother's life and giving up my pride, shame, privacy and myself. Having sex with son and then now, the father. It's only five minutes but it was a lifetime. A memory I would re-live every day, inerasable, re-live over and over again in my head. More importantly, I had no time, I had to choose now. Vance has till Thursday but my only shot left, Mr. Douglas, will be gone by tomorrow. My entire inside was tumbling down. The sky kept falling on me. I decided to shake hands with the devil.

He slid a hand on my leg. Sniffed my hair. My skin shrivelled at his touch, stomach turned over. I could hear Mom's voice saying to me for the thousandth time 'Pride is as invisible as words of gossip, and will hurt you deep, only when you decide to make them win. Doing the right sometimes is doing the lesser evil.' Forget what people will say, that won't save my brother's life, I had to do what I had to do, the lesser evil for a greater good.

I cast all my pride, shame and everything away. He stroked his hand up my dress, closer to my privacy. The fire flies flashed less. The ribbits stopped. He switched off the van's headlight that was the only light in the wilderness. The mid-night blackness came, so black, it destroyed all the shadows. I couldn't see anything infront me. My nightmare begun. A howling dog sounding like a wolf 'Aruuuuu' was echoing above the creepy silence. 'Arrh –Arrh – Arruuuu!'. One fire fly blinked its light.

Everything was hard for me to swallow, like trying to swallow all the sadness of the world. My reflexes instinctively held on to his sweaty hand that was on me, on my leg. I held his hand still, wanted to push him off, but this was it, I couldn't. I inhaled, long and deep. Swallowed my inside. Breathed. Let go of his hand. Said to him with a crying voice,

"Remember Mr. Willie job ..." sobbed, "Please."

He grunted and grinned as his hand savagely roamed wherever on my body that he pleased, went under my skirt. Just this one time. For Vance. It will be over soon. Oh God please let it be over soon, I prayed. Please, God hear my cry, let it be over soon, let it be over. I felt clustered in the van, the air thickly smelled of him as he drew down his pants, a musty stale smell. I wanted to threw up.

I let go of the black pouch, closed my eyes. The van rattled as he waddled and fight with himself to climb on top of me.

'Ribbit'.

Blind, black darkness.

My bare-feet cold. So cold. So, so cold. Tears came to the brim of my eyes. His hand touched me there, a tear dripped from my lashes, his other hand molested my breast. My lips squinted, pressed together and trembled as I forced myself to muffle the wheezing sound of my helpless cry. Fighting the crying sound from coming out. My chest heaving with pain and disgrace.

It's too much, made no sense holding it back. I let it out. Let it go. Cried.

I slowly rolled my white underwear down my legs. His grotesquely hairy belly was belly to belly with mine. His breath smelled rancid as if his tongue was decomposing. His slimy drooling tongue went everywhere. My breast, neck, face and lips. He asked for my tongue. Kissed on it. He kissed my lips spitty. The gross scent of his mouth stained on my mouth. Everywhere that he kissed had his scent.

Two lines of silver tears stretching down my face. Flowing into my gun bruise under my eye. Wetting the blood that had bled from it. Crying, tears with blood. A most undesirable feeling. A feeling that will remain with me, forever, to re-live, a feeling just like being molested. Like being raped. Like being raped by a father-in-law. I felt like dying.

'Ribbit.'

Blood and tears poured down.
 Down.
'Ribbit'.
Poured down. Down.
Down my face.
I'll have my REVENGE.

END OF BOOK 1

IMPORTANT NOTE TO ALL READERS

Please keep this book. You'll need it to make reference for book two when things start turning completely upsidedown. If you do lend out this book, lend to responsible persons who you're sure will return it or just don't lend at all. This is just the tip of the iceberg. Trust me, I'm the author, I know.

Read excerpt from book 2 at **RichieDrenzBlog.com/THOR2**

Remember to Join our official facebook page at **facebook.com/EroticBlissByRichieDrenz** and let me know what you think of what you have read so far. Come on and chat with us. Looking forward to see you there.

Also Remember to check out a sample of my True Sex Story, CLIMAXES at **RichieDrenzBlog.com/Climaxes**

And if you enjoy laughing I have a belly busting comedy titled THE JAMAICAN NINJA Read samples of it at **RichieDrenzBlog.com/The-Jamaican-Ninja**